The Liz Reader

A Collection of Shorter Works by Elizabeth Daniels Squire (1926-2001)

Edited by C. B. Squire

With an Introduction by Margaret Maron

An Imprint of
The Overmountain Press
JOHNSON CITY, TENNESSEE

Photo on front cover by John A. Miller
Photo on back cover of Liz and C. B. Squire by Hiram Cody
Photo on back cover of gravestone by Catherine Schultz

Table of Contents

INTRODUCTION

It still seems unbelievable to me that Liz is gone, that I will never again see her warm smile across a hotel lobby or conference room. Because we lived on opposite sides of our native North Carolina, we seldom saw each other physically; and when we did, it was usually on the fly at crowded mystery conventions or literary gatherings halfway across the country. Happily, we both belonged to Sisters in Crime and, since she collected regional news for the national bulletin, I'd get little nudges from her whenever an issue was due. Her voice was so distinctive that all she had to say was "Mar-garet!" and I knew instantly who was calling. She was a letter in my mailbox, a voice in my ear, a cheerful E-mail on my computer screen. I suppose that is why I am still having such a hard time coming to grips with her loss.

One of the first times we met face to face was in 1989 when her initial mystery novel was published. Since Kill the Messenger was loosely based on her illustrious grandfather, longtime editor of the Raleigh News & Observer, the book's launch party was held in Raleigh and she invited me to come. That night, surrounded by friends and family, Liz fairly glowed with happiness at the fulfillment of a personal dream.

When the Southeastern Chapter of Mystery Writers of America was being formed, Liz immediately jumped right in and offered to do all she could to help, agreeing to serve on the board of directors. She also edited our newsletter for several years, all the while grumbling that she had forgotten to do this or overlooked that. She laughed about her leaky memory and made us laugh, too, when she capitalized on that endearing quirkiness and created an absent-minded sleuth, Peaches Dann; yet one senses that her self-deprecation was a learned defense to cover the hurt of a dyslexic childhood before her dyslexia was diagnosed. In a family where reading and writing were so important and came so naturally, the young Liz's struggles and frustrations with the printed page are wrenching to contemplate.

Coupled with the loss of her mother before she was three, there must have been deep scars from those years, but she was not a confessional writer and seldom alluded to them. "Fragment" and "Funny Story," both printed here for the first time, are probably only the tip of a very large iceberg. Self-pity was not in her make-up though. With her dry, sly, self-effacing wit, she made book talks and signings a delight, and I never came away from dining or lunching with her without a new memory trick.

"If you absolutely must remember to take something with you when you leave the house," she said, "then put your car keys with it. You can't drive very far without them." It works for cell phones, library books, or if you drop in on a friend on your way back from grocery shopping and stick your ice cream in her freezer. Your keys may be cold, but you will not forget your ice cream.

Practical and good-humored, and valiant, too. That was Liz, and it is that Liz which we find between the lines of this last collection of her work—a tart comment here, a trenchant observation there, and always that kindly spirit that empathized with human failing.

I miss her E-notes, I miss her phone calls, I miss seeing her at the conferences she so enjoyed. She was a very special person, and I do not need any of Peaches Dann's memory tricks to know that I will never forget her.

Margaret Maron
Johnston County, North Carolina
January 2002

PREFACE

Elizabeth Daniels Squire, who died suddenly on February 25, 2001, published six short stories in the mystery genre during the 1990s—not enough, she thought, to make up an anthology. Before she left for her last promotional trip, Liz mentioned that she was going to have to decide whether to write—and publish—more mystery short stories, or to continue concentrating on full-length novels.

On February 24, I talked to Liz on the phone—she was stopping over at our son Mark's house in Sebastopol, California, on her way home from Alaska—and she told me she had reached a decision on an anthology. But she didn't tell me what that decision was.

Liz had written extensively for many years, and, thanks to assistants such as Gigi Derballa, Julie Burns, Ann Everett, Melissa Lewis, Lisa Franklin, and Catherine Schultz, we were able to locate many unpublished writings—fiction, poetry, and non-fiction. And Bonnie Kettner, our office manager, managed to keep us all headed in the right direction. This collection is the result.

Included are several short stories featuring Liz's memory-challenged sleuth Peaches Dann, a short biography written immediately after her death, and articles on writers and writing, on food, and on other topics. A number of comments and anecdotes have been sprinkled throughout.

Liz's mystery short stories are taken from a number of anthologies, as indicated before each one, and are reprinted here by courtesy of the anthology compilers: Jan Grape, Dean James, Ellen Nehr, Nevada Barr, Elizabeth Foxwell, Martin H. Greenberg, Carolyn G. Hart, Claudia Bishop, Nick DiChario, Jeffrey Marks, and Emyl Jenkins. Thanks are due to Margaret B. Tenney, archivist at Ashley Hall in Charleston, South Carolina, for providing us with stories and poems Liz wrote while she attended high school there. I also thank Emyl Jenkins for letting me include Liz's profound "Summation of a Life" from The Book of American Traditions, an excerpt from which appears on Liz's tombstone.

My sons and I also thank the incomparable Margaret Maron for writing the Introduction and for many other kindnesses.

So this is a celebration of the life and work of Liz through the years. Comments of others, including my own, are in italics, whereas roman type has been used for all words that were actually written by Liz. While these pieces have been arranged very roughly in chronological order, they have also been grouped to reflect various phases of her writing career.

I must note that nothing in this book would satisfy Liz—she would have wanted to rewrite much of the previously unpublished work before allowing it to see the public light of day. But on the other hand, I have restrained my own editorial proclivities in an effort to preserve what Liz referred to as her "voice."

But this isn't all. There is still an unfinished novel, a novella, a children's book manuscript, and other material. Also, Liz's mystery novels are all in print in one form or another; her agent, Luna Carne-Ross, is still arranging for new editions, and The Overmountain Press has issued new editions in both hard-cover and paperback in its Silver Dagger imprint.

If you knew Liz, read her books, or just met her at a mystery convention or a library reading, you will have a good read!

C. B. Squire

Autobiography

In the 1990s, Liz wrote two pieces that, taken together, amount to a short autobiography. They describe the influence of books on her life and a self-interview on how she wrote, including tips for aspiring writers and an account of her own efforts to overcome dyslexia. The first is from an interview with Gwen Hunter for her nationally syndicated column, "Writer to Writer":

Half a Fiction-Writer's Work

The last person who interviewed me in my office described it as a sunny, well-organized office at the edge of the woods. It's true I look out one window above my computer at woods. I look out the window on the other side of the room at green fields. I am surrounded by pigeonholes and standing files, and walls of bookshelves. There are also stacks of paper waiting to be dealt with that the interviewer kindly didn't notice.

How can writing fiction generate so much paper? Partly, of course, because these days half of a fiction writer's work is promoting books, going to conventions, talking in bookshops and libraries, and such. I think this is especially true in the mystery field. I have a whole standing file of places I'm going to speak or be on a panel in the coming months while I talk about my new book, *Is There a Dead Man in the House?*. Fortunately I am a little bit of a ham. Another standing file relates to research and to bits of memory lore donated by readers, God bless their hearts. Because my absent-minded sleuth, Peaches Dann, has been writing a book called *How to Survive Without a Memory*, they send me memory tricks, jokes, and even serious research which is very helpful. But back to the office.

I have happy memorabilia standing around such as the tea pot with a skull and crossbones thereon. A rose is between the skull's teeth. That is the Agatha Award for the best traditional short story written in 1995. I have a rock collected from a nearby cave in which I set a rather scary scene in *Whose Death Is It, Anyway?*. And so it goes. I live out in the country outside of Asheville, North Carolina, and I walk up the hill to my office in a separate building. That separation is a wonderful thing. When my office was in the house I was constantly distracted by thinking of things I ought to do. Now I go to work every morning and come home in the evening. I get more done.

I grew up in a writing family and began telling stories before I was even literate. I wrote short stories in college and after, and even briefly had an agent trying to sell them. I became a newspaper reporter, which may or may not count, but was great training. About 30 years ago I sold a syndicated newspaper feature on the hands of celebrities like Salvador Dali and Carl Sandburg. That led to a book on how to read your own hand, which is still in print. Since we mystery writers never waste anything, my sleuth learns to read hands and uses Salvador Dali's handprint as a clue in *Whose Death Is It, Anyway?*. Every bit of writing experience you ever have will be useful.

I wrote one novel during the time I was a reporter. I rewrote it about once a year. I got an agent to send it around but the word came back it didn't fit a niche.

It never occurred to me to give up. I had the idea that to be the real me, I had to write novels. If I never had one published it would mean I was nothing. This is the wrong attitude but it kept me writing fiction.

My first writer support group was a joy. A wonderful novelist and poet named Sarah Litsey Nye was our head honcho. She made us all feel like we were bound to publish fiction if we kept writing, and the members of her group had a high success rate. I felt almost real. Since all the members of the group were serious about getting published, we had a high level of criticism. Never destructive. We talked about what worked and what could be made to work better.

I never had time to take a formal class or go to writers conferences while I was a reporter. But I saved my notes—about a flood I covered, for example—and one of the best scenes in any of my books is the fictional flood that is a highlight of *Kill the Messenger*. Advice to young writers: Save notes, interesting ideas, and memory joggers even if you don't keep a formal journal.

I was lucky. I managed to get agents. I let them screen the rejection letters and tell me only what I needed to know. Meanwhile I kept my mind on my writing. What's that old expression? "Keep your eye on the donut and not on the hole."

Finally St. Martin's Press said it would buy a mystery I'd written in which the head of a newspaper family gets murdered, if a few revisions were successful. Fortunately they were. By the way, that was not the book I rewrote once a year, but a new one.

When I sold that novel, *Kill the Messenger,* my husband and I went out to a fancy restaurant to celebrate. However, when the revisions were finished and accepted I became depressed. Now I know that when I am all through with a book I get postpartum blues, just as some women do after they give birth! I get over those blues by throwing myself into writing the next book.

Networking is the best way I know to find an agent. When I left my job as a reporter and began seriously writing books, I did everything I could to meet other folks in the writing community. Through a friend in the North Carolina Writers Conference, I found the agent who sold my first novel.

I still love to write as much as I ever did. It's hard work but it's a kind of meditation, too. I get up and write early in the morning, and if I miss a day I feel deprived. When I wasn't under contract, I might not write if I wasn't in the mood. To get novels done on deadline you have to learn to keep working, whatever your mood.

I do a lot of rewriting because I am simply incapable of writing an outline. I know the beginning of a book and the end, but the middle comes intuitively as I go. I post a calendar of the book on the wall. Across the top are all the dates, down the side the name of each character. I write in where each character is and what he's doing at each time as soon as I know it. This came about because I somehow managed in rewriting *Who Killed What's-Her-Name,* the first in my Peaches Dann series, to have the killer somewhere else at the same time he was supposed to be committing the murder. I go cold when I think of it. Thank goodness the copyreader caught it! I also keep an address book with each character and his age, appearance, birthday, car make, and anything else I might need to know. I do careful research not just in libraries, but physical research. For *Is There a Dead Man in the House?,* for example, I got the head State of Tennessee archaeologist to show me a skeleton buried in 1849. That's the year a skeleton in my book was buried, also in Tennessee.

I am part of a critiquing group that includes other published writers as well as serious wanna-bes. The group includes two English professors, a psychiatrist, and a trained nurse. They are more lighthearted than that sounds, but their advice is usually right on the mark. My mysteries are meant to entertain, to keep the reader on the edge of his chair, and give an occasional chuckle. So the serious care I give to writing them might surprise. Even the memory tricks my sleuth includes in each book really work. Mystery readers like to learn as they escape into an adventure.

Since I have been writing mysteries I travel more to conventions and such, and I have a great excuse to learn more about anything that interests me. The book I am working on right now includes scenes on a cruise. So I had to go on a cruise, right? Somebody has to do this hard work! *Is There a Dead Man in the House?* is set at the renovation of a house built in 1795. So I watched just such a renovation and learned all sorts of fascinating stuff about old houses. Did you know they mixed hog bristles in the plaster?

The awards I have won have been very important to me. A 1998 calendar with an outstanding dyslexic for each month hangs in my office. On the front are outstanding dyslexics chosen over the years like George Burns and Whoopi Goldberg and Cher. I was chosen as a mystery writer for August this year. Yes, I was one of those kids who had a terrible time learning to read, and I still can't spell. Like the sickly kid who works out and overcompensates to be in the Olympics, I was simply determined first to read and then to write. Nowadays there are wonderful methods for helping dyslexics, but kids still have to work extra hard to learn the basics. The purpose of this calendar (put out each year by the Los Angeles branch of the International Dyslexia Association) is to encourage kids by reminding them that for some reason dyslexia frequently goes hand-in-hand with great determination and creativity. I am touched to have been chosen.

Then there is this most recent bit of news—my TV movie option! A film company has optioned my first two novels for a possible movie, and though I am excited about it, I try to contain myself. I know that film companies option more material than they finally use. Still, it is a first step to a Peaches Dann film. In my dreams, Goldie Hawn plays the part! Ah. . . . Dreams!

Of course, my Agatha award is my pride and joy. I won it for a short story about my absent-minded sleuth: *The Dog Who Remembered Too Much.* Winning was a complete surprise, and every time I look at the award I glow. One effect of dyslexia, which was little known back when I was a kid, was that I was constantly told I wouldn't try. I look at the Agatha award and think to myself, hey, I not only tried, I succeeded!

My family have always been great supporters of my writing, God bless them, and they still are. A career as a mystery writer would have been very difficult otherwise.

I wish I had enjoyed each step of my career more and not worried about the future. But perhaps I would not have been so determined if that had been so.

The main tip I have for aspiring writers is to remember that every life experience is grist for the mill. I don't keep a real journal, but I keep a weather journal. Appropriate weather does great things for a book! Save notes, newspaper stories, interesting ideas. You think you will remember all this later when you need it, but you may not. The chances are that you can use it more effectively if you keep it all in a shoe box or a computer file. Newspaper stories don't have to be the big flashy ones. Small intriguing bits can add texture to a book or story.

A year or so ago there was a story in the paper about a man whose dog brought home a human leg one day and another one the next, and nobody could find out where they came from. I worked that into a paragraph where my sleuth's outrageous father is berating her for finding dead bodies. He recalls the newspaper story about the legs and says, "At least you don't have a dog!"

To the wanna-be trying to get published, I say that the most important thing is to keep on writing. It's a tough sell out there, and you won't make it unless you are unusually lucky or have staying power. Also, writers groups really help if you get into one where people have a positive attitude. I have heard of groups where people tear each other down. Nobody needs that.

* * *

The second of these pieces was written by Liz in 1994 for "Writers' Bookshelf," a regular feature in the newsletter of the North Carolina Writers' Network.

Books Writers Depend On

The books that set me on the path toward becoming a writer were rip-roaring page-turners. I had trouble learning to read. I had to go to summer school in the first grade. Had there been ability reading groups in second grade, I would have been in the lowest.

But as I grew older, my aunt Ann Bridgers, who was a playwright, gave me books that were so exciting that I had to read them whether I could or not: *Tom Sawyer, Treasure Island, A Tale of Two Cities, Moby Dick, The Three Musketeers, Twenty Thousand Leagues Under the Sea* and *Les Miserables,* as well as short stories by Edgar Allen Poe and Arthur Conan Doyle. These were original unabridged. Most were complete with long Victorian words.

But nobody stood over me and insisted that I read every word. Nobody told me I wasn't trying if I read a word backwards. I slipped over long words. They were musical mystery. Gradually, as I kept coming across the same word, I learned it from context. If I read something backwards, context kept me on track.

I began to see how a writer could keep the magic going. Because the bones show in a page-turner, even a great one. To any would-be writer, I recommend this whole school of books, modern or ancient, from the works of Homer to the novels of Stephen King.

I'd never heard of a hook, but I soon knew that a great grabbing sentence was the right start. Okay, I admit I went back and checked and some of those great starts that I remember were preceded by a lead-in of Victorian philosophy. But the hooks were there. For example, Poe caught me with: "The sentence—the dread sentence of death—was the last of distinct accentuation which reached my ears," in "The Pit and the Pendulum."

As I read by flashlight under the covers at night, I could see that it was those end-of-the-chapter cliffhangers, put there partly because Dickens was published in installments, that never gave a poor reader a chance to slip away.

And those first few sentences about a new character could be grabbers, too. Such as the description of the released prisoner in *A Tale of Two Cities*: "The faintness of his voice was pitiable and dreadful. It was not the voice of physical weakness, though confinement and hard fare no doubt had their part in it. Its deplorable peculiarity was that it was the faintness of solitude and disuse." Suspense needed to be about people who mattered.

By the time I was 15 years old, I had made up my mind to write some kind of adventure. My father, Jonathan Daniels, wrote editorials that made some people mad and others chuckle. He wrote books about contemporary history. He said writing was a great career and adventure was okay. I was pleased at my choice, and happily oblivious to the difficulties. (Like getting published.)

Then my aunt introduced me to Eudora Welty—first to her writing, then in person. I was inspired. The wonderful gentle Southern comic touch in her writing really got me. I wanted to write stories that would make people smile with recognition at how things are. Even later while I wrote my first mystery, *Kill the Messenger*, I wished I could write like she did. I still do.

I want my readers to do something a little bit like patting their heads and rubbing their stomachs at the same time. I want them to lack the will to stop turning the pages, and I want them to pause and smile. Which means that I, as the author, have to both pat and rub, too—right?

Maybe I have the knack in my upcoming book, *Who Killed What's-Her-Name?*. It's the first of a series about an absent-minded sleuth who has to use her memory tricks to save her own life and solve the crime.

A Tale of Two Cities it's not. I couldn't fit in the French Revolution. I did put in the network of newspaper computers with access to news stories all over the world, and also other information like coroners' reports. Madame Defarge would have liked one of those.

Nobody writes like Welty. I haven't managed that. But I say right-on to reading wildly different kinds of books. Then in the end you have no choice but to be yourself.

(To everyone's loss, Eudora Welty died in July 2001, five months after the death of Elizabeth Daniels Squire.)

If Liz was as gracious and kind to everyone else as she was to me, she will be sorely missed. I had met her—sat next to her once—at a mystery event, but my memories are about something else entirely. Shortly after that event, I saw her letter in Newsweek, *discussing her experiences as a child with undiagnosed dyslexia. This was just after we had learned that our daughter, who had a very good record in high school, but never seemed to care or try, and who then had a series of disasters in college, had herself been struggling with dyslexia all those years. We were in a storm of emotions—relief that it was a problem that could be addressed, terrible guilt that we hadn't recognized it, practical issues of getting proper help—and so I wrote to Liz. Her response then, and later, when I ran into her at a Sisters in Crime event, could not have been more kind and encouraging. I will never forget it.*

Triss Stein

The Early Years

Liz, of course, had a wicked sense of humor and saw the funny and ridiculous side of almost everything. But her life, especially the early years, had its tragic moments. When she was two, Liz lost her mother, who was giving birth to a second child (both mother and child died). After four years of being raised by her aunts and grandmother in Switzerland and New York (after her father, Jonathan Daniels, received a Guggenheim fellowship), Liz went to live in Raleigh with her father and his second wife. Two years later, Liz's half-sister Lucy was born. Lucy is now a novelist, psychologist, and head of the Lucy Daniels Foundation in Raleigh, North Carolina. In 1994, she started off a foundation workshop session with a reminiscence of Liz—as a small girl and Lucy's older sister—who was called "Bibba" by her family. And here it is:

The Magic of Sublimation

From: Dr. Lucy Daniels
March 5, 1994

. . . I've had a lifelong wish to be a sorcerer. It grew out of the contrast between me as a shy, cross-eyed tongue-tied little girl confined in a walled yard, and my eight-years-older half-sister who could come and go as she pleased and loved telling me about all the wonders she witnessed in her travels. These included walking in the storm sewers under Raleigh's Glenwood Avenue, killing a copperhead at the creek, and glimpsing the body when our great-uncle Henry died at our grandparents'.

But even more than that, Bibba—assisted by the audience of trapped and gullible three-year-old me—could do magic on the spot: Make daffodils appear where there'd been none before or make my doll or shoes or other things vanish in thin air. She could see elves that I couldn't see in the hole under the roots of our pecan tree. And if I hadn't been such a scaredy-cat, she'd have made me small *enough to go down there with them.*

As a little girl, Bibba's magic filled me with envious wonder. Only as an adult did I come to understand its basis. Bibba's mother had died suddenly when she was two, and immediately afterward her aunts and our father had changed her name to her mother's. So Bibba's sorcery had really grown out of her intense need for power and control in a world careening out of control. She was driven to feel herself the cause of disappearances and of people turning into other people.

But between the wonder of childhood and the somewhat deflating understanding possible as an adult, Bibba's example had had yet another benefit. Even as she performed her magic, I could glimpse the sadness and anger that motivated it. And therefore, she'd pro-vided my first experience of sublimation, which I'll now define as simply the expression of unacceptable or unbearable feelings in an acceptable and sometimes idealized form. *In this way, sublima-tion allows a means of dealing with emotions that might well be unbearable otherwise. It's a process that I suspect is active in all of us as we struggle to achieve success with our creative products.*

Sublimation has to do with using our pain to make life better. And what's so valuable about this is that we all have pain—at one time or another, in one way or another. There's no escaping it. *Per-haps this is what we most have in common: suffering and trying to rise above suffering while still acknowledging it. Personally, subli-mation has been the basis of my writing. It's also the reason behind the Lucy Daniels Foundation and the Lucy Daniels Preschool. Both are efforts to free people to use their pain to make life better rather than being crippled and blocked by defenses against recognizing that pain.*

. . . Life is hard. That's why it's wonderful when we can find a way to make it better. Sublimation—using our pain to creative ends—is the best example I know of this. It makes me feel like there really is magic in the world such as Bibba showed me in the yard. Only Bibba doesn't have it cornered any longer. The magic of subli-mation is magic available to all creative people. Not just sorcerers. . . .

* * *

Liz wrote about these childhood experiences—the death of her mother, her name-change from Adelaide Ann to her mother's name, Elizabeth Bridgers; the reluctance of her father to tell her about her mother's death, the departure from her aunts' home to live with her father and her new stepmother—in two pieces written while she was in high school, one of which she revised about ten years ago for a writing group she worked with.

First of these is clearly non-fiction and uses the actual names of Liz's aunts. It is entitled "Fragment" and was written (as best we can tell) in the mid- to late-1970s:

Fragment

First memory: I am looking out from behind a set of bars—on a crib, I believe. I am afraid because my mother has gone somewhere. An adult I do not know is half-amused, half-annoyed that I am upset. I hate her—I think it is a woman. I hold on to the bars.

Yet, if I stood in a crib in that glimpse of the past, it must have been from a time before my mother died. About her death when I was two-and-a-half years old, I remember nothing at all. She died in childbirth and my infant brother died with her.

I do remember my father trying to tell me. I was playing with my toys—new toys, I guess, because my mother died on December 18. And my father couldn't bring himself to talk to me about it right away. That is what I learned from my aunts 33 years later when I finally asked. My father wanted my mother's sisters, Emily and Ann, to tell me what had happened. But my two loving aunts had a puritan streak: "She's your child, and you must do it yourself."

"All I remember about that Christmas," my father told me (also 33 years later) "is that I bought you every toy I could lay my hands on." And then finally he came to tell me what I must already have known—that my mother was gone in some mysterious upsetting way. I often knew things that had not been put into words, often knew without knowing that I knew. I understood after my father married my tall, determined stepmother when I was nearly six, that I was never to bring up the subject of my mother. He could occasionally say with tears in his eyes that my mother had been a fine and beautiful woman. But I was to ask no questions, and was to act as if my stepmother had become my mother in every way. My father would have been shocked to know he wanted that. And I only realized it after my own children were born, after they reached the age for asking questions. Then I had to find out more.

For memory is only a shadow on the back wall of my mind: I am absorbed in my world of play. Then my father stands seriously in front of me. I see feet and legs planted too heavily on the floor. He says, "Adelaide, I want you to know your mother has died and taken your little brother to heaven with her."

I want him to go away and leave me alone with my toys. I am annoyed. He tries harder to explain. I feel his intensity, his sense of drama. His desperation. He stands so heavily on his feet. He wants me to understand. "Yes," I say. Don't I have any questions? "No." I only want to continue my make-believe, perhaps with "Bootsie," the smiling baby-doll, even now still in the back of a drawer, cracked and bandaged—but how could I throw her away?

I remember no grief. I do not even remember my father's face.

A picture of him at about that age—about 25—probably from before my mother's death, now hangs on his display wall with signed photographs of three presidents and other memorabilia.

The photographed face is eager, brightly alive, like a confident racehorse at the starting gate. The dark curly hair irrepressibly a little out of place, the eyes ready to snap up any irony, any amusement, any useful fact—like the eyes of a swooping eagle, ready to pounce on dinner. One half of the mouth is almost laughing; the other half turned down with a small tic of impatience. It's an infectious face: even the slight weakness of the chin adds to his charm, makes that face so obviously need love.

There is no charm as part of my memory. I stand with a toy in my hand and try to say whatever minimum thing will make him leave me alone. And there the memory hangs, incomplete. The feelings stronger than the outlines.

I did not give my father what he wanted: a moment of shared grief, a catharsis. I am sorry even now, almost 50 years later. But even now, I also resent his having wanted to use me to sentimentalize his grief. To make it more theatrically satisfying. I'm sure his grief was real. Why do I feel I know what he wanted so many years ago? Ice crystals harden in the eighth vertebra of my spine.

And yet I adored my father. I remember the trap for the maid. That was when we lived in Switzerland with my aunts Emily and Ann after my mother's death. Perhaps I resented being in Switzerland. A later clue from Ann: I went to walk with her in a park. "Let's feed the squirrels," she said. "No," I said, "these are not my squirrels. These are not my trees. The leaves are a different shape."

Also, I did not like the maid. The good-natured, easy-going one I did like had been fired for letting me eat a piece of raw bacon as she prepared a bacon-and-potato casserole. I resented the new woman. So one night, I tied a string across the hall so she'd trip when she came past, a string about a foot off the ground.

Then the doorbell rang and my father was home, full of enthusiasm and laughter. I ran to meet him, down the narrow, brightly lit hall and smacked my face against the floor, hard—so glad to see my father that I forgot everything else, even my own trap.

* * *

And now this short story, written at about the same time as "Fragment." Liz's writing group made comments on the story, especially noting the irony of the title. Liz carried out some of the suggestions in longhand, and we have incorporated this editing but otherwise left the story pretty much as we found it. The cast of characters—and Liz's mother's family were certainly that—includes her grandmother Annie Cain Bridgers, a Christian Science practitioner, a large woman who was the widow of Robert R. Bridgers Jr., son of the founder of the Atlantic Coast Line Railroad; her aunt Ann Preston Bridgers, an actress on Broadway who co-authored a play called Coquette that was Helen Hayes's first starring role on Broadway and later made into a movie starring Mary Pickford; her aunt Emily Norfleet Bridgers, who wore leg braces and walked with crutches due to a childhood bout with polio, ran the WPA Writers' Project in Raleigh during the Depression, and later wrote study outlines for the North Carolina State University's library; and her uncle Robert R. Bridgers III, the inspiration for Liz's short story "In Memory of Jack" (which appears later in this anthology). Liz's mother, Elizabeth Bridgers Daniels, had died in 1928.

A Funny Story

Augusta's large dark eyes under her black bangs seemed too wise for a five-year-old's and gave the impression of being larger than a second look showed them to be. She was a frail child but stood firmly on her feet in her good laced leather shoes from Best & Co.—a lovingly dressed child in hand-smocked pink.

She stood by the small table at the end of the blue couch in her aunts' and grandmother's apartment, in the light of the lamp that glowed because the afternoon was gray outside, and pretended to draw a picture of a dragon. But really she was watching the woman who had come with her father. Augusta understood her aunts Mary and Joy were pretending not to watch the woman too. Her grandmother Lauralee never pretended anything. Her father watched the woman as if she were magic. They all ate Lauralee's dark chocolate cake, served by Joy on the good plates with the gold rims, with silver forks from Lauralee's father's plantation. Augusta wasn't hungry and continued to draw.

She'd been so pleased when her father came. He swept her up in the air and looked at her and laughed. They said she got her black hair from her father. His hair came down on his forehead in a point and waved back. His blue eyes were always looking for jokes.

Augusta watched the woman, who crossed her silk-stockinged

legs one way and leaned that way so the china winged horse on the mantel seemed to sprout from the top of her head. Then she crossed her legs the other way and leaned toward the glass-front bookcase with the sparkly cloth on top. The woman's smile came and went, like the light in the brass lamp with a loose wire that needed to be fixed.

The woman said polite useless things that the child did not bother to listen to. And then, suddenly, she said something in a true voice. She said, "It's important to me to be a successful mother." And then, "Children need discipline. They need to have it made clear to them how they are expected to behave. I intend to do that."

Augusta was so surprised she held her purple crayon perfectly still. She had known as soon as she met the woman that this was somebody who didn't know how to behave. She wore party clothes in the daytime when there was no party.

Maybe the woman was pretty, but she moved too much. If Augusta had been sitting in the straight chair next to Aunt Mary and moving this way and that way all the time like the woman, Aunt Mary would have reached out her cool, calm hand and touched Augusta, and would have said with a quiet smile, "be still."

Instead, Aunt Mary said, "Augusta's things are all packed. We'll mail the toys the way you asked." And the first flutter of panic made Augusta's stomach turn over. She held on to the magic of the apartment, where she had lived since the death of her mother. The green and white winged horse on one end of the mantel, the unicorn on the other. Aunt Joy on the couch, always sitting so straight and sure in her familiar good black suit, her face almost like a valentine. Grandmother Lauralee rocking in the big rocker with the moon face carved in the back—the chair where she sat when she wasn't in the kitchen baking cakes or at her desk studying about God.

But now, what could go wrong while Aunt Mary was so calm in her upholstered chair with padded wings? Even if the woman who'd come with her father now sat opposite Mary's chair and the small dark table where Mary kept anything she might need. She always sat right there, mending or making lists or listening. Her cane hung on the edge of the table and her wooden crutches leaned on the wall in back of her chair. She was beautiful. Not her face, which was too pointed, but her blue-green listening eyes.

"We can't stay but a few minutes," the woman said in her clipped voice that didn't roll and sing like Aunt Mary's and Aunt Joy's.

Augusta rubbed the toe of her right shoe back and forth on the magic rug next to the couch. She wished the woman would be struck by lightning. Augusta was afraid of lightning. The rug was magic to Augusta because the colors were not the same all over the repeated designs, but varied as if the rug had a mind of its own. It was exactly straight on the unpolished wood floor of the living room. Each time Aunt Mary passed it, she stopped and straightened the rug with the rubber tip of her cane.

"We can't stay but a minute," the woman kept saying. And Augusta's father said, "We've only been married three weeks and Nancy arranges all the details of my life for me. I don't know how I got along without her."

The magic of the rug wasn't enough. Even the magic of the cloth on top of the bookcase wasn't enough. Small mirrors were sewn into the embroidery of the cloth. Some were missing but that only made the cloth more exactly itself and not like any other.

Augusta grabbed hold of the day—the day which had been so normal, that began with familiar magic noises. The trashmen down in the street yelling back and forth to each other as they emptied trashcans into their truck, the click of Aunt Mary's crutches as she moved around the apartment straightening up. Mary made a rhythm—thump-and-thump-thump with a click. The first thump was her two crutches together, then the foot in the black shoe without the brace under the bottom, then the foot with the brace. As long as Augusta heard Aunt Mary's crutch-rhythm she felt safe.

For breakfast earlier, Aunt Joy had bought big golden oranges from the fruit man down the street, and Augusta and Aunt Joy had had a race to see who could peel her orange faster as the spicy smell of the peels rose in the air around them.

Then Aunt Joy had taken Augusta to walk on the windy sidewalk, pointing out things that were fun to see—the fat lady walking three dogs on leashes that were getting tangled, or Mr. Jones, who ran the newsstand on the corner, showing off a pumpkin his son had cut for Halloween.

And Aunt Joy had explained the sad things, like the man in the rumpled suit with the collar turned up, selling pencils. This was a hard time, Aunt Joy explained, for people to get jobs. "A depression," she said.

Augusta and Aunt Joy gave a nickel to the organ grinder on the corner, clinking the coin into a dented cup held out by the organ-grinder's monkey in black jacket and cap. Then the old man turned a crank on the barrel organ and music came out.

But when Aunt Mary took Augusta to walk, she would not let Augusta give a nickel to the organ grinder because she said monkeys had fleas. Augusta understood that each person in her life could do some things but not other things. Lauralee could bake cakes but could never find anything. Aunt Mary always knew where everything was, and whether it was important to hurry in order not to be late. And Aunt Mary always had things in her pocket-book that Augusta might need, like pins. And Aunt Joy was in charge of nice surprises, like the record she brought home last week of music to learn to clap your hands in time to. To learn about rhythm.

And her father was in charge of laughing. He was no good at all if Augusta lost her shoes or if she were sick on the floor. And if he was expected to arrive at a certain time, he'd likely come at another time—but he did make everybody laugh.

Sometimes Augusta wasn't sure why what her father said was funny except that partly it was his voice. He had a special voice for funny stories. Yesterday he'd said that whatever Joy couldn't put in the soup, Mary used to mend her underwear. And they all laughed. Laughing felt good.

"The monkey will miss you," Aunt Joy said on that morning walk, "but it will be good for you to be able to live with your father again, now that he is married. Your mother always said that if she died he should remarry."

Something was not right about Aunt Joy's voice. But Augusta had not been too alarmed. Her father came and went. Sometimes he stayed in the apartment with Lauralee and Mary and Joy for several weeks. He came and went in bursts of fun. He had a top hat which he sometimes wore out in the evening—a hat that collapsed into an accordion pancake. He would let Augusta push the cloth so that it would spring up into a hat, and then push it flat again.

But lately he was not always fun. Not when he took Augusta to visit the family of his new wife. An unfamiliar place where people were too polite. Augusta broke out in a fever and her father brought her quickly back to Mary and said, "Here—you take her," as if he were accusing Mary of something. Aunt Mary and Aunt Joy were always here to come back to.

Augusta could barely remember her mother, but sometimes her father became serious and told her she was named Augusta for her mother who had died. Once he leaned back in Lauralee's rocker, where he sat because Lauralee was in the kitchen, and acted as if he were seeing something far away. His hands were loose and dead on the arms of the chair. His voice was shaky, and he said, "Your mother died bringing you a little brother, who died too. . . ." And then he seemed not even to know Augusta was there, and said, ". . . because a doctor made a mistake." And tears came into his eyes, which made Augusta squirm. That wasn't what her father was supposed to be like.

Lately he'd made Augusta uncomfortable again, talking about how she was going to love her new mother, who must never be called a stepmother because that would hurt her feelings.

The new mother, only obviously she wasn't a mother, put her gold-rimmed plate down on Mary's table and stood up. "We have to hurry," she said. "We have errands to do on the way to the train."

Aunt Joy fetched Augusta's small black suitcase and handed it to her father. Joy stood very straight. Sometimes Joy stood straight like that when she was angry. But Augusta's father said she stood that way because she'd practiced walking with a book balanced on her head and her stomach pulled in so she could walk right on stage. Then, when she could walk like a saint, they'd given her the part of a cigarette girl. She'd left the stage to take care of Augusta.

The woman reached down and took Augusta's hand in her long nervous hand. That wasn't right. Augusta waited for somebody to say so—somebody to say stop, don't go. Augusta felt like grabbing the couch and not letting go. Aunt Mary and Aunt Joy each kissed her as if she was supposed to go. Lauralee heaved up out of her chair and gave Augusta a large hug. "Goodbye, darling," she said, "we'll miss you so much." Lauralee smelled like chocolate. She was shaking.

Augusta's stomach went hard at the bottom. Her father smiled as if everything was all right. The woman tugged at Augusta's hand. "We have to hurry," she said. Augusta was numb all over. She pulled away with a quick jerk and said, "I want to take one of my toys." She had to take something from the magic, something to make her a little bit safe.

"You'd only lose a toy," the woman said. "There are a lot of nice toys where we are going. And your toys will be mailed to us."

Augusta's voice raised to a strange high pitch. "I have to take a toy."

Aunt Mary came close, with her familiar rhythm—thump and thump-thump. "How about a very small toy?" she said as if she were commanding.

Augusta's father gestured with his gray felt hat, already in his hand. "O.K., get it quick," he said, and Augusta ran back to her familiar safe room. She looked out at the back of the tall stone building next door. She looked at the picture on the wall of St. Francis feeding the birds. She sat down on the bed with the blue Indian spread with birds in whirls. What would become of her room?

The woman's shrill voice called to Augusta to hurry. The woman might follow her here. Augusta grabbed a golf-ball—she couldn't even remember where she had gotten the ball but it was part of the magic—magic she could carry in her hand. Hard and dimpled and round so she could feel it without looking at it. She hurried back before the woman came into the room.

On the train, Augusta's father and the woman talked and laughed about the place they were going. They touched hands and kissed. Augusta became lost watching people out the window of the train still standing at the station. Black men in uniforms pushed carts with baggage on them. Families followed. One girl Augusta's size followed a woman the size and age of Lauralee. Two women in dark coats like Aunt Mary and Aunt Joy hurried after a tall pile of bags. A father carried a small boy in a snow-suit on his shoulder— the boy smiling as if he was going somewhere he wanted to go.

They were all like framed pictures through the glass window. Then a porter in a white jacket came and made up the berths in their small compartment. He showed them how the toilet was hidden under the seat and the basin hidden in the wall.

And then the porter left and Augusta felt for the safe magic of the golf-ball. Her hand was empty. "When do you remember having it last?" her father asked in what Aunt Joy had called his I-am-being-reasonable voice. There were almost angry lines between his eyes. Augusta could not remember. They could not find the ball. There weren't many places to look—not many unders in the compartment. Everything was built in. Augusta began to cry just as the train began to jerk out of the station, with framed people out the window waving—at who? Augusta began to sob loudly.

"I knew this would happen if we dragged along a toy," the woman said. She sat smoking a cigarette between her long fingers with the red painted nails, legs crossed, frowning. One leg bouncing up and down on top of the other.

Augusta's father tried to change the subject, to tell her a story. He told her she was being silly. And finally, while the woman frowned and shrugged, he told Augusta that in the morning he would buy her another golf-ball. "Look, just please don't cry. We'll buy you another ball." His voice cracked.

And Augusta couldn't help sobbing even harder. "I don't want another golf-ball. I want *my* golf-ball."

Finally Augusta agreed to get in her berth. She climbed a ladder and slid between cold, unfamiliar sheets in a small dark place. She agreed it was unfair to cry so loudly that she kept other people awake. She softly cried herself to sleep, swallowing sobs.

In the morning, the train was passing a new kind of country. The trees had different leaves. The houses were small and far apart.

And her father was doing what he always did when things were wrong—he was trying to make a funny story. Some stories he told over and over again and people still laughed. Augusta could tell by his voice that he was shaping a story he liked. "Can you imagine?" he asked the woman. "She kept us awake all night over losing a golf-ball!" And then he laughed out loud, his blue eyes glowing with light. And he mimicked Augusta's voice: "I don't want a new golf-ball, I want *my* golf-ball!"

* * *

And another story, written in the late 1970s when Liz was working with a writing group led by Sarah Litsey Nye in Redding, Connecticut, reflects on life at a fictional school, obviously modeled on the very real Ashley Hall in Charleston, where Liz graduated in 1944.

In Memory of Wickedness

Did we misunderstand Sally Hite because she was not like us? Her worst sin, perhaps, was arriving at Miss Beauregard's School at mid-term after cliques were already formed. Her second sin was a double-header: being too small-town and too dressed-up all at once—certainly too dressed up for a girl of 15.

Otherwise, her bragging about what she did with boys wouldn't have set us to baiting her.

We had never baited Delight Devore when Delight told us about answering the front door wringing wet and wearing nothing but a bath towel and carrying on a flirtation with the telegraph delivery boy right on her doorstep—and all that when her parents were out. "Oh, Delight, you didn't!" we squealed, admiring her daring.

By contrast to Sally, Delight was one of us. We would never have thought of telling on Delight when she rolled the toilet paper down the school's ornate three-flight circular front stairway, so that the tube, trailing paper like a comet, bounced into the front hall just as the boys from St. Simon's Military Academy were arriving to call on Sunday afternoon. We could always use a little excitement.

At Miss Beauregard's, we were carefully sheltered from all wickedness, and in the South in the early 1940s wickedness still existed. We enjoyed knowing about that, and were convinced that the reason two street-level windows in a classroom on a back wing were painted and nailed shut was because there was a whorehouse across the street, and God forbid that we should see the red light glowing or the customers coming and going after dark. The city had grown around the school, and the side street really was seedy. We laughed at the senior who insisted the windows were painted so that people on the street couldn't stare in on us as we studied math, and we never walked around at night to find out what was outside the windows, because to get outside the large walled garden of Miss Beauregard's required a signed pass entitling this or that girl to be allowed to leave with this or that approved adult. Also, if we had found out there wasn't a whorehouse, we would have been deeply disappointed.

By March we were bored and restless in our walled garden. Then, into the mid-term doldrums of Miss Beauregard's came a large black Cadillac bearing two fat, fluttering women and Sally Hite from Paris, Kentucky. Sally had on a short black jacket of some long shaggy kind of fur that I had never seen before and therefore assumed must be fake; bangle earrings and high heels. And she was chewing gum. Her dark hair was curled too tightly and her black eyes darted about like bugs afraid of being swatted. When I discovered Sally was to be put in the huge, airy four-girl-sized room I shared with Bucky and Annie, I was appalled.

Bucky and I had been at school the year before. We were well-established. Bucky, who was blonde and precociously good-looking—even without the lipstick that was forbidden at Miss Beauregard's—knew lots of boys at St. Simon's. She was a fountainhead of blind dates and giggly discussions about boys. I could tell ghost stories, and sometimes a group of girls would slip into our room after lights out, being careful not to get caught. I'd tell stories until we were all happily scared to death. This was before television even existed, you see.

As for Annie, she was new that year and shy and hard working and followed our lead.

Bucky and I, and even Annie, had had status. Now we had Sally Hite smelling up our room with 220-volt perfume even after she took off her high heels and fur and was told firmly that chewing gum was against the rules. She was not about to subside quietly and follow our lead. First, she sat on her bed and surveyed the room. Then she walked over to Bucky's dresser and picked up the picture of David, who was Bucky's favorite right then. "He's nice looking," she said, without much enthusiasm. "I left the pictures of all my boyfriends at home."

And then Sally began to tell us about her boyfriends: the one who gave her the amethyst ring she was wearing; the one who brought her white orchids for the country club dance back in Paris. Over a period of a week, each story got better than the last, and in spare moments all the girls on our hall, and then girls from all over the school, began dropping in to listen and encourage Sally to tell more and more. My ghost stories had never been so popular.

But there was difference. Sally wasn't accepted. We half-believed her stories and half-expected that she was making them up to impress us. And perhaps that is why we were without pity as we led her on and on to tell more personal and damaging stories about herself. We were daring her to go deep into swift waters, and she was accepting the dare every inch of the way.

I particularly remember her rape story, although that was fairly early on and innocent. Still, it was the first story where she admitted she was not a virgin. Even at 15, we knew that some of us might not be virgins, but we certainly never knew which ones. That was secret. Taboo.

"George was the one who gave me the gold chain I told you about," Sally said. "We were walking out on the golf course between dances, and all of a sudden he pushed me down and made me do it. I was so embarrassed because he broke both my slip straps, and when I came back in the country club you could see where they were knotted because I had on a see-through blouse."

Gradually, the 220-volt perfume and the stories and the eyes that moved around like scared bugs made me think of Sally as less than human. I guess that happened to most of us. We were not really cruel girls at Miss Beauregard's—naïve, protected, inexperienced, boy-crazy, but not bloodthirsty. We laughed at each other unkindly sometimes. I remember when little Lue Bell arrived at the beginning of the year. Her mother had died, so her father sent her to boarding school at 14. We duly noted that her mother was dead and her father was an undertaker. That made her colorful and interesting. At a place like Miss Beauregard's, you needed color and interest. But no pity over her motherless state could keep us all from laughing one hot September evening when the windows were open and the street smells below rose unpleasantly. Lue Bell sniffed carefully, then she turned to her roommate and said, rather loudly, "I smell embalming fluid." Never again did anyone at Miss Beauregard's say "I smell fish." Ever afterwards, it was "I smell embalming fluid."

Now, that was mean enough. But, with Sally Hite, we became bloodthirsty. At a time when a girl of 15 was either a virgin or an accomplished liar or trash, we sat wide-eyed and egged her on to tell us stories about sex with at least six men. Bucky and Annie and I should have warned her to stop. She was our roommate. But then, it was our room she was taking over.

Then, on Saturday, Annie came down with a rash. Did we really believe that it was possible to catch a venereal disease by sitting on a toilet seat right after a woman who had contracted it from a man? Perhaps we were that naïve, or perhaps we wanted to believe it like we wanted to believe in the whorehouse next door to Miss Beauregard's.

Anyway, we persuaded poor little naïve Annie to go down to the infirmary because she might have contracted syphilis from sitting on the seat too soon after Sally. In terror, Annie blurted the story out to the nurse while all the rest of us waited for whatever dramatic development should come next. Syphilis contracted at Miss Beauregard's? It was unthinkable. There were bound to be violent repercussions. We quivered with anticipation.

While we waited, I was even nice to Sally—I mean, really nice instead of polite. I admit she still seemed a little bit sub-human to me. She was so much keener on putting on perfume than washing. But I decided that she was human enough to be hurt and we had thrown our weight towards hurt instead of help. Oh, she would deserve whatever happened to her, and maybe we'd get our lovely airy room back to ourselves. But I was sorry for Sally.

At four o'clock, a teacher went around and asked all the girls in the school except Sally to meet in the parlor. Miss Beauregard welcomed us in a cool, quiet rage.

Every new class of girls discovered with surprise and pleasure that Miss Beauregard looked almost exactly like the picture of Robert E. Lee in their history books: tall, erect, blonde, idealistic and unbending. She was impressive. "First of all," she said, "there never has been a case of a social disease at this school and there never will be. You should know that. How many of you heard a rumor that there was?" Timidly, we all raised our hands. "How many passed that rumor on?" The hands stayed up. "Any of you who have written letters home about this will see me after the meeting." She added crisply, "I am ashamed of you all. One girl who should have known better has said things about herself which make her no longer welcomed at this school. This girl will be isolated in the infirmary by the time you leave this meeting. While we are in church tomorrow, her parents will pick her up. Now, Miss Ernheart will explain to you why it is not possible to catch a social disease from a toilet seat," Miss Beauregard added, pointing to the school nurse. Then she left the room like a general who had done his duty.

I pictured Sally in the Infirmary crying. How awful she must feel to be thrown out of Miss Beauregard's.

About a week later the postcard came. I suppose Sally sent it to me because I had been nice to her that last day. I turned it over guiltily. "Hi," said a scrawling, violet-inked message. "On the train home men brought me my lunch, dinner and chewing gum. Nice to have known you. Sally."

* * *

We have no idea when this essay was written, but it was in Liz's computer at the time of her death. Opinions vary as to what Liz was trying to say here. But here it is, with hardly any editing:

One Southern Family

The nomad of the desert follows a set course—to certain springs and tribal grazing grounds in certain seasons. But the modern American nomad moves at the whim of the tides of opportunity without the advantage or tragedy of a set course. We forget the fatal flaw that can infect a whole family. We have little opportunity to study families, for by the time our neighbors become familiar to us, half of them have moved to the company's branch office in Peoria, or to a new job in Texas, or to Kathmandu.

But 30 years ago in the South, birth had such sway that invitations to parties could be secured by pedigree alone. One impoverished frail old lady survived on the refreshments she studiously devoured at aristocratic parties.

Families had a semi-feudal significance in the South, and a flaw or a virtue infecting a whole family could throw it high into the limelight and crush it in the resulting fall back to earth. Both together, because unusual flaws and unusual virtues go most often hand in hand.

Thus it seemed first a great blessing and then a subtle but deadly curse on one particular Southern family that its members were never able to recognize or share their own despair.

They were brave, gallant, gay—almost all of them. The women carried themselves proudly into the wind like the maidens carried on the prows of ships, but they went barefoot when they pleased—even beneath the glittering shelter of evening clothes in receiving lines.

The men were charming above all else. They had a talent for enthusiastically listening, which flattered and pleased everyone they met. But their enemies claimed that, however charmingly they listened, they never heard. They had the arrogance to be truly democratic in manner—to treat the garbage man with the same courtesy and ironic humor they reserved for the governor. Hence their friends were many, but their enemies were powerful.

Above all, members of this particular family were envied by friends and enemies alike. The poor envied them their money and power, and the rich envied them their popularity—ill-gotten, they felt, for in any political showdown, the loyalty of the family went to

— 22 —

the broad base of hardworking people who formed the largest population group in the state and rarely to the rich and powerful.

It seemed that power came to them almost from God Himself in defiance of the usual early conceptions. Therefore, every member of the family heard one phrase more than any other: "You are so lucky!" They heard it like a symphony—the treble notes of flattery, the melody of sincere belief, and the base notes of anger and envy from everyone they met. Even from each other they heard it, from the time they were small children—"You are so lucky, lucky, lucky."

This was the most damning criticism—of the head of the family in particular, and all the rest of them in general—so those who did not believe they were lucky, out of hypnosis from sheer repetition, came to believe it out of pride as a defense against criticism.

"Oh, Miss Agnes," cried a trembling, fluttering little cousin sitting on the wide porch under a drooping purple clump of wisteria blossom. "Oh, Miss Agnes, you are so lucky! You have everything you want!"

Miss Agnes, the matriarch of the family, smiled regally across the heavy silver tea service set out on the white embroidered linen tray cover on the ornate Sheffield tray. So heavy that only the Negro butler could carry it. She glanced across the wide flagstone verandah into the comfortable house decorated with the cheerful baby pictures of her three sons and the mementos of honors granted her husband—a picture of him arm and arm with a president.

Miss Agnes held her head high, as if facing cheerfully into a storm. "We want what we have," she said simply—and immediately the phrase passed into the mythology of the family.

How can a family know despair if it wants what it has?

Some of you may recall the Thundering Herd booksigning tour that Keith Snyder set up for some of the authors attending the 1996 Bouchercon in St. Paul, MN. I was the driver of the infamous blue minivan with the wood paneling and the short-circuited ding-donging door. To make a long story short, I did fine until we were leaving the last store. We were late, I got lost, I nearly rearended somebody. Liz sat way in the back and stayed the picture of calm. After apologizing profusely to all the passengers, Liz finally piped up and said, in her soft, Southern drawl, "Now, don't you think that we, as writers, deserve a little excitement now and then?" I will never forget that. She always had an interesting perspective to add to the mix.

Anita Slate aka "Smokey" Brandon

Clocks and Demons

"The little old shop on Clark Street was a watchmaker's when I was young," said Grandma. "You think it's dingy, small, and out of place among all the big modern stores, but it wasn't shabby in the old days.

"Thomas Mailan, the owner, had an imagination tucked somewhere under his white wig, and an amount of luck which startled people. Legend had it that the luck was in his grandfather clock, an ornate old piece which he never would sell.

"On Friday night, people said, he opened the mahogany front, and talked to the three demons who lived on the pendulum. Wong, Bong, and Gong, they were called, and if you listened closely while the clock struck, they really did seem to be talking through the chimes.

"Mailan's shop was as strange as the legend. The outside was covered with cuckoo clocks, and although none of them told the correct time, they were set so that one chimed every three minutes. Mailan sat up nights, setting the clocks and winding them, some people said; but most of us believed it was the work of the three demons. 'They take care of all the clocks in the shop, on Saturday nights,' the watchman told my brother. 'I've seen 'em,' he said, and he winked like one who knew.

"When old Mailan died, his son took over and modernized the shop. He had plate-glass windows put in, and he featured expensive wristwatches and those fancy little watches on pins, or on gold chains. He put the cuckoo clocks on a shelf in a corner, and I think the demons must have disliked Mailan the younger because they never wound the cuckoo clocks, or helped in any way.

"Of course, the son had promised his father to take care of the old grandfather clock, and to wind it regularly. For a while, he kept his promise and wound it every Saturday, but he was a careless young man, without much love for superstition. After some weeks, he left the winding to his assistant, a funny little hunchback who wore thick green glasses.

"Mailan supposed himself to be a dashing young man and, accordingly, married one he thought a dashing young woman. He had invited his assistant to be the best man. They had a large and flashy wedding on a Saturday night, and in the rush the assistant forgot his duty as clock-winder. Just as the organ welled into the wedding march, the man remembered.

"Perhaps he was more superstitious than Mailan Junior, or maybe he recalled how his former master would have felt; anyway, he tapped the groom on the shoulder, just as the wedding ceremony began, and he whispered something in the groom's ear.

"'Wind it tomorrow,' said the young Mailan, laughing; and the wedding went on.

"I think the most nervous person there was the best man. I remember that I was sitting in one of the front pews with my sister, and she remarked to me at the time that he seemed unduly fidgety.

"After the wedding, the bride and groom went back to the shop for a suitcase that the groom had left there. They say that just as the wedding party opened the door, the clock tolled forth, slowly and dolefully. Its chiming seemed almost like a curse.

"Mailan tried to laugh, and the assistant turned very pale. They both knew that the clock had always been wound at seven-thirty, and it was then ten o'clock.

"The bride finally spoke. 'The clock's stopped ticking,' she said. 'You'd better wind it.'

"Mailan took the key himself, but nothing would start the old clock. He wound it until the spring was very tight, all to no avail.

"Then a strange and almost funny thing happened. The twenty cuckoo clocks all chimed, one after the other.

"Mrs. Mailan laughed; Mailan looked angry. 'Who wound those?' he almost shouted. There was no answer except the ticking of the cuckoo clocks, and a silence, which should have been filled by the grandfather clock.

"Mailan tried to repair the old clock himself," Grandma concluded. "Then he called in several other watchmakers. They all came to the same conclusion: a vital and irreplaceable part was missing, and had been for a long time. No one could figure out how the clock had run for so many years—that is, they could think of no *rational* explanation. But I thought I knew!

"After a week of useless worry, the young Mailan and his wife went off on their postponed honeymoon. We never saw them again. They say that he lost all his money gambling and drinking. And the shop fell into disuse. The clocks were sold—all but the grandfather clock. No one would buy it. They say that even now, on a windy Saturday night, you can hear the three demons chime the old clock."

* * *

At Ashley Hall, in the early 1940s, Liz wrote a number of poems—which, thanks to the folks at the school, we were able to locate after Liz's death. There is no doubt Liz had not seen these poems in many years. Her official biography mentions that Liz won the South Carolina poetry prize while she was at Ashley Hall, but we have been unable to pinpoint which of these not-very-cheerful poems—if any of them—was the prize-winner.

Murder

How could you know as I was knitting there,
Beside the hearth, in lace cap, and in shawl
That I would kill you when you slumbered off
And close your laughing mouth for once and all.

And yet I saw your eyes were pale with fear
And when you stirred the coals, the poker shook
There for a while I laughed, and laughed aloud
To know I caused that pinched and frightened look.

The wind that whispered in the eves
The coals that cracked and crashed before they died
Were all that sounded as I cut your throat
You slumbered on and never even cried.

Oh, I have washed your blood up off the floor
And now I sit and relish with a smile
The thought of how you fainted dead away
After I had laughed a little while.

Snake Charmer

Thin pipe, a devil's drum,
And a gray snake wavering.
Climbing, dancing, undulating,
To the pipe and a Muslim's hum,
To the song of a beggar savouring
Of sweat and opium;
Circling after the charmer's gaze,
In a dizzy, swerving, graceful maze,
But waiting only to strike and kill,
When the Muslim's haunting tune is still.

Suicide

Drumbeat of rain growing,
Thin song of wind blowing,
Loud splash of waves pounding,
Deep crash of thunder sounding.
Sing me a louder song,
Fiercer and free.
Yell, shout, the night long;
Wail, cry to me.
Rude storm take me;
Rough winds break me;
Throw me dead on a lonely isle,
Where only the buzzards can see my smile.

Greener Grass

Oh, I will stay with you a while,
   drink your reddest wine,
   and watch you smile.
I'll nibble at your choicest food,
   and take for mine
   those things about you that are good.
But when the evening blushes and is dawn,
You may look surprised and hurt
   to find me gone.

                  * * *

There is a house beyond
Where both the wine and conversation are more filling.
I will tarry there to dine if only they are willing.

Disillusion

There were some little hurts I cherished then,
Familiar piquant pains that tore my heart.
I scorned their homely nuisance when
The world was gay; I laughed away their smart.
O little hurts that fled before my scorn,
I was much happier when my heart was torn.
How can I catch your earthy joy again
To fill this aching emptiness called heart.

Summer Sea

The wind is high, the tide is low
And all along the beach,
The shells are left like Neptune's bones
In wind and sun to bleach.

And in the gusty solitude
Are mermaids sitting there,
With the sea to wash their faces,
And the wind to comb their hair.

Contrast

She was warm and full of fun,
We could laugh together;
She was like a swig of rum
O'er the wild heather.

I would ride her lilting voice,
She would smile at me;
Redolent of poppy leaves,
O'er the deep sea.

Now with white hands folded
And eyes straight ahead,
Yellow, waxen, moulded,
She sits and nods her head.

Lullaby

When I am dead and they bury me
Under the soft black ground,
I want the skies to be raining
With a sleepy drizzling sound.
I want the rain drops dripping
From leaf to leaf above me
And singing a sleepy lullaby
To the tears of those who love me.
For only the peace of a slow warm rain
And the peace of a dull grey sky
Can make me fully willing,
And even glad to die.

Christmas 1942

There is no irony in Christmas
Coming to a blood-soaked earth;
In reds of blood and holly mingled;
In tinseled wealth and censored worth.
Nor is there irony in carols
Raised among the bombs by night,
Nor Christmas prayers from toughened fliers
Leaving on some midnight flight;
There is no irony in children
Looking to the Christmas skies
For guiding stars and Nazi bombers,
Gazing up with practiced eyes.
Now in the gaunt, cold face of terror
We look full and laugh aloud;
We love the humble joy of Christmas.
Irony is for the proud.

Slow Dusk

Daisies sway,
A red bird sings,
Flying this way
To test his wings.
Tourists eat
On red checked cloths,
And dusk is sweet
For summer moths.
Lightning bugs
Go on and off;
Sailors wink,
And matrons cough.
The summer night
Is full of sound;
Life and laughter—
Gay, profound.

Landmarks

Here is a power wily, like live hair
And crisp as new straight grass.
Here is a strength, a live white quivering flare
Of self-assurance. Here a dare
To tear up old conventions, wreck the plan—
Built up by self-restraint—that binds a life.
Here is a recklessness that spares no man
As the wild pent-up torrent hurdles forth
Mixed with a strange sweet laughter of release.
Here is a careless, willful scorn of peace—
Glory of ruin and violence and despair.
Now let the rain pelt down like sparks of steel,
Ripping to lifeless shreds the small green leaves.
Now let the wind's dark violence whip the air
Into a furious sea. Oh, let it tear
The old familiar landmarks down.
If I am damned to wear a passive face
And check the flow of passions, watch the glory go
Of willful drunkenness—to change my soul
Into that meekness which the world calls "whole,"
Oh, let the rain erase with brutal hands
These weak dumb objects that have seen my hour
Of unrestraint, with whom I glimpsed brute power.
Let agony of vines blown loose from walls
And splintered trees and bruised and beaten grass
Be all that stays to face the realistic night.
With fierce brutality and massive chaos of sound of day,
Rip the old prosaic worn-out landmarks down.

I am the high school English teacher in Skagway, Alaska. Elizabeth came to our school on February 22, and was kind enough to work with the entire 7-12 grade population that was present. She gave our students some very positive feedback and great pointers on how to write mystery novels, as well as encouraged them to get published. It isn't very often that people of such caliber visit us, as we are fairly remote. She was a very enjoyable person during her visit here. It came as quite a shock to me when I received notice of her untimely passing.

Cheryl May
Skagway English Teacher

The 1960s and 1970s

After her graduation from Vassar College in 1947, Liz worked in New York for a while—first as an editorial assistant at American Home Magazine *(where I had worked years earlier) and then as a psychometrist with Johnson O'Connor Associates, a New York psychological testing firm housed in a mansion on the east side of Manhattan. At this job, Liz specialized in giving tests such as wigglyblocks to the paying customers.*

*In the summer of 1948, we met one weekend in Ridgefield, Connecticut, at the home of Pat McQuaig, who had met Liz at Henry Wallace headquarters in New York—where Pat, Liz, and her aunt Ann Bridgers were all volunteers. We were married in December 1948 and she moved into an apartment I was renting in a remodeled silo in Wilton, Connecticut. Liz immediately discovered that being the wife of the local weekly newspaper editor meant fielding a lot of phone calls, many complaining about stories in the latest issue of the paper (*The Wilton Bulletin*). In 1949, we moved into a small house in Georgetown, Connecticut, where our first son Jonathan Hart was born in 1950.*

In 1952, Liz, Jonathan, and I set forth on the great adventure in Beirut, where I had been invited by Kamel Mrowa, publisher of an Arab-language newspaper, Al Hayat, *to be the founding editor of* The Daily Star, *an English-language daily paper. I stayed with the paper for a year, wrote a report on what I thought should be done to improve the paper, and left to freelance, mainly for* The New York Times. *Subsequently, I joined a group that was planning to publish an English-language weekly paper. It was called An-Nida—that being the name of the newspaper whose license we were using. Liz started writing features for* An Nida, *but we finally closed the paper down for financial reasons. In the spring of 1956, Liz and I returned to Connecticut with our son, six-year-old Jonathan Hart, and his two younger brothers, Mark Mustafa and Worth Paul.*

While I returned to work for Acorn Press, the company that published The Wilton Bulletin, *and later for McGraw-Hill, Liz began working on a project called "Helping Hands," a newspaper feature* about handreading that General Features distributed to more than 100 papers. This evolved into a weekly feature based on celebrity handprints, including those of such people as Carl Sandburg, Eleanor Roosevelt, and Salvador Dali.

Liz loved to tell the story of her encounter with Dali, which took place in the lobby of the St. Regis Hotel in New York. When Liz arrived at the hotel for the appointment, with red-ink stamp-pad at hand, she asked the concierge to please let her know when Dali appeared in the lobby. "Don't worry," the concierge said, "you'll know him when you see him." During the resulting handreading, Liz made a print of Dali's hand and asked him to autograph it. Dali being Dali, he scrawled his inimitable signature across the entire handprint—and this was the way it ran in the column.

In addition to the newspaper feature, and of course raising children, Liz began work on a book based on the feature. Titled Fortune In Your Hand, the book—Liz's first—was published in 1970 by Fleet Press, an offshoot of General Features Corp. It is still in print from three different publishers including an edition in Italian.

In the early 1970s, Liz went to work for a new weekly newspaper, The Redding Pilot, published by Acorn Press. She doggedly covered auto accidents, floods, murder trials, and board of education meetings. Later, her work evolved into feature-writing for the Acorn Press papers in western Connecticut and eastern New York State. But she was already at work on another non-fiction book—this one based on interviews with American Field Service exchange high-school students from a number of foreign countries. AFS International was started by AFS ambulance drivers (of whom I was one) at the end of World War II. AFS now arranges something like 10,000 such exchanges each year. Here is the introduction to that work, never before published:

Growing Up Around the World

When students learn how it feels to grow up in a place with different weather, with a different kind of land—maybe an island, maybe rough mountains—or with different history and customs, they see the world and their own lives in a more meaningful way. High-school exchange students from other countries agree about this. Students become more aware of exactly the way in which their own countries are unlike others.

During his year in Connecticut, Hiroyasu, who came from Tokyo, found that Americans often asked him, "Why are you so quiet?" That set him to thinking.

"In Japan, we have a different philosophy, which originated in ancient China—'think before what you say,'" said Hiroyasu. "But here in America, you speak before you think, and then watch people react."

After his school year in Connecticut, he said, he could see why Americans "express thoughts while thinking—because you have to communicate with people from all over the world with many different ways of doing and thinking, and you need to talk and discuss it. Japanese, though, have so much in common that they don't need to talk so much."

Growing up in an island group where the same basic racial group has lived for thousands of years, this boy from Japan is more aware of how this has shaped his way of looking at the world. He spent a school year in an area of Connecticut where many families have moved from other parts of the States, and where many people are the sons and grandsons of those who moved to the United States from other countries.

An American boy who lived in Japan for a time saw much the same things both about Japan and his own way of growing up, but from the opposite side of the coin. He said:

"In America, we all came over on different boats from different parts of the world, and are united only by patriotism. But in Japan there are such strong bonds of sameness."

Then he could understand the Japanese manner of humbleness which had made him uncomfortable at first. A Japanese schoolmate would say to him, "I can't speak English well, but you are good in Japanese," when plainly the opposite was true. A Japanese mother, he found, would never brag about her children but, instead, brag about her friends' children. This was quite unlike the United States, where even some of our folktales glorify bragging. One of the heroic deeds of Davey Crockett, the American frontier hero, was to win a bragging contest.

A common American expression is, "If you don't place a high value on yourself, who will?"

The American visitor to Japan came to the conclusion that the Japanese manner of humbleness grows from the cultural unity of the Japanese people. For, he decided, "the personal ego is not as important" in Japan because of the "sharing of thought on all kinds of things." There seems to be, he said, "a feeling for the whole family, the whole culture—rather than 'me, me, me.'" He could see that in Fukui, the part of Japan where he visited, people carry their sense of loyalty to the group so far that often the people in a business firm would all take their vacations together.

But are there really many great differences among people who grow up in varied places? Aren't people basically all alike? Students interviewed for this book agree that people are better able to see how alike they are when they come to understand their differences.

How would a man who had spent his life in Vermont feel if he passed a house and saw the family run out the door naked in January, roll in the snow, and then run back indoors again? A polite hostess in Mississippi would not be likely to feel she was insulting a guest by crossing her legs in a comfortable position with a toe pointed toward the visitor, would she? Yet there are parts of the world where a naked dip in the snow in January is utterly respectable, and where a toe pointed at a visitor is the greatest of insults.

In Finland, the sauna bath is a widespread custom. When children are small, whole families take saunas together. When they are older, boys and girls generally bathe separately. Water is thrown on hot rocks to create steam. When everyone in the sauna is perspiring freely, the group runs out to roll briefly in the snow or, in summer, jump into a cold lake. Then, back to the sauna. "Exhilarating!" says an American visitor. If someone should be passing by when the family is rolling in the snow, no immodesty is involved because the person passing will discreetly turn his head away, according to Jarmo, a Finnish exchange student. In fact, he adds, if someone stares at people practicing the national custom of sauna, he would be considered "something weird."

An American girl who stayed in Finland and took saunas at her host-family's lake cottage agreed that the Finns are so unanimous about not staring at sauna bathers that she did not feel uncomfortable rushing out of the sauna naked and jumping in the lake. She knew that if a boat happened to be passing on the lake, people in the boat would look the other way. Yet she would never have practiced the same custom in the United States, where staring at people who rush outdoors naked is not considered weird at all.

As for pointing your foot at someone, even inadvertently—that is considered such a disrespectful and insulting gesture in Thailand that the first thing an American must learn if he goes to live among the Thais is to avoid this absolutely. The gesture is considered far worse than thumbing one's nose at someone in America, a girl from Bangkok explains.

And an American girl who lived in Thailand explained that during her year with a Thai family she saw the proper gesture for each kind of person carefully practiced. In contrast, on her return to the United States she became aware of a kind of social chaos— that Americans have few set guidelines on how to treat anyone, except, of course, that they would not go around thumbing their noses too often.

Each country is unique in ways other than the usual ways we learn—what it imports or exports, what its form of government is. This book is about exchange students from other countries who lived in the United States and tell what it was like to grow up, by comparison, in their own countries. "Of course," says a Turkish student, "none of us can say she represents her whole country, any more than I can say the family I stayed with in America is like all Americans—I can only represent myself and my family."

But while each student is shaped by life in one family in one economic class, in one city or town, in one country—and tells about it from the point of view of one person, boy or girl—he can indicate the marvelous variety of ways of learning how people of other cultures live.

In Morocco, said a student from that country, "children have the freedom to take responsibility when they are very young." If a girl's mother is out, the girl will consider she is the head of the household and take responsibility. Young boys are often left in charge of their fathers' shops. So this girl considered Moroccan life "freer," in a way, than that of her American contemporaries, although she was not allowed to date boys when she was a senior in high school in Morocco—a restriction that would have made many American seniors feel they had no "freedom" at all.

The exchange students discovered that, not only do they have to learn exactly what people in other countries mean by the words they speak, but that gestures don't mean the same thing everywhere, either. In Yugoslavia, when two boys who are friends meet, they often kiss each other as part of the greeting. Dragan, a Yugoslav exchange student, quickly learned that, in New York State, a boy who kisses another boy is doing something regarded as odd. Nikita, a girl from Ghana, discovered that when she stood as close while talking with a friend in Pennsylvania as she would in Ghana, the friend backed away. At first, Nikita felt insulted, and her friend was thrown off base when forthright Nikita said, "Hey, what's the matter—do you think I'm going to spit in your face?" Then they both realized that how far you stand from a casual friend to talk is different in the United States and Ghana. And they saw, further, that this difference could make an American student—used to standing at a greater distance—feel crowded, and a Ghanaian student—used to standing closer—feel hurt, unless both know that the normal distance for conversation is not the same everywhere.

And the normal way to express feelings can vary widely. A New England girl who lived in Finland said she had to learn to figure out what her reserved Finnish friends were feeling. By contrast, her New England friends seemed very outgoing. But Yvette, a Bolivian girl who came to New England, said her family and friends in the United States were extremely reserved compared to Bolivians, "who laugh and cry easily."

In fact, when Yvette first met her American family, she rushed over and hugged her new mother and father and kissed them on both cheeks, in the Bolivian manner of greeting. She was about to do the same to her new 16-year-old North American "brother" when she noticed the look on his face: pure alarm. He had expected a handshake.

It is not just words or gesture or posture that may have a changed meaning, depending on where and how a person grew up— even the conception of time varies. People say they do not feel time passing in the same way everywhere. To a boy from Afghanistan, the rapid pace of life in the United States was a shock. And an American girl who lived in Afghanistan for a school year said, on her return, "Time means nothing to people there—if a plane is twelve hours late, it is no problem."

A boy from Morocco says people there take time to enjoy life, while an American who visited Morocco saw this perception of time as related to a more fatalistic view of life than the American. "Americans feel you have to get hold of yourself and make something out of your destiny," he said, "while Moroccans take a more relaxed attitude toward the way they use time because they believe a thing will happen only if it is Allah's will, anyway."

Several exchange students who lived in suburbs in the United States expressed amazement at the way some Americans use space. "Everything is so spread out that you can't go anywhere without a car, while at home I can walk almost anywhere I want to go," said a girl from Turkey's capital of Ankara.

An American girl who lived in Thailand noted that privacy, as she knew it, was not valued there. People did not choose to be by themselves, and when she indicated to her hosts she would like some time alone once in a while, they worried that perhaps she was ill. Yet a French girl found some matters she considered very private were not considered so by her United States friends. She was shocked when they asked "Do you have a boyfriend?" soon after they met her. In France, a boyfriend is a very personal matter and no one would ask about that, she said. A person's family life is private, too, and members of a family do not ask acquaintances to visit in their homes, but take them to cafés. Only close friends visit at home. By contrast, she noticed that her American family liked her to bring friends home.

There are places in the world where, except for the biological fact that girls grow up to be mothers and boys fathers, there is little difference between a girl's life and a boy's life. Yet in some places, quite the reverse is true. Japanese students recommended strongly that the chapter in this book on growing up in Japan should be based on interviews with both boys and girls—so differently do they perceive and experience life. A Japanese boy found it hard to get used to the fact that American girls are sometimes noisy and forthright, for a Japanese girl who behaved that way would not be considered feminine or a desirable mate. By contrast, in Finland, boys and girls do not live sharply contrasting lives. A Finnish boy says he believes the northern town where he lives is typical in the custom that boys and girls usually share costs equally when they go out on dates—fair enough, he adds, when they can expect to earn equal salaries.

Most of the exchange students we talked to said women receive equal pay for equal work in their countries, although some of the girls said women cannot always get the same jobs—or the same respect on the job—as men. "Why is it always the women who have to serve tea in some Japanese offices?" asked a Japanese girl whose mother and father are both successful in business.

A surprise to many American students is that boys and girls from countries where they have less freedom to see each other alone do not necessarily find this unpleasant. In fact, such students report some advantages. In Morocco, girls do not openly go out with boys because, a Moroccan student says, it would make the girl's parents unhappy. But some of the more daring girls have secret dates with boys. "It is simpler to go out with boys in the United States," one of the "daring" girls told us, "but there is something disappointing about it. Boys in America do not value the company of girls as much."

Some basic values take amazingly changed form from place to place. Take cleanliness, for example. Some Americans go to great lengths to see that they, and their clothes, are spotless at all times—so much so that the United States is nicknamed the "bathtub culture." Yet these very bathtubs amazed two Turkish students, who said that in their country you are taught that, to be clean, you must bathe in running water, or else you end up sitting in a pool of your own washed-off dirt. "But I have to admit," said one of the Turkish students, laughing at how shocked she had first been at the U.S. way of bathing, "that Americans do get clean" in bathtubs. But by contrast, an American who lived in a Turkish village said she felt at first that things in the village could not really be clean because of all the flies there. Then she became aware of how the Turks' religion requires them to wash five times a day, before prayers, and how people take off their shoes on entering a house, to keep the inside clean.

Another surprise was to find that what students said they liked about their own countries was not always what someone from another country would expect. What one person regards as a drawback is seen by someone else as a great advantage. A student from Bolivia saw how her American family enjoyed television in the New York area, where there were a variety of channels and many good shows to choose from. But she was pleased that there is just one Bolivian television channel and that does not come on the air until 10 a.m. The wonderful variety of U.S. television shows means that TV "is replacing your friends and your goings-out," she told her friends in the New York City area. By contrast, Bolivians still visit a lot and play golf or tennis or basketball or other sports almost every day.

A student from South Africa who had considered the schools there too strict approved of those strict schools after a year in the U.S., saying, "They are so nice and quiet!" A boy from New Zealand told with pride how few social activities there are for young people in his town, making them resourceful.

The many ways exchange students perceive the world, while they search for greater international understanding, is what makes their comments interesting. While there are now a number of international student exchange programs, one of the earliest—and still the largest—is the AFS International scholarship program, and the interviews in this book are with students taking part in the AFS program, either as foreign students in the United States or as Americans studying abroad.

AFS has set up also an exchange program within the United States, where students live for a time in a community with a cultural heritage unlike their own. For, as a Turkish student observed, there can sometimes be as much diversity in ways of life within the borders of a large country as between that country and another.

But while we may be aware of some of the varied kinds of citizens in our own country—from Mexican Americans to Maine lobstermen—often our knowledge of the many ways young people grow up in other countries is almost nonexistent.

Liz was as sweet a lady as I've ever known, and also had one of the most sly senses of humor.

Toni L. P. Kelner

---

*At about this same time—the early 1970s—Liz joined Sarah Lit-
sey Nye's writing group in Redding, Connecticut, for which she wrote
a number of short stories. Here are several of them:*

Solutions

"You are going to get in trouble some day opening the door to
any stray sad person that comes along," Mr. Hanlon told his wife.
But she never did—until October 5.

Then, the man who stood at the door polishing his glasses
looked frail, worn out, but basically high-minded like the pictures
Mrs. Hanlon had seen on television of Woodrow Wilson in his last
illness. The stranger pushed his pale-rimmed glasses back astride
his thin Roman nose and said good morning in such a gentle,
courtly, old-fashioned way that Mrs. Hanlon half expected him to
bow.

"How do you do," he said. "I am collecting a fund to help start a
colony on Mars."

If he had not looked so earnest as he held forth a coffee can
with a picture of an assortment of celestial bodies painted in gold
and blue on the outside, she would have laughed.

What a morning! First there had been a seedy-looking man with
bloodshot eyes looking for work. Since the mill had closed two
months before, that was not such a surprise, but Mrs. Hanlon lived
in a small apartment that was part of a two-family house. Her land-
lord took care of the yard as part of the arrangement. She took care
of the apartment herself and thought it was good training for the
two children to help. There was no work.

The man looked so desolate and hung-over that she imagined it
would be hard for him to get work at all. She was reminded of her
own father, hangdog and hungover on occasions and rarely managing to get work. Of course, he had been under painful pressure,
unable to support his big family properly during the Depression.
But it hadn't helped any when he spent part of his meager pay-
check on cheap liquor and stood on his head in the middle of the
main street and crowed like a rooster. The memory was so painful
that Mrs. Hanlon had gotten indigestion from fried chicken ever
since.

"I have three children," the man at the door said, and Mrs. Hanlon realized by the way his eyes clung to her face that this was his
way of asking for a handout.

"I can't bear to think of you and your family hungry." She sighed
dubiously. She gave him the money in the cookie jar that she was

saving toward a good waffle iron. There was not a great deal. Mrs. Hanlon always gave it to somebody before it mounted up. She looked the poor man in the eye and emphasized, "Promise me you won't spend it on drink," and all the force of a lifetime backing temperance movements rang out in her tone of voice.

At first glance, the Woodrow Wilson type, though possibly insane, seemed less depressing than the man with bloodshot eyes. At least he was trying to do something, not drowning his fears in a bottle. His brown suit was worn at sleeve and trousers cuff, his shirt was frayed at the back of the collar, but he managed to look eminently respectable. Even his celestial coffee can was painted in muted tones of gold and blue. There was nothing flashy about the gentleman.

"A colony on Mars soon is the only pleasant way to save the human race from itself," he explained in his gentle cultivated voice.

Mrs. Hanlon smiled kindly. "I'm sorry I can't help you, but I really like to give to things close at hand, like the fund being raised in our church to send Bobby Upchurch to Scout camp. Mars seems a little out of my line. I have enough trouble just coping with the problems on this block. I'm going to leave outer space to the government." She noticed there were only two dimes in the coffee can.

Nothing daunted, the gentleman took a step closer. The leather on his polished black shoes gaped slightly where it was cracked at the side of the toes. "This great nation is built on the cornerstone of individual initiative," he intoned. "When the going gets difficult we have to get out and help the government. Our government has a great problem which will soon be too difficult to manage—people!"

Mrs. Hanlon was slightly alarmed—after all, she was a person herself—but the man looked so sensitive and well-intentioned that she could hardly suspect foul play.

"People are multiplying too fast! Soon, we shall have too many people in the world for the space and the food supply; and soon," he added, taking a deep breath, "even too many for the air available to breathe! I used to be a college professor, and I have done a comprehensive study of population trends. And I know better than any man in the world what trouble is engulfing us. Why else do we have war scares and international crises? Too many people!

"And multiplying all the time." He glanced apprehensively at the children playing tag in the yard next door.

Poor man, a little off his nut, but not dangerous, Mrs. Hanlon decided. He looked so tired, so discouraged. "I can't give you any money," she said, "but I just made some cupcakes. Why don't you have a cup of coffee and a cupcake?"

He looked as grateful as if she had offered to donate a rocket ship. He sat down diffidently at the chrome-legged table, eyeing with admiration the cupcakes in their pleated yellow paper cups. "You are very kind. Chocolate is my favorite flavor, as a matter of fact. . . ."

Then he continued with his chosen subject. "There are only a few possibilities that can save us. I've done a survey on that, too. What do people do when there's a surplus? I started with islands, that is the best way to do any study. Microcosm, you know."

"Excuse me if I begin cooking supper," begged Mrs. Hanlon. "My children get in a terrible humor if they have to wait for supper."

"Exactly," the man said. "It is the same on islands. Now there are several possibilities to keep people in line with the food supply. A crash program of starting colonies is the pleasantest. But there are others that have worked quite effectively. War, of course, but we can only indulge in civil war these days—global wars are too dangerous." He wagged his forefinger at her. "We want to see the population reduced, but not entirely. Then there is cannibalism— effective, though sometimes people's eating habits are the hardest of all to change."

Mrs. Hanlon wished that he would not bite into the cupcakes with quite such gusto. She could not truly grudge the poor man the fact that he was eating the whole plate she had planned for her own family's dessert, but she wished he would not bite with such ravenous deliberation and talk about cannibalism at the same time. His long white front teeth sank savagely through the brown icing and into the pale heart of each cake as though he had not eaten for a week—which, of course, was possible.

Fiercely as he ate, he paused after every few bites to continue his lecture. "Of course, there is human sacrifice, and legal enforcement of birth control. I tried to work for compulsory birth control, but so many people think that is a personal matter. Also. . . ." He lowered his eyes, carefully flicked a crumb off his dark blue tie, and added with some embarrassment, "Some housewives get the wrong idea if you knock on the door and start right in to talk about sex.

"People enjoy lotteries," he added.

"Yes," she cried eagerly. Any change in subject, however irrelevant, would have pleased Mrs. Hanlon, who was so naturally tenderhearted that it made her feel sad to put out poison for the ants in this spring, and so naturally modest that she would walk around the block to avoid two dogs breeding on the sidewalk. "Our church raffles off a car every year to help raise funds. Oh, I do think lotteries are a wonderful idea."

"If my efforts fail to raise funds for a crash program for a colony on Mars, I am going to propose human sacrifices based on a national lottery. People love to gamble. Look how they play the numbers racket even when it is illegal. This will be legal. You will have the chance to win a lot of money or lose your life—the essence of adventurous gambling. That will make people cheerful about it. Motto: Double or nothing.

"Of course, you have to be fair about these things." He talked more loudly. The supper preparations involved noisy pounding. "If the lottery fails because people do not like that big a gamble, I will work for cannibalism based on security. A certain guaranteed life span to each person. Base the whole thing on an age span the way you do with chickens. Everybody gets to live until he reaches the perfect baking age." He finished the last cupcake, sighed deeply, and said, "You have been too kind. How can I thank you enough?"

"Why, think nothing of it." Mrs. Hanlon wiped her hands on her apron. She had been pounding veal for Veal Parmigiana, half hoping to miss some of the gentleman's comments. But she had not missed the comments and now had the uncomfortable feeling that she had splattered blood on her hands. Totally unfair, this feeling. Lady Macbeth deserved it, but Mrs. Hanlon's greatest sin was being too kind. "I'd be glad to do anything to make you feel more cheerful."

"You are right," he said. "I get too easily depressed. I keep feeling I am going to fail in this crusade, and the alternatives do depress me. I am going to keep at this no matter what for six more months, though the response has not been encouraging." He looked sadly at the two dimes in the coffee can.

"If I come around again, I'll be raising money for the next least depressing idea—the national lottery."

By the following spring, Mrs. Hanlon had nearly managed to forget the man who had stricken Veal Parmigiana from the menu. A cruel chance, since her Italian mother had given her an especially good family recipe, and she had been famous for it. Her husband kept begging her to make it.

One balmy day when the leaves were greening and the birds were singing, she answered the door, and there, frailer and seedier but just as dignified, just as Woodrow Wilsonesque as ever, stood the sad old man.

"No," said Mrs. Hanlon, "don't say a word. I couldn't bear it. I'll get my pocketbook." To three dollars from the pocketbook she added six from the cookie jar. The old man's hand shook with feeling as he took it, and she could see he was searching for phrases to show the degree of his gratitude. Probably nobody had ever given him that much before.

"Not a word," she repeated. "I am giving you this money on one condition, and I want you to promise me one thing only. Don't spend it on one of your causes. Go to the nearest tavern and get yourself some supper and above all a couple of good stiff drinks."

* * *

I relate especially to the following story because it's largely based on descriptions I fed to Liz every weeknight on my arrival home in Wilton, Connecticut, after traveling on the nearly defunct New Haven Railroad in the 1960s. Those who did not go through that period of commuting from Connecticut to New York (and, one hoped, back again) can hardly believe what conditions were—but I can say there's no exaggeration here:

Khetu and the Branch Line

Alfred P. Arthur and the plain neat woman with the store-bought pie missed the early train on February 4, 1962, Doomsday. Naturally, Alfred was not a Hindu. He was a Congregationalist. He did not believe in astrology—well, not really. But he suspected that if an officially declared day of doom arrived for anybody, it would include him. There was an invisible planet called Khetu which, according to the Sunday *Times*, nobody at the Hayden Planetarium took seriously. Nevertheless, astrologers, and especially Hindu astrologers, said it was reaching an alignment in the constellation Capricorn which would cause disasters, possibly the end of the world.

Khetu planet could certainly spot Alfred as a natural for any disaster it had in mind. In the last year his pump had collapsed, his furnace had exploded, the Canadian stock on which he had hoped to make a killing out of his savings had fallen flat. To make ends meet, he secretly took peanut butter sandwiches to work in his brief case and ate them behind the closed door of his private office. Those were the dramatic troubles, the suns in the constellations of worries, but there were thousands of lesser troubles orbiting the larger ones. The fender on his car was dented, for example, because he had been thinking about his troubles when he should have been concentrating on the traction between the wheels of his car and the ice on Pitchfork Road. And so on.

Until lately, Alfred had thought of himself as a pleasant and promising young man. His two plump blonde little girls had squealed with joy over his bedtime stories—they preferred the ones about choo-choo trains. His gentle, innocent-eyed wife had taken great pains to show her pleasure in his homecoming every night by looking her best in a luscious colored sweater, hair freshly combed, smelling of carnation soap, because as he turned in the drive she always washed her face and combed her hair to arrive dewy fresh at the front door. She had always laughed at his jokes with the overflowing glee of a happy child—until lately. This year a worry line was engraving itself between her eyes, and the new baby on the way left her exhausted at night.

It was foolish, but as he got discouraged he began to think more and more in terms of omens. Once, he found himself tempted to walk from the office to the station without stepping on the cracks of the sidewalk in order to bring himself good luck. It was a game he had played with himself as a child on the way to school in the city. "Really, pull yourself together, man," he told himself.

"And, you know," he said to tall cheerful John Wiesser, friend and neighbor who sat next to him on the late train on Doomsday, "the worst thing is that I have come to think of the train as a sort of an omen of the fact that my world is disintegrating. Every week that I commute the train looks more patched together with duct tape, and it depresses me because it looks exactly like I feel. The train and my state of mind are the same."

"Good lord," said John, "not that! I get discouraged myself because people who don't ride the train won't believe the stories I tell about it. They take it all for a good old American tall tale like Paul Bunyon's blue ox. You mustn't let the train affect your state of mind. That would be fatal! Besides, your world isn't disintegrating. You've just had a streak of bad luck."

Involuntarily, they both looked around at the familiar train. The rail line was having its troubles, and it was economy proud—quite happy to have its efforts at frugality blatantly obvious. Duct tape did seem to be the favorite mending material. An X of it criss-crossed a small hole in the window that looked like a bullet hole, though more likely was witness to the large number of children who lived near the track and too frequently threw stones at the train. Splits in the window shades were mended with the same tape.

The floor was pockmarked composition in squares, probably once black-and-white checkerboard, now variations of worn and eroded gray. Two by two, the seats were bound together by their chrome trim like Siamese twins fastened at the backbone. The windows too were set in chrome, and all this silvery trim was beginning to be crusted with brown lacy spots of rust. The lights in the ceiling cast a yellowed flicker strained through the bodies of hundreds of tiny bugs which had somehow crawled inside the china globes that covered the lights, and there died.

"You mustn't take the train as an index of your state of mind," John repeated. "That would be fatal."

"Maybe that's the effect that Khetu had on me," Alfred gloomed. "Fatal."

His friend looked alarmed. He had known a number of commuters who had found the pressures of working in the city in very competitive jobs—and living in the country in very competitive houses—too much. There had been a suicide and several nervous breakdowns in the peaceful-seeming little country suburb where they lived.

John assumed the manner of a kindergarten teacher on a rainy day. "Look how pretty the lights out the window look."

At that moment, a distraught man carrying an old gray trench coat came marching down the aisle to the water cooler, stomping his feet so loudly that the two friends turned and watched him even before he reached their line of vision. He had the narrow-eyed, panting look of one who crosses the desert closely on the heels of a watery mirage. Just behind him the tired black-suited stoop-shouldered conductor was punching tickets.

The man took one of the white conical cups out of the holder, sighed thirstily, and pushed the proper button to produce cool clear water. Nothing happened. He pushed it in little jerks, as though to loosen it up. Nothing happened. He banged the water cooler with all his force, reminiscent of a stage hero who is shouting "Let me in, let me in!" Nothing but the conductor appeared.

"You can see there's no water there," the conductor said with annoyance. "Go try in another car."

The man turned purple. "There are nine cars on this train," he shouted. "This is the last car. I've tried them all."

The conductor shrugged. "Well, I was afraid of that. There hasn't been any water on this train in months."

The possible murder of the conductor was averted by another catastrophe. Was Khetu warming up for something big? A train wreck? The end of the world?

The scrubbed faded little woman held her pie on her lap, in a thin white cardboard box with a cellophane window in the top. Forward of her sat an extremely elegant couple—the man in a blue pinstriped suit, the woman with a large and expensive artificial rose on her hat. Suddenly, with no warning, the back of their double seat completely collapsed so that they lay virtually in the lap of the frightened little woman with the pie. The couple lay for a moment rigid with surprise, as elegant and still as if they were laid out for their own funeral. Then they sat up and began to apologize, declare their innocence, and hurl biting insults at the railroad all at once with the staccato gestures of an old silent movie. The plain woman's pie had been custard. It had spurted all over her, looking entirely out of place as one spurt dripped down like a sad mustache on her clean thin-lipped humorless face.

The elegant couple flushed with embarrassment and anger, while the pale little woman merely looked resigned and surprised, touching a drip of custard on her black dress gingerly, as though she hoped to find that it was not really as gooey as she expected.

"It is unfortunate," said John, "that the train is out of paper towels." Alfred said nothing.

Fortunately somebody had a package of facial tissues to lend the little woman. The car rearranged itself. The conductor hid in a corner. Peace descended. Newspapers rustled.

John was just wondering what effect all these failings of the train would produce on Alfred when he noticed Alfred's mouth rounding into a horrified circle, his eyes staring in alarm. Alfred jumped up as if he had sat on a bee, and shied out of the seat. A column of hot steam rose from the floor where his feet had been and hissed toward the ceiling. Two young girls with schoolbooks in the seat across the aisle began to giggle uncontrollably, and somebody said, "This trip beats all!"

As they moved to another set of seats, Alfred turned red and his mouth set in a grim line. "This is the last straw," he whispered to himself.

One of the things that bothered him most was that, like most of the commuters, he had to dress with great propriety to keep his job. A dark suit with the knee creases sharp, dark shoes. His uniform was quiet good taste. So he took part in the calamities of the train dressed in his best—like the wives of Henry VIII who carefully powdered their noses in order to look regal in the eyes of the world at their executions. The steam, if greasy or gritty, might have ruined his pants, his indispensable uniform.

They were almost to the familiar causeway that arched the track at their own station, before the electric flash. It was at the front end of the car. A gangly nervous young man sat there, too old to be strictly adolescent, too young or possibly too inexperienced to look entirely comfortable in his tan suit, which was still new enough to have the original stiff store pressing.

There was a yellow spurt of light and a report almost loud enough for a homemade bomb. The young man sprang so high and so straight into the air that he suggested the automatic ejector seat on a supersonic airplane. It was too much to expect that a flat-broke railroad had installed automatic ejector seats, no matter how great the need. Plainly the young man rose on the wings of sheer terror. And plainly he stuttered.

It must have been a long-standing stutter—no mere fly-by-night stutter could have gained such magnificent momentum: "Je Je Je Je J J J J J Jesus H H H H aich C C C C C C Christ." He landed back on his seat open-mouthed to find himself virtually unharmed. And, still stuttering as rapidly as an electric cement breaker, he began to tell his story in the soprano voice of hysteria to anybody who would listen.

Alfred P. Arthur got off the train with his friend John Wiesser and stood in the moonlight next to the beautiful stark black outline of a bare tree. And right there, watching the train sway into the distance, he began to laugh. He laughed so hard he could hardly stand. His dark overcoated figure bent almost double under the pale station lights.

"Are you all right?" John asked tensely.

"Yes!" he cried. "Yes! Look, the whole world is not like the railroad car! The moon is still shining."

Somewhat to the horror of the other passengers, the two friends went off singing, only slightly hysterically.

The two young girls had left the train at the same station. They stared after the two gray-haired men singing in the moonlight. "I wonder," said one to the other, "if it was all too much for them, if their minds have snapped? You know what they say about today? It's supposed to be a day of terrible disasters."

But the next morning Alfred P. Arthur was back on the train. The *Times* reported Khetu had moved out of the critical alignment in Capricorn. There had been no world-shaking disasters. The outlook for the future, though dark, was improved.

Alfred picked off a piece of duct tape, intended to mend the train seat, from his carefully pressed pants.

"On the whole," he said, "I think I'll miss Khetu. It was rather nice for one day to think this all made sense."

Liz and I sat next to each other at the Saturday night LEFT COAST CRIME dinner. We talked mostly about her trip to Skagway the following week, as I'd been there previously. Liz was really looking forward to the visit and we made a date to get together at Malice to chat about Skagway.

I'm deeply saddened by her death. Liz brightened every room she entered and made a friend of everyone she met. Peaches Dann may have a memory problem, but Liz will long live on in mine.

Kate Grilley

And written at about the same time is this somewhat more ambitious story:

The Man Who Collected Himself

"You wouldn't think being born could be an anticlimax, would you?" Chester emphasized the word *born* in his cynical, insinuating, heavy voice. He raised an eyebrow in a bored arch and waited.

He usually got a laugh, or at least a grin, with a remark like that, if only because it was so obvious he expected it. But the tan-suited doctor, in his brown leather chair backed by the weight of a wall of varicolored books, listened as quietly and seriously as a stuffed owl, moving only to jot down a note in his black notebook.

A note of bitterness sharpened Chester's voice. "Being born was a disappointment, a complete anticlimax like everything else that has ever happened to me. At least I've been consistent—the same boy since I was red and bare and ugly and only a foot-and-a-half long. My mother says I looked like I wasn't quite done, too rare. They should have kept the afterbirth, and thrown me out." He glanced up hopefully to see if the doctor looked shocked. Another disappointment: The doctor looked politely sympathetic.

Chester gripped the arms of his red leather chair, then suddenly jerked his head around and glanced over his shoulder. "Nice couch you've got there." He was sitting in front of the brown leather couch.

Then he turned back toward the doctor and arched his bushy eyebrow again. "My father had expected that if I didn't look like him, at least I would look like the president of the State Bar Association, but I didn't, I looked like the chauffeur. Of course," he added, "that showed good taste on my part because the chauffeur was the best looking of the three."

No laugh. Chester twisted in the chair uncomfortably. He was slightly too fat, slightly preposterous looking, with curly blond hair, a receding chin, and a nose which seemed to have outdone itself, grown extra-long as though to make up for the lack of a chin. His eyes were more appealing—alert, attentive, and crinkled at the corners, so that when he smiled they seemed to laugh ironically, and when he looked sad his blue eyes seemed to darken like a stormy sea and stare far into the distance with an air of painful but great wisdom—all the more unusual since Chester could not have been more than 22.

"Since I embarrass my father and mother," he said, smiling, eyes crinkling at corners, "I have gone out of my way to be amusing. I can even make my father laugh. My mother laughs, too, but then she'll laugh at anybody, as long as it's a man. I collect funny or shocking stories about people who get what they deserve." He straightened his grey pinstripe tie carefully like a man taking stock of himself before going up to make an after-dinner speech.

Chester was well dressed, with only a bizarre touch here and there like the royal purple handkerchief in his pocket, and the purple argyle socks. He held his head high with an indefinable air of style that made it obvious that he was used to commanding attention. But the way in which he alternately composed his hands in his lap in a study of limp-fingered nonchalance and jerked them up to grip the arms of the chair as though he absolutely expected somebody to pull it out from under him; the way his eyes kept darting up to the doctor's face to catch his reaction to every remark, made his stylishness seem a self-cheering device, like the proverbial whistling of the man who passes the graveyard at night.

He was quite a contrast to the quiet, listening doctor, who had no idiosyncrasy of manner or dress that would have been easy to remember or describe, except his very studied lack of personality clues. "You will not find out about me," his plain exterior said. "You are here to find out about yourself." A male sphinx, careful to keep a balance between formality and sympathetic interest. He had, in fact, exactly the manner that Chester regarded as stuffy and hence in need of a little shaking up.

"My favorite story," said Chester, "is the one about the king who collected himself."

"What is that story?"

Chester paused, looked quickly over his shoulder, then back at the doctor. "Interesting view out the back window," he said, though there was nothing out the window but grass, trees, and a garbage truck. He stared at the doctor as though he was seeing something tragic beyond and in back of him.

After all, this self-collected gentleman with a red volume entitled "Case Studies in Delinquency" by his right ear, and a black volume called "Sadism in Six Cases of Schizophrenia" by his left ear, might not even appreciate the story. Maybe like Chester's father he would laugh in a cornered way, making it obvious that he thought the story was too embarrassing to be taken as anything but funny, yet not really worth the physical effort of a healthy *ha ha*. "A mechanical man would laugh like you do if the spring was beginning to wear down and needed winding up," Chester had once said, and his father looked embarrassed, then laughed again the same way: "Hahaha, haa, haa haaa—"

"There was once a king," Chester said to the doctor, "who had a terrible temper and a great knack for revenge. When the courtiers or peasants made him mad, he liked to pinion them on a long spear and watch them die slowly. In fact, he had a whole row of spikes set up, impaling a cook who had burned his roast boar, or a courtier who had given him the wrong advice, or a general who had lost a battle, or a Lady who had refused him—a nice assortment of people, all in different stages of dying slowly on the long sharp spikes. Now, every morning, right after breakfast, the king would go out on his balcony and gaze down to inspect the stage of agony of each of his enemies and see which were done to a turn and ready to be thrown out on a hillside for the buzzards."

The doctor made a note in his black notebook. *Which at least proves,* Chester thought, *that he's listening. I wonder what he's saying about me?* "Can smile even in discouragement"? *Or . . . or what?*

The doctor was actually taking notes on exactly the bare facts sorted from Chester's remarks. But he had a habit of writing in parentheses little tentative notes to himself with question marks or exclamation points. So far the only parenthetical note he had written was "(purple!!)."

Chester whirled and looked behind him again. "Interesting picture," he said. "I like still-life pictures. I have a picture in my room of a lot of dead fish on a marble slab at the fish market. The blues and greens are lovely. But I'm forgetting to tell the story.

"Now, the only trouble was that the king's subjects didn't like to see their relatives and friends dying slowly on spikes, and they hated even worse to think they themselves might be next—they might be wriggling like a worm on a hook if they rubbed His Majesty the wrong way. So the king was not very *popular.*" Chester had a way of emphasizing the last word of every sentence as though he were reluctant to let go of it.

"One day he went out on his balcony and leaned over the edge to see who was still wiggling, and somebody gave him a push. He fell onto a particularly long sharp spike that was already holding the Lady Guinevere Alice, who wasn't insulted because she had just died.

"Naturally, nobody bothered to pull the king off the spike. His younger brother wanted to be king, and everybody else was glad to be rid of him. And thereby," said Chester with careful emphasis, "he became the first collector in history ever to collect himself."

He was at last rewarded with a wry smile and a thoughtful pause. "Why do you suppose you like to collect these amusing macabre stories?" the doctor asked.

"I don't know," said Chester. "My whole life seems to be one big joke. Even the problem that I came to tell you about is rather funny, but it would be a lot funnier if it happened to somebody else. It seems unfair since generally I've worked my life out very well—I don't know of anybody who has so much to worry about but who manages to stay so cheerful and amusing."

There was a tense pause, and Chester glanced over his shoulder again. "The strange thing is there's nothing wrong with me, I'm sure, except. . . ." He stopped, chewed his lower lip, and frowned grotesquely, gripping the arms of the chair until the blood was forced out of his stubby fingertips.

"It sounds rather silly, so I hate to say it." The corners of his eyes crinkled into a forced smile. He swallowed before he spoke, and his Adam's apple danced up and down. "I have the feeling that a horse is following me around."

All of a sudden the doctor showed real interest. He sat up straighter in his chair so that the top of his head came in line with a four-volume set of blue leather books lettered in gold, and he gave the distinct impression from Chester's vantage point that he was balancing them on his head. "And is this horse that follows you a particular horse that you know?"

"Well, no." Chester frowned in thought, and his Adam's apple bobbled again. "I haven't exactly met this horse, but I know what it looks like."

"What does it look like?"

"Sad, just sad and rather mean, like a bloodhound with a nasty temper."

"Like anybody you know?"

"I don't pick out friends who look like horses. My friends are all rather more stylish and self-collected than a horse. Anyway I have never seen the horse. I simply have the feeling that if I don't keep looking back over my shoulder every few minutes, it's going to sneak up in back of me and take a bite."

"Where is he going to bite you?" It was obvious from the way the doctor leaned forward slightly that he had high hopes for an illuminating answer.

Chester gripped the arms of the chair with alarm, and glanced nervously over his shoulder. "He's not really there." His voice was temporarily an octave higher. "He's not really going to bite me, I just think he is. He's not there. So how can he bite me any particular place."

Then he gave the doctor a knowing stare. "I'll bet this means something dirty to you. I know about psychiatry, and I wouldn't consult you if I could get rid of my horse another way—it all goes back to sex."

The doctor smiled enigmatically. His last parenthesis said,

"(Horse???—rape???)"

"Actually," said Chester, "I always behave properly, but my thoughts are quite sophisticated. I've read a lot."

There was a long silence while Chester recomposed himself, arranged his awkward hands nonchalantly, and finally smiled.

"At first the horse was a good joke. My friends just nearly died laughing about it. But after a while it bored them, and then it bothered them—and at the same time it began to seem so real to me that I had to keep looking. People were tired of the real reason— the horse—so I had to keep thinking of excuses to look over my shoulder every few minutes. Can you imagine the work involved in thinking of a new reason to look over your shoulder every five minutes?" Chester drooped, then tensed and looked over his shoulder quickly. "Besides, suppose I get a crick in the neck? And the funny thing is that if a real horse really bit me, it actually wouldn't be so bad—just another anticlimax. It's the sneakiness of this horse that bothers me, like somebody creeping up in back of me to say 'BOO!'"

Chester pulled his face back into a smile. "Do you suppose if the horse bit me he would give me a horse laugh? My brother used to say 'Boo' and then laugh at me, but this horse is not at all like my brother. My brother has never had to be sneaky because everybody likes him the way he is."

There was a clap of thunder in the distance. Chester leaned back in his chair in a heavy parody of nonchalance. A fly buzzed futilely against the inside of the window screen. The doctor waited.

"Of course my older brother Robert is one of the reasons why I am always an anticlimax. He looks like my father, which is an unfair advantage. He's very earnest and determined, like my father, so he does well in school. He wants to be a lawyer like my father, so they have long talks about it. Teachers always get him first, then me—from the sublime to the ridiculous. But I can't complain, really. Until the horse business started to bother them, people found me more amusing, and after I lick this foolish little problem, they will again.

"In a way, my mother likes me best because I'm more fun. For instance, I collect those little cards with funny sayings on them and give them to people on the proper occasions." He crossed his legs comfortably, and his well-tailored grey flannel slacks rode up to show an even larger expanse of the purple argyle socks. His plump face seemed to grow fatter and more chinless as his cheeks puffed out in a smile of contented self-satisfaction. "When my mother went on a diet, for example, I presented her with a card that said, "Want to lose ten pounds of ugly fat? Then cut off your head!'

Chester's shining smile tarnished a little around the edges. "Of course in another way," he said, "she prefers my brother because he doesn't cause trouble with my father. She was rather upset at Father's reaction my senior year in high school when I learned to make bathtub gin in the cellar and sold it to my friends. But the funny thing is that they never get really mad and shout and get it over with, but then of course that wouldn't be dignified. It's like those storm clouds out the window—heavy and dark like bunches of poisonous purple grapes. At my house there is never a real storm and then a clear sky."

There was another faraway thunderclap, and the air took on that pre-storm oppressiveness that makes animals pace their cages in the zoo and humans snap at each other over trifles.

"Smoke, by all means," said the doctor as Chester pulled out a cigarette case. "Need a light?"

"Won't you have one of my cigarettes?" Chester offered.

"Thank you very much," the doctor replied, "but I have some of my own here."

Infuriatingly impassive, Chester thought. "No, please have one of mine," Chester said. "I would like that."

"Thank you, but—"

"No, please," Chester begged. "I want you to take it to prove something."

The doctor smiled tolerantly, took the cigarette, and lighted it. "What does this prove?" he asked.

"I want to see if you act like my father did when I gave him a cigarette yesterday."

The doctor took a puff. There was a silence. Chester glanced quickly over his shoulder, then both of them sat waiting expectantly.

"Am I acting like your father?" the doctor asked politely. He was interrupted by the explosion.

"I also like practical jokes," Chester said as the doctor, struggling between a gasp and his professional manner, wiped his face carefully with his white handkerchief and picked up the bits of the trick cigarette which had fallen on his desk when it exploded.

"I put those together myself," Chester said with pride. "My father says that I have a perverted sense of humor. He says that's why nice girls won't go out with me. But that's not true. I'd just rather go out with a group than with one girl. Girls come to my parties and die laughing at some of the things I do. The girls think I'm shocking, but they obviously like to shriek and giggle. I have a line that stops the younger ones cold. I say, 'Will you spend the night with me?' If the girl says, 'Yes,' I say, 'Oh, really—I just wondered. I'm making a survey.'"

"In other words," the doctor said, "you have a great need to make other people feel foolish."

"You might say that," said Chester, "but really people don't mind—they have such fun at my place, and I don't think it's just because I always buy the liquor." He quickly changed the subject.

"I don't think I'm illegitimate," he said with sudden annoyance. "I think Father just uses me to make Mother feel guilty because she always wants to have fun, and because everybody likes her better than they like him. She says I'm his, and I believe it. My mother just loves to have fun. Is that so bad? With anybody—the mailman, the garbage man, my father's friends. There's always music, popular music, in my house, and people laughing. It's funny that I think of it as a discouraging place. She loves jokes, like those wineglasses that have spill holes in them.

"It's a funny thing, sometimes I feel like I'm older than my mother. She looks so young, with blonde hair and big, round, blue eyes. When I was eighteen, she got me to take her out dancing at a teen hangout to see what it was like. She flirted with all my friends like she was sixteen, and made me promise not to tell Father she went out on the golf course and necked with one. Yes, I think my mother likes me—lots of times she tried to cheer me up. But. . . ."

"But," the doctor repeated encouragingly.

"But that's not much help when Father begins to talk to me about my inadequacies—*inadequacies*, that's his favorite word." Chester perked up. He had thought of another joke. "You know the old story, Doctor, about the father who said to the little boy, 'Jump, Ikie, I'll catch you.' Then the little boy jumped, the father didn't catch him, and the boy fell and skinned his knee. 'Now let that teach you a lesson, Ikie. Never trust nobody, not even your own father.'

"Now sometimes it seems to me that growing up was as if I had no father at all, and my mother, like the jump-Ikie story, wouldn't catch me if I fell.

"It doesn't pay to take life too seriously—or even death, for that matter. I thought of that when I got locked in the museum with all the dinosaur bones. My father was on some sort of board of a museum once. He went to a meeting after regular hours and told me to look around and amuse myself while he was busy. And then he forgot me. That was when I was still rather young—about eight.

"A museum is so empty at night—full of glass cases of dried remains and imitations and bones. It's as empty as your head feels when you have a high fever. First I was scared to death and then, all of a sudden, I felt rather at home. I went in and studied the wax figure of the Neanderthal man wearing its real animal skin, and thought to myself that, at least, being extinct was rather peaceful.

"And then my father remembered me, and came back, which was thoughtful of him.

"To tell you the truth, I've made a little deal with myself. If you can't help me I'm going to hide in the museum after hours on Saturday, and when everybody has cleared out for the weekend, I'm going to remove the life-size figure of the Neanderthal man from its pedestal and put it in the storeroom in the cellar. Then I'm going to dress myself in the bearskin and curl up on the pedestal above the "Stone Age Man" placard, and take a combination of rat poison and sleeping pills. I wonder how long Monday it will take them to notice the difference?"

"I don't think that will be necessary," the doctor said crassly. "I think I can help you."

Chester lowered his eyes to his shoelaces, fidgeted with the buttons on his grey-flannel suit, and bobbled his Adam's apple. "But really," he said, rallying, "I'm being a bore about all this. My only real problem is my horse." He looked behind him again. "I wish you didn't have that old English hunting picture in the waiting room. I don't really believe in omens—but I feel like it's a sign of bad luck."

There was a knocking on the windowpane. Chester jumped. But it was not a horse. It was a sprinkling of hail.

"Hail in the summer," said Chester. It was plain that he took it as personally as the horse picture in the waiting room. The doctor got up and shut the window. "And I'm lucky to have so many friends," Chester said. "Now that I have my own room and job, I give a party every Saturday. It's a funny thing, I don't drink myself, but I like to watch other people get silly. Then all week I tell them funny stories about what they did on Saturday night. I guess I'm really a scream around the office."

Just at this point there was an unfortunate interruption, a tornado. Chester found himself surrounded by a roar like jet planes all swooping down on him. The back half of the room was crushed into splinters like a wooden strawberry basket crunched in an angry giant's hand. In the whirling spiral of wind, the books rose like a flock of many colored hysterical birds, their bindings flapping in the wind, pages flapping and torn, neuroses and psychoses flying through the air in wild abandon.

But Chester sat untouched. He was no more than scratched by the flying splinters and broken glass. At first he sat stone still, stunned. If he had been as naturally cheerful as he thought, he might have exulted in this unusual piece of luck—that the tornado came that close and yet missed him: Not only a miracle but a miracle in his favor. He had heard that a tornado could perform freaks, but he surveyed the splintered boards with amazement. The doctor was hung, like an old rag over a jutting beam of the lower floor, obviously dead, with his head stove in like a crushed egg. He was dripping blood, Chester observed with mild revulsion. It seemed to him that this was exactly the sort of situation he was likely to be a part of, but alive, of course. Death was probably comparatively painless—at least, since he had never died, he could think so if he chose. Naturally he had been left alive to appreciate the nightmare.

He sat in the same chair he had been sitting in before the tornado, staring into space. But not just ordinary space—emptiness framed with jagged splinters and the flat icicles of broken glass. He could hear people shouting somewhere out in space. They didn't seem real. Then his eye was caught by a small black notebook near his feet. This bird had come home to roost. It was the doctor's notebook.

His heart started to beat fast. Were these the notes about him? In all his life, he had never really been sure of anyone's opinion about him. Was he really funny, as he hoped, or an over-cheerful bore like Mr. Smith, the postman, who told the same joke every time Chester was in the yard when he delivered the mail on Saturday. "Think fast," Mr. Smith would say, throwing a letter through the air to Chester. "Airmail special-delivery from me to you."

The doctor's notes seemed disappointing at first glance—merely a condensation of Chester's own words. Then a few comments sprinkled down the page leaped out at him with the violence of another tornado.

Seductive mother—infantile—more like a sister or ?
Father never blows up—fears own ability to control his rage
    at son if he once gets angry?
Incestuous feelings toward mother?

Chester gasped. *Incestuous* was not a word he had ever heard applied to anyone he knew socially.

Fear of reprisal from father (symbolized by horse) behind?

"My God," said Chester, "this is pretty rough." But he had gone too far to stop. His eyes raced down the page picking out the parentheses between the playback of his own words.

Overwhelmed by father—identifies with mother—thinks "If I
    become like ineffective woman, I will not desire mother"—
    Attack from behind protects him—yet now lies near to be
    raped by father. Loses whichever way he turns.

"Good God," said Chester again, "and all I've got to pit against all this is a sense of humor!" He read on.

Grisly stories—sense of humor??? Mostly acting out own rages—openly yet with make-believe. Provokes disaster (cigarette) and contempt. But never quite enough yet—

Chester felt physically sick. His eyes opened wide and bulged with shock as though he were so full of desperation that he no longer fitted into his own body. It did not occur to him that the notes were fragmentary impressions, and might have a completely different and less horrifying meaning for the doctor than they did for him. It seemed to him they contained the essence of all the most terrible things he had ever feared about himself and pushed to the back of his mind in panic. He pulled out the large royal purple handkerchief. His face contracted into the tragic mask, and he held the purple handkerchief in mid-air before it as if he were about to sneeze. A shudder shook his body while a huge sob tried to break loose like a volcano erupting. But no tears came, not even a sneeze.

He brought down the purple handkerchief with an air of defeat, lowering a flag in surrender. He folded it carefully, concentrating every ounce of attention on it, and stuck it back in his pocket at the habitual jaunty angle. Then he caught a glimpse of his own still wildly horrified face, above the well-cut jacket and jaunty handkerchief, in a large broken pane of glass that had fallen on the dark brown rug. He looked like a burlesque of a shocked young man. And at last he laughed, steering himself back into the shallow waters where he could hope to navigate. He bowed to his wry reflection formally and said, "So you collect stories with shocking endings? Well, this is a good one for your collection. The story of you, you bastard!"

Then he smiled at his reflection, which smiled back like a grinning pop-eyed gargoyle. "You were wrong, you know, to think that you could get away from anticlimaxes. Here you are again, Chester, not the first, but only the second collector in history ever to collect himself."

At a Sisters-In-Crime breakfast for librarians in Washington D.C. several years ago, Liz was one of the guests and panelists. As the moderator called the panelists to the podium, Liz made it all the way to the front of the room, and then squeaked when she realized she had forgotten her name placard. It was such a perfect response from the author of the Peaches Dann mysteries. I'm sure she won dozens of devoted readers that morning.

Toni Walder

The Boa Constrictor

"I think, on the whole, the thing that bothered me most about the boa constrictor was that it had a smile exactly like my Cousin Euridice Bricknel back in Cross Bend, Mississippi," Mary Spratt said brightly.

It proved the extent of Anna Orange's iron poise that her only reaction to this turn in the conversation was to arch her snow-white left eyebrow a sixteenth of an inch. Actually, the conversation had taken a turn for the better, or at least the more cheerful. We had been discussing how nerve-wracking it would be to spend two weeks or more in a cramped fallout shelter with a mischievous small child. All very pointless, since Anna was the only one of us with a converted cellar, and all her children were grown. But it was a new variation on one of her favorite topics—that children nowadays aren't taught the proper way to behave.

We sat on Anna's old brick terrace, at the shimmering glass-topped white iron table, four women and a child, framed against the huge gnarled lilac trees at the end of the terrace. I was there, of course, and Mary and Anna and Anna's daughter-in-law, Barbara, with Susan, her little girl.

Anna, at the head of the table behind her silver service, which sparkled in the late afternoon sun, turned to Mary on her right. "I am not surprised that rearing your children by a book could lead to almost acquiring a boa constrictor. What happened, my dear? Did you take the occasion in your stride, as usual?"

Mary was small and red-haired. Her clothes breathed girlishness—well restrained ruffles and vivid blue slacks. It amazed me that when she listened, all the motion in her body could concentrate itself in her attentive blue eyes, which burned like powerful pilot lights. Yet ask her one question, as Anna did, and her face, body, and especially her hands, flamed into expressiveness. Then her red hair and lips and fingernails seemed merely the brightest part of the dancing, glowing rush of the story she was trying to tell, even if the story was trivial.

"I did the best I could." Mary paused and glanced around Anna's formal little garden with the high evergreen hedge to hide the neighbors whose six children went barefoot in summer and made mud pies, by Anna's report, while the 150-pound mother, wearing shorts, hung out tons of wash to wave in Anna's direction, and their father mowed his huge lawn in his undershirt. Anna could not bear to watch such a degree of unrestrained comfort.

In front of the graceful undershirt-proof screen of hemlock was an old-fashioned formal border of flowers, all white except for a few prize purple bearded iris and blue delphiniums. There were white roses, peonies, azaleas, sweet William, and a tree rose at each end of the bed, an exclamation point. A tiny lily pool was centered against the flower bed, with a little white Italian marble statue of a cherub leaning over its sunny reflection in the still water—the focal point of the garden.

"In a snake farm, of course," Mary continued her story, "it was not as simple to stay calm and collected as in your beautiful garden, Anna, but I tried. I think that the most discouraging thing about a boa constrictor is that big friendly smile when it's swallowing some poor little animal. Of course it doesn't mean to smile, but the only way it can swallow an animal bigger around than it is, is for its throat and mouth to stretch and stretch—and the mouth stretches around into a huge deep curve. While maybe the leg and foot of some little animal hangs out one corner."

Anna flinched almost imperceptibly as though she wanted to cry out, "Please! Not while we're eating!" but the lifelong habit of courtesy restrained her.

Mary stopped, and two vertical wrinkles creased her fine-skinned brow, evidently at the painful reptilian memory. "The next time anybody gives me a mean-pleased phoney smile, I won't say he looks like the cat that swallowed the canary, I'll say he looks like the boa constrictor that swallowed the cat!

"Whenever Cousin Euridice told a piece of gossip that would ruin somebody back in Cross Bend, she smiled just like that boa constrictor. We didn't get on very well. I didn't live up to her ideas of how a Southern young lady should act. I was a tomboy, you know, and I liked to try everything new. And I left Mississippi of my own free will and accord. She still can't accept that."

"But it's important to try new ideas and to travel," protested young Barbara Orange, who sat across the table from Mary on Anna's left. She probably hoped to change the course of the conversation because she felt the boa constrictor story was bound to make raising children by books sound foolish. The story would help to prove Mother-in-Law Anna's theory that the younger generations were going to the dogs.

Barbara was about 22 and married to Jeremy, the Orange family maverick. She wore a full gathered Guatemalan print skirt and a man's shirt, a tense girl, with her long blonde hair ruthlessly scooped back from her face and elastic-banded into a ponytail.

Her manner was polite but essentially challenging. "On guard," her blue eyes said. "I have an offensive play to match any of yours." At the same time her smile seemed to say, "We will observe the rules of the game. We will not draw blood."

We often met in the library. Barbara believed so firmly in following the advice of books that I wondered what she did when two books disagreed. Now her mouth was bent into a Cupid's bow smile but so stiffly that you expected the words to be part of the act of defense—arrows.

Jeremy had not married a woman much like his mother. Anna Orange matched her house, which adjoined the terrace. Both were perfectly preserved and beautifully appointed gems of construction. The house was colonial, small, but beautifully made. Inside, where we had stopped to admire the old ceiling beams, the rooms were tiny, but the fireplaces were huge, heavy-beamed, and authentic. The furniture was antique and choice. Brass and silver and old polished mahogany gleamed, oriental rugs gave richness and color to the floors. The pictures and the bric-a-brac spoke of Anna's cosmopolitan, wandering life. There was, for instance, a signed photograph of an Italian countess. There were not many books, a few faded leather tomes which I believe belonged to her husband.

With her fine-skinned slender aristocratic hands, her chiseled features, and commanding manner, Anna seemed poetically in place in front of her perfect little house. Even her lilac scent mingled with the scent of the lilac bushes blown across the terrace by the slight afternoon breeze. Her lavender dress brought out blue lavender tints in her carefully waved white hair. She had been sitting here by the lilacs the week before when she complimented me on my doctor husband's honesty.

"He told me as soon as he knew that I had inoperable cancer," she had said. "Don't tell anyone. I only wanted you to know how I admire his forthrightness."

So she had not told her family, certainly not Barbara or Jeremy, because she said she did not want to burden them with her problems. It was part of her conception of self-discipline, and I'm afraid part of her difficulty in reaching her own children. She was gracious and unbending when they might have preferred her blunt.

Now Anna was trying not to look at her two-year-old granddaughter Susan, who was making a beautiful pattern with chocolate icing on the shimmery tabletop. Like most bright children her age, Susan liked to tease grownups. You might have guessed to look at her elfin snub-nosed face, framed with unruly sandy curls. At home Barbara simply removed Susan's food when she got too messy. Here on the terrace she was too proudly aware of Anna's condemning eye to act. So Susan smeared chocolate with great glee and no interference while mother and grandmother politely worked at not noticing.

"When I was young all nice people knew how to raise children," Anna intoned, "and I consider it one of the signs of the lack of any meaningful standards in the younger generation that they must go to books to learn what should be a matter of instinct, or something they learn from their mothers or other older wiser women."

As she spoke, she poured the coffee into blue-and-white Wedgwood cups from the silver coffee pot, with faultless sure movements like a trained dancer executing a classical and much practiced movement. Position No. 1: the invitation—head graciously and quizzically inclined toward one of her guests, silver pot poised above the cup. Position No. 2: coffee poured with an elegant gesture. No. 3: white cube of sugar plucked with silver tongs, a quick pinching gesture like the dancer who leaps and touches the toes together before she lights again. She passed the cup to Mary Spratt.

Mary put the cup down and rested her heart-shaped, sharp-featured face on her small amazing hands. You could never fail to notice her hands, since she gestured with every sentence. They were the pointed tapering hands with knots at the finger joints that I might have expected on a philosopher or a priest—rather like Durer's etching of praying hands, except for the blood-red fingertips.

"Well, sometimes I think you can raise children by a book, but then again I have doubts," said Mary. Her twin boys were in college and out of sight, if not out of mind. They were now two intense dark-haired young college sophomores whose eyes glowed so brightly with interest in any subject that I felt sometimes, as they discussed Zen Buddhism or the possibility of lichens on Mars, that there must be too much wattage for the wiring—a possibility of short circuit. "I liked the book I had fine until I had to figure out where in the house I could put that thirty-foot snake."

"You're joking," said Barbara, who clutched her book on child care which recommended "permissiveness." That very "permissiveness" that Anna said would make fallout shelters so unpleasant. In contrast to her mother-in-law, Barbara did not believe in fallout shelters. She often quoted an article she had read saying that any sort of shelter, even public, encouraged atomic irresponsibility. No mere physical force which could cause nothing worse than death frightened her as much as a challenge to her carefully selected how-to systems.

"How could a book on how to raise children produce a boa constrictor?" she demanded. "And anyway, aren't they dangerous at thirty feet? Wouldn't they swallow children?" She looked protectively at Susan, then quickly away to avoid recognition of the creeping chocolate that streaked the little girl's pink dress and circled her mouth.

"Well, yes, I think boas are dangerous," said Mary. "I know I was afraid it would swallow me, if it got a chance, when I saw it took five strong men to hold it." She held up five fingers. "I learned to admire snakes because I liked to share experiences with the boys, but there was a limit to the experiences I could enjoy sharing."

"Like being swallowed, for instance?" asked Anna Orange dryly, patting her white hair more firmly into place. Anna was a kind woman, so she was capable of enjoying the company of her undisciplined ponytailed daughter-in-law and her friends, even though they were a shock to her system. Just as she belonged to the League of Women Voters with Mary and me, though that was sometimes a shock too. She argued cheerfully but she could not quite control the critical innuendoes that crept into her cultured voice.

Anna tried to be nice to Barbara in order not to emphasize what I knew she felt—that Barbara had married the nearest thing to a black sheep that the Orange family could produce. Almost all the Orange men were stockbrokers and lawyers. Not Jeremy. He was interested only in automobile engines and violins. He used to come in from working on his car, covered with grime and oil, wash his hands in the most perfunctory way, which is to say mostly on the embroidered hand towels, and there, his mother told me, they'd find him in his early American chintzed bedroom at suppertime, still as grimy as the innards of his car, playing heartbreaking music on the violin, and looking ecstatically happy. It was not a surprise when he flunked out of Yale.

"However did you get mixed up with a boa?" Anna asked Mary. "I didn't even know there were any in Connecticut."

Perhaps because Mary was small, I always thought of her as "cheerful as a bird," and she pecked at a new idea with the concentrated excitement of a robin pecking at a worm.

"No, no, I'm sure there are none just loose around in Connecticut, but my boys used to have a little zoo out in the barn, lots of snakes. Of course, you can't keep a boa constrictor in an unheated barn. He wouldn't feel at home. He's a tropical snake."

"So your child-rearing book implied you ought to let your children keep a thirty-foot boa in the house?" Anna's eyebrows were entirely out of control.

Barbara never stopped smiling, but she must have felt her friend was subjecting her methods to ridicule, and she was not self-assured enough to endure that. She cradled her Wedgwood cup in her hands so tightly I was afraid it would break.

She was only 22 and her mother and father, both economics professors with strong socialist leanings, looked decidedly askance on her married life. They felt that her mother-in-law was immorally rich, or had been, and that her husband was shockingly unbookish. Barbara and I knew each other well, for she and Mary and I were active Democrats in a 90% Republican town. She told me she had married Jeremy partly because he looked like a poet. In fact, before they were married, he had actually written some poetry to her under the inspiration of love. To support poetry with the craftsmanship of his hands—that seemed romantic.

After they were married, when she went down to look at the grease-spotted back room of the garage where he loved working, and saw the sweating, swearing, laughing men and the nude women on the wall calendars with bosoms as large and carefully bulls-eyed as archery targets, she had been let down. Perhaps being married to a mechanic who wrote poetry was not so ethereal after all. She became a book snob. She did everything by the printed word—cooking, fixing up the house, raising Susan, gardening—and frequently she carried the book around with her, as she did that night, tightly clenched in her hand as though some of the good from it might be absorbed by physical pressure.

Jeremy was considered to be a mechanical genius, got work to do on the most complicated custom-made sports cars, and made more money than some of the men who owned the cars, but that did not impress Barbara. If he had been an airplane pilot she would have felt backed by reading Antoine de St. Exupery. If he had been in the hotel business she could have read Bemelmans. But mending broken cars—what serious writer glamorized that?

"You are exaggerating about the boa constrictor, aren't you, Mary?" she demanded.

"Why, this story doesn't need to be exaggerated." Mary threw her arms wide. "It's bad enough as it is. Of course, I was perfectly sure it would be impossible to buy the snake. I was sure they wouldn't let us do such a silly thing. So I thought I might as well let the boys go on and try and find out for themselves. And I've always encouraged them to find out about anything. Though that does lead to the problem of sampling, and I haven't entirely licked that yet."

Barbara was given to sudden shifts of mood. She clicked down her coffee cup suddenly in her emphatic, tense way, and said quietly and evenly, but with surprising passion, "That, of course, is what I'd like to have: the sureness of my convictions and the nerve to seriously consider buying a boa constrictor and to decide not to do it strictly on the facts and the merits of the case. And then to know I was right."

I remembered the stories she had told me about her family: her father glancing up from a book with a far faraway look, and saying, "Hmmm—?" when she asked a question; and her mother arriving home late from work, with an assortment of cans and frozen packages to produce a quick meal before a meeting, and saying, as she threw together a nationally advertised jiffy assortment of food, "It's more important than anything else for a woman to be an active member of the community."

I didn't suppose Barbara got any feeling of self-assurance from her married life either, with an Alfa Romero engine dismantled in one corner of the living room while she was trying to decorate the room in tan, gold, and black out of a book called *Sophisticated Interiors*. Poor Barbara—she probably felt as much at home with her formal mother-in-law and adventure-loving Mary as with any other assortment of people.

And we were an odd assortment. Barbara pulled out some knitting for Susan, and watching her frown to see clearly, it occurred to me there was only one thing Barbara and Mary and Anna Orange had in common, and a rather coincidental thing at that: a tendency to nearsightedness and a prejudice against wearing glasses. Anna never wore glasses out of a slight vanity, I suspect; Barbara, because she had read a book by a California doctor recommending eye exercises instead; and Mary, because she felt they were a sign of weakness, not proper Southern feminine weakness which might make her more appealing to other people, just deficiency. But, I'm lucky to have unusually sharp eyes, especially at times when many people find it hard to see, at dusk for instance, so perhaps I'm being intolerant of my friends.

I was glad I did see Mary so clearly or I would have never believed she could contort her face into such a look of distaste.

"But if you are ever trying to do something like importing a snake in such a way as not to succeed at it," she was saying with scorn, "don't ever trust the Consular Service to be unhelpful. Why, I never got so much help. There we went, just off the ship, our last stop in South Africa—Bill and me and the twins. The man in the consulate looked annoyed at us, and lazy and hot, and I thought, hurray, he won't help a bit. And I said, 'Excuse me, but it's necessary to get some sort of permit to import a boa constrictor into the United States, isn't it?' And I all but winked. 'That's hard to get, isn't it? My boys want to take one home.' And do you know what happened? That unpromising little man all of a sudden took notice and stood up straight and said, 'I don't know about a permit for a minor importing a snake, but I'm sure I can help you!'"

"Why," said Anna, "you underrate our Consular Service. I have always found them so helpful when I was traveling. We brought some beautiful paintings and statues back from our European trips, and whenever we had the least trouble we found the consuls and the Embassy people so helpful.

"That little laughing cherub fountain down in the lily pond is the only statue I have bothered to move around with me all these years. But then it means more to me than most. It was a present from Howard to celebrate our twentieth wedding anniversary in Rome. He said the cherub's smile was the symbol of our happy life, and I never look at the little statue but I think of that. That was the happiest year of our lives. The year before the Depression."

And the year before Jeremy was born, I thought. For Jeremy had surprised Anna by arriving after his brother and sister were nearly grown.

"Why," said Anna, "I have only to look at my little imported cherub even now and I have a feeling of warmth about our helpful foreign service."

Mary's forehead frowned but her twinkly eyes and gesturing, winking-ringed hands remained as vivacious as ever. "I underestimated the way the man would help with the snake, all right," she said. "He went in the back room to look it up and came back beaming, just pleased to death with himself. He said, 'Madam, we can work it out, but there is something more wonderful than you could expect. The very man who can help you is here in this building. Imagine that! He is my cousin and he is in the reptile-exporting business. He sends big snakes to all the American zoos. I am sure you have seen his snakes. They are magnificent!'"

Mary was an expert mimic, and we all but saw the man expanding into the general benefactor who would help his cousin and Mary into the happy completion of a deal. She fingered the lace on the ruffled cuffs of her white silk blouse and said, "That was the beginning of my adventure."

Most people admired Mary's ability to go out and have adventures without any apparent effort, and without any show of panic when they turned out badly. I did. Nothing ordinary ever happened to her. Even her children never seemed to suffer from the usual dull troubles like runny noses or skinned knees. One had been arrested for painting a rude picture of Kilroy with his nose poking around the door of a police car while the policeman was making a phone call. His only excuse, that he didn't usually get that drunk, was true but inadequate.

One had shot himself when he was 18, with an antique pistol for which he had made bullets himself with melted lead and a mold. That was the only time I ever saw Mary look frightened, not primarily because he was hurt, I suspect, but because she wondered if he had been trying to kill himself. Afterwards, I decided it had been my imagination. Mary and the boy, George, joked about it and said it just proved you couldn't trust homemade bullets to do a thorough job.

Mary could extract every ounce of color from a story, too. Once she told me about losing her underpants in the middle of I Street in Washington, D.C., and when she added a traffic policeman to stop the cars so she could pick them up, I accused her of exaggerating. (She didn't tell that one to Anna Orange.) She had smiled engagingly and said, "Well, I do like to embroider a little."

Barbara did not trust embroidery and kept trying to pin down Mary's facts. "What kind of permit do you have to get for a boa constrictor, exactly how did you have to go about it?" she asked. But when anyone tried to pin Mary down, she said, "Well, I don't remember that, exactly, but what I do remember. . . ." and she held out some particularly fascinating tidbit of information which made you forget what you'd asked. You were never sure whether she had forgotten or wanted to skip the details for some reason of her own.

"What I do remember," she said to Barbara, "is that snake man. The fattest man I ever saw." She inscribed a circle in the air. "He didn't walk, he bounced. And had a big greasy mustache. Somehow I didn't feel he was very clean, but then I was just being awfully American. He didn't speak any English, but the man at the consulate said it didn't matter; we could pick out the snake we liked and come back, and he'd translate the haggling over the price."

"But, my dear," said Anna Orange, "certainly you didn't go to a strange place with a man who spoke no English to buy a snake you didn't want! And drag along your husband and two impressionable boys. We women must set the standards for our men."

"Yes," said Mary, "that's exactly what I was doing—setting standards." She folded her hands primly in her lap. "I remember what my mother always said: 'We must show them what to do but we must never let them know.' Why, I can hear my mother's voice now talking about my father's vacation. Every year he wanted to go to the mountains. 'Dear, I want to go where you want to go but it always seems to me that while you think you prefer the mountains, you really have more fun at the beach. And you look so distinguished with a tan.'

"So I was setting standards for the boys when we went to the reptile farm, but I had to see that they decided themselves what was impossible."

"But about the snake," I reminded her.

"Yes, well, we came to a yellow stucco wall with purple bougainvillea all over it and an iron gate—why, it was a lovely wall. And in back of that gate a long narrow series of gardens—well, yards, not gardens—stretching back goodness knows how far—and snakes in pits and cages."

"What kind of cages?" asked Barbara earnestly. "What did they look like?"

"Well, I don't remember the details," said Mary, "but I'll tell you what I can't forget—those big wormy monsters! They had small, mean, glittering eyes and thick heads, but the head was kind of long too. And long sharp teeth that slanted back toward the inside of their mouths, and lots of small scales all over them. Really, I didn't think they looked very friendly. And one had a lump in the middle." She inscribed a small circle with her index finger. "He was still digesting the last animal he ate. And the smiling one had an animal half swallowed."

Anna Orange looked up from her coffee. "When I was in London on my honeymoon, there was quite a stir about a boa constrictor at the Zoological Gardens that had swallowed his rug. Some of the best people went out to watch him slowly unswallow it." It seemed to comfort Anna to get the conversation around to the best people. "It was a large rug and quite a sight, but we were presented at Court that day and didn't see it."

Anna was nobly ignoring Susan, who had gone to dig in her formal flower bed with a silver tablespoon, near a clump of rare lilies.

"The snakes I saw didn't have any rugs," Mary went on. "That might have made them look more civilized and respectable and British. They looked entirely wild and scaly and wiggly. There were also pens with rabbits and one with a pig. . . . And the smell! I don't know what smelled. Maybe they didn't keep the cages clean.

"But the fat man beamed and beamed and got a skinny little assistant, and they took out a boa three feet long and pulled it to its full length to show it off. I thought I knew a couple of words of Spanish that I'd picked up from a book about a little Spanish boy when the boys were small. I thought they meant 'too big.' Well, the boys looked at that snake, and I could see they were stunned but pleased. They kind of grinned and nudged each other and walked around and looked at the snake from all sides, and I could see them thinking what an impression it would make on their friends in the seventh grade. So I summoned up my feeble Spanish and said, '*Tan pequeño.*'

"The big fat man looked disappointed and a little sad. He looked up and down as if he was trying to figure out what kind of people we were, and then he shrugged and led us into the next yard. He and the skinny assistant began to pull out another snake, and he began to shine with pride again. That snake was even bigger." Mary's red-tipped hands were held far apart.

Anna Orange, without leaving her seat, had begun to collect the empty coffee cups on a tray. "I would say, my dear, you were in danger of being strangled by your own theory."

Barbara glowered and pulled a strand of her ponytail around to chew on it. She hugged herself as if she were cold, but though the sun had deserted us it was still a warm afternoon. "I think you're making it all up," she said. "Your boys are smarter than that."

Barbara got more belligerent the longer she worked at ignoring Susan. And since I was the only one who could look at the child freely (Mary would have felt it was tactless), I decided we were going to be in for trouble. The power to make both grandmother and mother sit up so straight and allow such liberties was going to Susan's head.

I knew the look in her eye. My old dachshund gets the same look when he's looking for something to do that will be shocking enough to stir up excitement and get a little attention. One Christmas he got that expression and then chewed up the Christchild out of the creche under the Christmas tree.

Susan could be charming with her grandmother when her mother wasn't there, though she had had a fit of the giggles when Anna tried to teach her to curtsy.

"Well, I figured the boa constrictor man had misunderstood me," said Mary, getting back to her story, "so I looked at the two men struggling with the snake. They had to tussle a little with that one. So I spoke very clearly and loudly, and I said, "*Tan pequeño.*" But that just set them off on a long discussion with each other, and every time one of them let go of the snake to wave his arm in the air, I was afraid the snake would get loose. I'm the kind who even gets nervous about accidents when Bill uses one hand to talk while he's driving in heavy traffic.

"They put the boa away and began to call somebody else, and another man came along, and the three of them went and got a bigger snake. And I'll admit it was magnificent, if your taste happened to run that way, though rather slimy—it had been in the water. The boys just stood there with their mouths open. They were past saying anything. And I thought about that smell in my house and felt discouraged."

"Exactly what sort of smell was it?" asked Barbara, interested in spite of herself. She probably wondered if it was worse than crankcase oil.

"Well, I can't describe it," said Mary, "but I sure was relieved when the boys changed their minds. George came over and said, 'You know, Ma, I don't think we really want one for our zoo. If we got a little one it would grow, and what on earth would we feed it?' George was very fond of our dogs, and I could see he had begun to put two and two together. So we waved our arms till the man understood and he was disappointed but I was saved."

Anna picked up the silver tray to carry it in the house, and Barbara took along a few stray dishes. Mary turned to me when they were out of earshot and whispered, "I wouldn't tell them because they wouldn't understand, not being raised as I was, but you were born in the South so maybe you can understand. That was one of the worst moments of my life. I've only lately gotten so I can talk about it. I used to wake up at night and think about it and perspire. I guess I'm too proud, but rather than admit I couldn't control my men by tact, I would have bought the damn snake. The captain might have saved me and not allowed it aboard ship."

"Sometimes," she said (and it was the only time I ever heard her so blunt and bitter), "I wonder if I've failed to control Bill and the boys, or whether I've controlled them too well, and the will to live has been squeezed out of them."

I knew Bill, her husband, drank too much. I wondered again if she thought George had really tried to kill himself. Maybe she thought that, as her doctor's wife, I knew more about her life than I did.

"Anna leads her life so beautifully," she said, "and Barbara is young enough to still hope to find the right track. I envy them."

She stopped abruptly as Barbara and Anna came back.

"If we could only go back to the good old days," Anna said suddenly, "when life really made sense."

This comment was obviously a reaction to the whole disturbing afternoon and to the contradictions in her own effort to live up to her former way of life without butler or maid. After the formal and elaborate meal, she would wash the dishes.

"Sometimes I think there is nothing left in the world to hold on to," said Anna. "Nothing left but standards no on can afford to live with. When I think of the way it used to be before this socialism, that gives all the money to people without taste, people with no standards"—she glanced towards the hedge—"and corrupts the poor so they won't do an honest day's work. . . ." She noticed Barbara's belligerent stare and collected herself.

"It seems to me," said Barbara firmly, "that there has never been anything worth holding on to but knowledge. Things," she said, glancing scathingly at Anna's exquisite house and terrace, "break and get lost, or they cost too much money. Knowledge is something you can afford and keep!" And she clutched her book as though it might sprout wings and fly away.

Mary laughed. "You all sound so serious."

Anna Orange came to heel immediately, remembered her social training, and recaptured her formal smile. Barbara laughed nervously.

"I wonder if there is anything you can hold," Mary said banteringly, "except a cupful of Anna's good coffee, or maybe an advance ticket for the first flight to the moon. I bet there aren't any snakes at all on the moon. The only thing you can really count on, I guess, are your own abilities—for instance, the ability to help other people decide what to do."

There was sudden silence. Perhaps Mary was remembering what she had said to me.

Just then there was a loud splash. It was beginning to get dark, so we couldn't see clearly, but the sound told us that Susan had fallen in among Anna's pink lilies and large goldfish. Anna and Barbara both jumped.

"I'll go," Barbara announced, and her tone added, *This is not your business, stay out of it*, and she ran to the foot of the garden as the splash was followed by heartbroken screams.

I hoped Anna would protest, and run and put her arms around little Susan or find some way to tell Barbara she was not thinking of Susan's fall in terms of Barbara's failure as a mother but was worried like any grandmother about whether the little girl was hurt. I wished Barbara could let her mother-in-law feel needed in the emergency.

But while Barbara ran to Susan, we sat in awkward silence, listening to the distant whimpers. Then Mary, always wary of silence, rushed to fill the gap.

"Yes, I reckon it was nice to live in the good old days when everybody knew what was expected of him and the problem of whether to buy a boa constrictor could never even come up. My mother never would have let us have one in Cross Bend, Mississippi—I know that! But she never would have had to say 'No,' because we would never have asked.

"Lordy, the world changes so fast now, how can children know what to ask, much less parents know what to answer? That's the whole key to the problem. Sometimes when I think of all the ways I was trained to act and how little those ways fit the world I live in, I just hope my children will be permissive with me while I sit down and figure what hit me."

Anna Orange may have hoped that the gathering twilight would help to obscure her unruly raised eyebrow. Over the little girl's approaching screams, Mary said, "Yes, I think it helps to have a book on raising children, but you have to be sure it's the latest edition."

"I'll get a blanket," said Anna. She turned to meet Barbara. "Is Susan all right?"

We had expected a Susan dripping like a baby mermaid, but even in the twilight the crispness of her clothes and hair made us realize she was dry.

"It was the little cherub statue," Barbara said flatly. "I'm sorry. It fell in, and I think it broke."

Knowing what the statue meant to Anna, I knew she wanted to cry. Perhaps she also wanted to cry because she had no excuse to hug her little granddaughter in a blanket. But she could never have cried except behind the closed door of her own bedroom.

"Everything breaks in time," she said briskly. "I'm glad Susan isn't hurt."

We were quiet: Barbara too guilty and proud to say anything more; Anna thinking back perhaps to the good old days when her husband gave her the little statue; and Mary caught, too, in the subdued mood of the falling dusk. I could still see my companions clearly, although it was obvious that without their glasses they could no longer see each other. Gradually, as each woman felt she could no longer be seen, except as a blur, her expression changed.

Barbara's polite belligerence gave way to confusion and inadequacy. She fingered her book as though she were tempted to look under "B" in the index to see where Mary had gone astray about the boa constrictor. *If not the theory in the book, if not "permissiveness," what, oh, for God's sake, what?* her eyes asked. She shivered and hugged her child as she might have hugged an old teddy bear for comfort.

Anna, no longer the socially well-armed aristocrat, became a wistful and lonely old woman afraid of the future on her formal terrace with its elaborate iron garden furniture—the trappings of a secure and serenely patterned past. Her face sagged. And Mary chewed her lip in self-doubting desolation.

Not the least of each woman's discouragement, I suspected, was that she imagined the other two sitting in the cool summer dark with the same bright cheerful manner with which each had challenged the third degree of the afternoon sunlight.

Journalistic Offerings

Most of Liz's writing career involved journalism. Here's an example—a piece about cemeteries, published in The Book of American Traditions, *edited by Emyl Jenkins. Included is a rare mention of an ancestor of Liz's, Edward Teach—better known as Blackbeard the Pirate. In a note to Liz on accepting the piece for the anthology, Ms. Jenkins wrote, "It really is one of the best pieces in the entire 650-page book."*

The Summation of a Life

A graveyard is full of mysteries waiting to intrigue. I learned that when I was a child. Wherever we traveled, my father would stop the car and go look at old cemeteries—the ones with tombstones tilted by time and grayed with moss. He looked for the history made real: tombstones for soldiers in the Civil War, or the stone for one entire family that died together in a yellow fever epidemic. And I understood from the large number of small carved lambs, and the tiny stones for babies and small children, that once it had been an accomplishment just to grow up. The people who came before me lived in a dangerous world, and most of their tombstones seemed to say they'd been brave about it.

A father (1808-1882) in a graveyard near Asheville, North Carolina, rates these words: "I have fought the good fight, I have finished my course. I have kept the faith." Not too far away, a tombstone bears a carved hand that points straight up to heaven.

Markers are so varied, from plain flat stones with inscriptions to large stone tree-stump-shaped markers for deceased members of the Woodmen of the World, from the stone angel carved by Thomas Wolfe's father, for example, to some homemade markers we found in a small family plot. Someone had cut squared-off holes in the ground above the graves, then poured in cement. Then the names and dates of the departed were written in the wet cement. Whatever their resources, these people cared.

I like to examine tombstones, which can hold the summation of a life or at least explain how it ended. I admire the explicitness of the story in the small space on some stones:

"Thad Sherrill, son of Jason (and) Clarissa 1846-1898. Bushwhacked on Mt. Creek by George Maney. Maney lynched by Mob in Murphy 1899. Hanging Him to Upper Valley River Bridge." So says an inscription in the Old Mother Church cemetery in Robbinsville, North Carolina. The kernel of a larger story of hate and revenge.

And more personal tragedies are spelled out too. In a small family resting place outside of Asheville, a large stone bears the almost-life-size picture of the motorcycle on which the young man buried there was killed.

But visiting graveyards has never depressed me. It's made me aware that I'd better make the most of my life. Because, as an old hymn says: "We are only here for a little while."

My father, who had a great zest for being alive, looked for something to laugh about on tombstones. He had a great affection for my aunt Emily, my mother's sister. But, almost as an antidote for the sadness at her graveside service, he found a joke on my great-grandparents' tombstone. They share a monument in beautiful Spanish-moss-draped Oakdale Cemetery in Wilmington, North Carolina. He died first, and so the stone said, "Here Lies Robert Rufus Bridgers." And his family put a Bible verse: "He rests from his labors." When his wife died, her name was added to the gravestone. So the stone now reads, "Here lies Robert Rufus Bridgers. He rests from his labors and his wife Margaret Elizabeth Bridgers."

Fortunately, that whole branch of my family seems to be endowed with a good sense of humor, so I didn't expect them to mind when I used that inscription in the first chapter of one of my mystery novels, *Remember the Alibi*. The mystery begins—where else?—in an old cemetery.

In real life, tombstones can solve mysteries. My husband, like my late father, is a tombstone aficionado. This helped him figure out his great-great-grandmother's Hungarian connection. You see, his staunch family had staunch Yankee names, except for several men in the family with the exotic name Bela, which is the Hungarian version of "Benjamin." How on earth, my husband wondered, had that name come down to him from his great-great-uncle? Perhaps, he suspected, his great-great-grandmother had had a secret affair with a wild Hungarian.

But when we went to the green and peaceful family resting place in Riverton, Connecticut, he found the gravestone of his great-grandfather's brother, Bela Squire. Nearby he also found the stone of Dr. John Bela, whose inscription made clear he had been community doctor for many years. So my husband figures the name *Bela* honors the doctor who brought an ancestor into the world. In gratitude after a difficult birth, perhaps. Stones often hint at more than will fit into the chiseled inscription.

Graveyards anchor family history for many people, I find. They make it seem more real than just the names in a county courthouse record book or a family Bible.

Sometimes, a burial place is a reminder of a painful mystery that changes the lives of those who are still alive. Not far from my ancestors in the Wilmington cemetery is the Kenan family plot. My husband found it, and called me over to look. Because there lies Mary Lily Kenan Flagler Bingham (1867-1917).

We'd heard her story. Rumors about her death were still around in 1986 and helped cause the rather public Bingham family dissension that led up to the sale of the family-owned paper, *The Louisville Courier-Journal*. Mary Lily was the widow of Florida real estate and railroad magnate Henry M. Flagler when she married Col. Robert Worth Bingham, publisher of the *Courier-Journal*. A scant few months later, she died under strange circumstances. Rumors said her husband might be to blame. The fortune she left to Colonel Bingham helped develop the paper. And that fact is said to have helped fuel family dissension. Meanwhile, Mary Lily lies in peace under the swaying Spanish moss. A mystery forever.

I, being Southern and aware of both near and far relationships, know that I am related to Colonel Bingham, who may or may not have caused his wife's death and who helped create a great newspaper. We are both descended from a far away ancestor who was a governor. And I come down from other creators of newspapers, and also from a pirate and other rather imperfect types. I can visit the graves of ancestors who flourished and those who definitely did not. I am a multitude.

I am the past as well as the present. There are graves to prove it. That's tradition, right?

And perhaps that is what makes a graveside service so moving at a time of loss. We need the comfort of the ritual—the hopeful words about the hereafter, the heads bowed, remembering. And there's also comfort in the fact that this particular loved one has now become part of the history and tradition commemorated in this place. So, comforted, we feel free to be glad to be alive, and even to laugh.

I ask friends what they remember about old graveyards, and often it's the funny stones, not the sadness. Like the one I'm told about in Beaufort, South Carolina, that says, "You see, I told you I was sick," and the one in Murphy, North Carolina, which says, "Thanks for the dance."

* * *

Liz was a pretty serious interviewer and was never happier than when she was interviewing a fellow author. Here is an interview she conducted in 1976 with John Toland following publication of his biography of Adolf Hitler. It was published in the Acorn Press newspapers. Coincidentally, Toland's wife, Toshiko Matsumura, had been Tokyo correspondent for some years for Platt's Oilgram, *of which I was managing editor. We discovered this connection years later at a party in Redding.*

An Author of Controversy

For any person who ever wanted to write a prize-winning best seller—and especially for those who write, and fall short—John Toland's story is enlightening and encouraging.

Today, Toland, whose *Adolf Hitler* (Doubleday, $14.95) is just out, is the picture of a successful author, with his nine published books among the many assorted volumes on the shelves of his informal barn-red country house in Connecticut. He has written on such varied subjects as *Ships in the Sky* (1957) and *The Dillinger Days* (1963), about the famous Chicagoland gangster. His last book, *The Rising Sun,* about Japan in World War II, began by causing a storm of controversy—some critics said he had been "Japanized" by his Japanese wife—but the book finally won all sorts of prizes, including the Pulitzer Prize for 1971.

Toland's newest book, *Adolf Hitler,* seems headed for the same controversial course, raising shock waves and probable sales to match.

But before John Toland had a word published, he had written 20 plays, half a dozen novels, and a hundred short stories. Then he finally sold a humorous short story to a science fiction magazine, and the well-pleased editor bought all of Toland's short stories for six months. Success at last? No. The editor was fired because the readers of the magazine did not like humorous science fiction—they wanted serious stuff about androids, Toland recollects.

But John Toland kept writing, cheered by the words of his original literary hero, Porter Emerson Brown, who said: "John, the worst thing that can ever happen to you is to be successful early.

If you are fortunate, you won't sell a word until you have written a million words."

Porter Emerson Brown influenced the way Toland puts together his books, too. In his relaxed early-American style living room, where he interviewed several members of Hitler's inner circle for *Adolf Hitler*, John Toland reminisced about how his father happened to bring Porter Emerson Brown home from the Christian Science Church one day when John was 14.

Brown had written a successful play, *The Bad Man*. He had traveled with Pancho Villa, and written some of Theodore Roosevelt's speeches. Brown stayed with the Toland family while recovering from a depression over his wife's death.

John listened to the playwright talk and said, "I want to be a writer, too." Together, they went to movies, and left halfway through. Then they would write the endings, and then go back and compare these with the endings provided by Hollywood. "Ours were nearly always better," John Toland recalls, "because they followed certain rules that Porter Emerson Brown laid down. 'Don't tell it, show it' was the most important rule Porter Emerson Brown said—'engrave this in your head forever.'

"My books are 'don't tell it, show it,'" says John Toland now. "I don't tell you why Hitler was so anti-Semitic. I give you 49 hints. Now, also, who knows what made him anti-Semitic? When you read Dostoevsky, does he tell you what made the man (in *The Possessed*) go mad? You see him go mad. That's better. And then everybody gets different conceptions of it. That is closer to reality."

Although Toland uses techniques he learned from writing drama and fiction, he believes switching to history made him a better writer.

Writing non-fiction immediately made clear where his weakness had been. "I could always write tremendous scenes, good dialogue, but I couldn't put it all together," Toland says. "I couldn't plot—but with history, God plots for me."

History imposed and added discipline. To find historical truth, Toland believes any writer has to be able to put aside all his preconceived notions.

Above his desk is a Japanese ideogram which says "cleanse you mind." He interviewed 150 top Nazis with that point of view. "Then you find out why they are what they are."

As a result of his ability to interview top Nazis, a woman called Toland a Fascist. "Oh gee!" he said, "I'm a Nazi, I'm a Communist, I'm a Christian Scientist, I'm a Catholic. You know what I am? When I interview a person, I am that person. And it doesn't bother me a bit what they did, because I am Dostoevsky with my little old recorder, taking down things for my next novel. I really don't listen as John Toland, the guy who was forced to go into the army and spend seven years because of a son-of-a-bitch named Hitler."

Dostoevsky wrote about people like the Nazis in *The Possessed*, Toland says. Yet "Dostoevsky never condemns. But you have the feeling, 'My God, how could human beings have done this?' I've seen how they do it—but you don't hate the people.

"I'm an excellent archival detective!" says Toland, with a twinkle of pleasure in his blue eyes. "Look at the stuff I've found!" His years of research and cross-checking with other researchers turned up proof that Hitler nursed his mother during her final painful treatment for cancer by a Jewish doctor—possibly a determining factor in Hitler's anti-Semitism.

As an interviewer and a researcher, "I work like a newspaper man. I'm a good leg-man," says John Toland. But his research would be considered beyond the call of duty by many "leg-men." To write about the Battle of the Bulge, Toland spent a cold winter night in a foxhole on the battlefield. As a result, Toland says, whenever his name is mentioned in a nearby town, people say, "Oh, that nut."

Yet being willing to work honestly in his own way, even to the point of being a nut, has brought him helpers—for example, Otto Skorzeny, Hitler's favorite commando. Skorzeny introduced Toland to many of the 150 top Nazis interviewed for *Adolf Hitler*, even though the commando and the historian disagreed about Hitler. Skorzeny thought Hitler a savior.

Now, John Toland has started work on a book about World War I—and, when he finishes that, he believes he will be ready to write fiction, plot and all. "I am a slow learner in the sense of writing," he said, "and as a human being. I think I matured late. I was not a natural writer. But you know what I had? I had guts. I didn't give up."

Then suddenly he said to this reporter, in a tone that suggested he meant all writers and reporters: "What I'm doing is what you want to do yourself, in thought process—don't do it unless you can stand the heat."

Of course we all knew what was most important about Liz: she was warm, witty, and a pioneer in helping us survive those pesky senior moments that we are lucky to live long enough to have. Liz didn't live long enough. One thing is sure, though: a lot of readers and writers will never forget her. I won't.

Carole Nelson Douglas

Another story based on an author interview featured Manly Wade Wellman, of Chapel Hill. It was published in the alas-now-defunct Arts Journal in Asheville in October 1982:

A Man of Many Words

"In a minor sort of way, I'm a regional Southern writer with a special emphasis on folklore and the supernatural," says Manly Wade Wellman, ignoring the fact that his *Rebel Boast* was nominated for a Pulitzer Prize, and the staggering fact that he has published 74 books and nearly 300 short stories.

And what kind of person is this man of many words who is probably North Carolina's most-published author? A man of strong opinions, raging interests, old-fashioned courtliness, loyal friendship and quick readiness for a fistfight with anyone he believes has unfairly insulted him or anyone he loves.

He is a man who can listen with such enthralled interest that when he was researching the Civil War, old ladies went up in the attic and brought down, for him to see, trunks of letters written from the battlefields. And he knows how to write books that hit the nerve of public interest.

"As is well-known," said Sam Ragan, North Carolina editor and poet, "Manly knows everything." There was a roar of sympathetic laughter from the members of the North Carolina Writers Conference, assembled to hear Sam and several others speak about Manly being honored at their 1982 session in Chapel Hill. Sam told how his wife Marjorie finally thought she knew something Manly didn't when she told him how to cook a rhinoceros hoof. But no, Manly told her how to cook it better.

Manly Wellman had some reason to know about the rhinoceros. He was born in Angola, West Africa, the son of a medical officer at a mission. Manly came back to the United States when he was six. By then, he already knew he intended to be a writer, and from the first he felt his subjects picked him, not he them.

"Something will jump up and hit you," says Manly. "You are possessed. It's a sort of a curse or a blessing."

For example, he is possessed by the old authentic ballads of the North Carolina mountains. He says, "I'd sit all day on a sharp rail to hear some of those people play," such as Obray Arlin Ramsey, "the best banjo I ever heard," or Tom Hunter, "the best country fiddler." Both are from Madison County.

"So, many of my 'John' stories come out of folksongs, like 'Little Black Train,'" he says. John the Balladeer is Manly Wade Wellman's most popular character in short stories and novels. John's manner and way of speaking come straight out of the mountains, and he carries a guitar with silver strings. He sings the old ballads to make friends, to quiet his mind when he's "a-studying" something out, and to remind himself of ways to combat bad magic and witchcraft—frequently the subject of ballads.

John the Balladeer is hero of Manly's latest published book, *The Lost and the Lurking* (Doubleday, 1981) and two other books.

On a trip to England, Manly found himself "possessed" by Stonehenge, almost as possessed as he is by ballads. He stood and thought, "my ancestors built that a thousand years ago." His next-to-be-published book, *The Hanging Stones* (Doubleday), deals with Stonehenge to some extent. That book and the "John" books are science-fiction fantasy genre and so is *What Dreams May Come,* the next book for Doubleday now in first draft.

Manly's writing has come full circle, for his first book, *Invading Asteroids* in 1932, was science fiction and his latest books are, too. In between, he's written about the Civil War and American Indians. He's written biographies, notably one of Wade Hampton, and local history—including *The Kingdom of Madison* about Madison County, and more. And for a self-declared minor writer, he has seen his books win a lot of prizes. These include several awards for science fiction, one for the best short-story collection of the year, the North Carolina Peace Award for regional history, the North Carolina American Association of University Women award for juvenile literature, and the Mystery Writers of America Edgar award for non-fiction crime study. In 1978 he won the state's top honor, the North Carolina Award.

For all this, Manly gambled. He quit a good newspaper job in the 1930s in the middle of the Depression to write books and short stories full-time. He lived in New York then, though perhaps because of his Southern heritage (ancestors to Jamestown, 1643) he didn't care for the manners of the local inhabitants. Men on the street would make provocative remarks to his wife, Frances. "Why don't you step out here," he'd say, "and," he explains, "they got the worst of it."

"It was dangerous to go out with him," laughs Frances, also a writer under the name Frances Garfield.

After a stint in World War II, Manly won a big cash first prize for a detective story—the Ellery Queen Short Story Prize. Then he and Frances could move to North Carolina, where he liked the manners of the inhabitants better.

Winning that contest was a close thing, he remembers. The three judges could not decide among the three top stories. At that point, they bumped into Christopher Morley and asked him to read and decide among the three. Morley chose Wellman's story with an American Indian detective. And so, Wellman explains, "I won first prize, and the second prize went to William Faulkner, whose shoes I am not even fit to tie." Shortly thereafter, someone insulted Christopher Morley in front of Manly. Said he to the insulter, "Would you care to step outside?"

With prize money in hand, Manly and Frances moved to Pine Bluff, North Carolina, then, in 1951, to Chapel Hill, where they have lived ever since. At 79, Manly is still writing full-time. And he has a long overview of North Carolina writers and writing. After all, he has helped a lot of them to get started. Some, such as novelist Mena Webb, were in his writing classes; some, such as science-fiction writer Karl Wagner, enjoyed his moral support getting started.

Times are getting harder for writers because people read less, Manly believes. "I know people who say they don't read and seem proud of it. It's like the Dark Ages. The baron in his castle said, 'What do you mean, do I read? Do you take me for a monk? I've got a very expensive suit of armor right there!'" When he first came to Chapel Hill, "you couldn't throw a rock on Franklin Street without hitting a writer." But now, "like the Indians, when the buffalo were gone, moved into the reservation," writers are taking other jobs in order to eat.

Are regional writers better off than general writers? They are if they happen to live in North Carolina, Manly Wade Wellman believes. Paul Green described North Carolina as having the right "climate" for writers. And Manly adds, "Paul Green helped create that climate."

Before he moved to North Carolina and wrote *The Sand Pebbles*, Richard McKenna did a little research to discover where writers were. He found there were two rich lodes, Manly says—one in North Carolina and the other in Oregon. North Carolina is still one of the best places in the United States to live if you want to be a writer, Manly believes. The North Carolina Writers Conference, which meets every year in a different part of the state, is one symptom that there are plenty of writers in North Carolina "doing something actual, as my mother used to say."

And Chapel Hill, though not so thick with writers as it used to be, may have the largest number of science-fiction writers for its total population of any city in the U.S., Manly believes. There is Manly Wade Wellman, still going strong; and Karl Wagner, who gave up practicing law to write. The last two have also started publishing collections of short stories. A collection by Manly, titled *Don't Look Behind You*, will be out soon.

At least in North Carolina, a writer who is cursed or blessed by a subject that cries out to be written about is not alone, Manly points out. "It is good here." At least here, "you write something, someone else will read it and the lonesome area you wrote in isn't quite so lonesome at that."

As for Manly Wade Wellman, he intends to stay right in Chapel Hill, and his friends in the Writers Conference say he will soon have published one book for every year of his life.

* * *

The following piece was commissioned by the Asheville Citizen-Times, *but at the time of Liz's death it had not been published. Thus it appears here for the first time:*

Mystery in the Mountains

I was six or seven, riding the night train from Raleigh to Asheville back in the days when trains went where roads could not go. Out the dark window I saw a mountainside with lights moving on it. With awe in her voice, my Aunt Ann said, "Those are the Brown Mountain Lights. Nobody can explain them."

"But why don't people just follow the lights and find out?" I demanded.

"Because you can see them at a distance, but if you get close they vanish," she explained.

This mystery thrilled me. Long before I read a mystery or wrote a series set here, the glamour of these mountains took hold of me.

My aunt took me to the Mountain Folk Festival in Asheville which swept me away with ballads about love and betrayal and Tom Dooley waiting to be hung for murder, the very heart of all mysteries.

Any mountain writer of novels that involve mystery is lucky to be able to draw on those raw ballad emotions. Sharyn McCrumb uses ballads as points of departure for books like *The Ballad of Frankie Silver*.

The Southern Appalachians offer much more: legends of "outlaws" of all sorts, mysterious features of the landscape from secret places such as caves to upright hollows, unusual folk beliefs, and also, though it's not always mysterious, mountain humor. These have colored my novels such as *Who Killed What's-Her-Name?*, *Remember the Alibi*, and *Forget About Murder*.

Mountains have been hiding places for fugitives back beyond even the Civil War. A cave hid deserters in Charles Frazier's *Cold Mountain*. Suspected bomber Eric Rudolph may still be here—maybe deep in a cave? Members of the WNC chapter of the national group that explores and protects caves tell me they helped search for Rudolph.

A newspaper story about a murder victim found in a cave six or eight years ago was my inspiration for a frightening scene in *Whose Death Is It, Anyway?* where my sleuth is nearly done in. (The real body was found in an old mine. Like my absent-minded sleuth, Peaches Dann, I tend to forget things.)

But to make my scene realistic, I went to visit a cave near the French Broad River in Madison County. I used the movement of the flickering light and dark in that cave, where a flashlight beam suddenly picked out a black hole—an entrance to another chamber—or a dark spot could hide a dangerous fissure.

Light tends to be dramatic in the mountains, and the shadows can build suspense until the writer's own heart is beating hard. Fog can turn light or dark and magical, with objects materializing as they come closer, disappearing as they retreat. Fog inspires eerie overtones in the book I'm writing now.

Few people visit narrow upright hollows—coves or fissures in the mountains where the sun shines in only at noon and the light is subdued. A scream for help might not be heard. So, an upright hollow was just the spot for my heroine to find herself in mortal danger in *Forget About Murder*. Never mind that I slipped and turned my ankle while scoping out the place. Research can be demanding.

Even place-names spark mysteries. Anne Underwood Grant, who usually writes mysteries set in Charlotte, and Patrick Bone, who writes young-adult books, are both at work on vampire stories—set, of course, in beautiful Transylvania County.

As a mystery writer, I get goose bumps when I see how closely death and beauty can be intertwined, especially in Appalachian country. Waterfalls can be lethal. Kevin Adams in his book on North Carolina waterfalls says it's easy to spot the people who won't fol-

low simple precautions. "They lie motionless at the base of the falls."
And who could tell if they were pushed?

With this in mind, I was set to write of murder at Linville Falls in *Where There's a Will*. But when it comes to murder, I discovered the accusing finger is more likely to point to overlooks than to falls. In fact, the Chestoa View Overlook near Linville Falls was fingered twice as a possible murder site. A man accused of pushing his wife and her friend to their deaths there in 1988 was tried twice and finally acquitted. When another body showed up below the overlook two years later, no killer was found.

I went to visit the site and took notes as we writers do. I found not only a breathtaking view but a boy and girl sitting on the low overlook wall, just one false move from oblivion. My stomach flip-flopped. Now, if they had been part of a ballad. . . .

Of course, I switched my murder to an overlook.

Legend has it that rocky places like falls or caves are where you might find all sorts of Cherokee supernaturals, for example the Yunwi Tsundi or little people, about a foot and a half high.

Sallie Bissell of Weaverville uses Cherokee legends, including one about an invisible lake that heals the wounds of warriors, in her *In the Forest of Harm*, a novel set in Nantahala and Cherokee.

In *Whose Death Is It, Anyway?* my sleuth, Peaches Dann, gets help from a Cherokee wise woman. Peaches reads hands—not to predict the future but to see character and potentialities. The wise woman explains a hand-marking that the Cherokee believe is one sign that a child can be trained to be a shaman, and this helps Peaches solve a murder.

Cherokee beliefs seem related to the magnetism of the mountains. Plainly there are certain people they charm in a strange way. These people pass through without intending to stay, and immediately go home, quit good jobs and move to the Asheville area, where they take any job they can get in order to remain. I have been amazed by them here, and I assume they probably show up in other parts of the mountains.

Our mountains nourish all kinds of secrets. Somehow, I have always bumped into lore about making moonshine, which mountain men believe is their right and heritage, and revenuers tried—and still try—to stop. As a reporter, I interviewed retired moonshiners and transporters in Madison County, where the art flourished during Prohibition. The Reems Creek valley where I live is the setting for *Thunder Road*, a Robert Mitchum 1950s cult film about transporting moonshine in the old days. An elderly moonshiner left from the glory days takes my sleuth on a chase scene in one of the cars modified to transport spirits and confound revenuers. That's in *Forget About Murder.* Some parts of writing are really fun.

And speaking of another kind of spirits, there's a large New Age community drawn to this area. Many of these people believe that Ley lines, or lines of mystic power, crisscross the Smoky Mountains. You can find practitioners of every mystic art such as tarot readers and pet psychics. In fact, both of those give me plot twists for the mystery I'm working on now.

Some folks in Weaverville, North Carolina, for example, and some over in the Tennessee mountains believe they have sighted flying saucers. There are chapters of the Mutual UFO Network and the Society for the Study of Extra-Terrestrials here in the mountains ever ready to collect data. Obviously that's where Deborah Adams, who writes mysteries set in fictional Jesus Creek, Tennessee, got the idea for the group of UFO enthusiasts in her *All the Hungry Mothers.*

These mountains have more different species of herbs and plants than any other place on earth, including ginseng, worth its weight in gold. Sometimes, it seems, we also have human beings with the widest possible experience and beliefs. That's an incredible resource for any mystery writer. Suspects and victims can come in wildly differing guises such as a New York actress or a fanatical back cove preacher or even a retired sea captain.

My forgetful sleuth has to be a memory strategy expert just to survive, so why do I enjoy thrusting her into mountain dangers and confusions? In mysteries, justice always triumphs. And if she can come out on top pursued by killers in caves or cornered by rattlesnakes, so should my readers and me.

But for writers and others—especially visitors and tourists—just two words to the wise: Watch out! These mysterious Appalachian Mountains can get a hold on you when you don't expect it, and not let go.

> *Over the last couple of years I have enjoyed getting to know her when she came to Raleigh. We had a wonderful lunch one afternoon talking about memory devices for Peaches Dann . . . and also for a non-fiction book she was thinking about writing regarding memory devices (I wrote a book about Alzheimer's).*
>
> *She was incredibly supportive of young writers and generous with her time. She was fun and accessible and "Lady" in the true and good sense of the word.*
>
> Carrie Knowles

Still another piece by Liz celebrates the aging process. It's in the form of a dialogue between Peaches and Liz. While she was mulling this idea over in her head, Liz asked me what I thought, saying "It's not falling together just right—I guess because I can't decide whether to tell this in Peaches's voice or my own."

"What if," I suggested, "you try doing a dialogue?" Here is the result, as published in Deadly Women, *edited by Jan Grape, Dean James, and Ellen Nehr. A quotation from this piece is on the tombstone that marks where Liz's ashes are buried in Buncombe County, North Carolina.*

The Older They Get. . .

Characters of all ages tend to talk to their authors. And, because characters live inside our heads, they have access to everything we know. On top of which they know even more than we do about themselves. Which makes them uppity or else helpful, as the mood suits them. Or even philosophic.

So I wasn't surprised when Peaches Dann, my 58-plus absent-minded sleuth looked me straight in my mind's eye and said: "You don't know how lucky you are to write about a well-seasoned wiser sleuth like me."

Now, I knew Peaches's on-off, on-off memory had nothing to do with age. She made it quite clear back when she first appeared in *Who Killed What's-Her-Name?*. Furthermore, with the passage of time she's learned the memory tricks that help solve murders. So she says.

"Every age is interesting," I said, not wanting this older-wiser thing to go to her head.

"Exactly," she said. "And it's great to have lived through all the earlier ages plus the present. You are all of yourselves rolled into one—the young, the middle-aged, the well matured. I mean, look at Henrie O. She tells Carolyn Hart all sorts of ways that her earlier experience as a newspaper woman can help her solve crime, right?"

"Or take Mrs. Pargeter," Peaches said, switching to the British detecting scene à la Simon Brett. "Mrs. P. admires the fact that her late crime-lord husband believed in honor among thieves. She knows how to use his underworld connections to solve crimes without-honor and actually make the world a better place. So even experience of a very dubious sort can be used with wisdom. And sometimes compassion."

Peaches had a point. "What I like about an older sleuth," I said, "is the same thing I like about being older myself. You reach an age where you're willing to do what works best for you even if it looks eccentric to other people. Where you respect the real deep-down differences in the way people's minds work, including your own. And if some folks think that's outrageous, so be it."

"I, myself, am not outrageous," Peaches said firmly. "I'm a prag-matist, pure and simple in every book."

"Except perhaps the time your dinner guests found an upside-down bowl with two toilet paper rolls on it and at the very top a half-eaten apple, all on the kitchen counter," I said. "You know folks always come in the kitchen."

"Temporary Found Sculpture!" Peaches cried. "Made of what came to hand, to remind me to take the rolls out of the oven at eight-thirty. Because my timer broke. And soon as I explained that the apple half eaten meant half after eight as in *a-t-e*, they all reminded me when the time came. Temporary Found Sculpture works. So it's not eccentric."

To spare Peaches's feelings, I talked about her peers. "Well, how about Dorothy Gilman's Mrs. Pollifax. She's sixty-something, and she outwits Bulgarian terrorists, African assassins, Albanian thugs, and other dangerous types with totally unconventional ploys. Like the time she substituted a can of peaches for a can of uranium and thus prevented mayhem."

"Don't give away plots," Peaches said. "It's not fair."

"And how about Father Brown," I said, to get more classical. "He was a Roman Catholic priest, and yet he solved crimes by step-ping in the killer's shoes. What was it he said? Something like 'When I'm quite sure I feel like the murderer, I know who he is.' What would the Vatican think of that?

"And how about Miss Seeton, who has already outlived her senior status?" I asked. "Miss Seeton doesn't even bother to find out why her sketches contain clues that help other more-law-enforcement-minded folks solve murders. She just draws cartoons and there the clues are. Now how is that for odd?"

Peaches retorted, "It's wise. You do what you can to be useful. And by the time you are fifty or sixty or seventy, you have learned all sorts of surprising things because you've had to. And anything you've learned can be helpful if you can just figure out how. That's the mystery. How to use it."

But Peaches isn't like Henrie O, who covered murders and wars and other disasters as a reporter. She's not even like Stephanie Matteson's Charlotte Graham, an older Oscar-winning actress-turned-sleuth with all sorts of fancy connections to help her out. When Peaches worked, she helped her first husband run a moun-tain craft shop—hardly apprenticeship to find killers.

"Of course you collect memory tricks," I said, "but aside from that. . . ."

She felt my skepticism. "My experience," she said, "is partly in figuring out what makes people tick. Back in my craft-shop days, I could tell—just by the blouses they wore—a customer who would want cute little carved wooden mice from one who wanted lovely traditional pottery. Mice go with ruffles. Men rarely buy cute mice, except when kids demand it.

"And," Peaches continued, "since I forget things, like who I put aside the toby jug for, or who I should know by name because they came in last week, I have more know-how in getting around what I don't know—in figuring it out. What else do detectives do? I have learned how to get folks to tell me what I need to know without letting them find out I don't already know it. Older sleuths have had to learn all kinds of things like that."

"You mean," I said, "that just as Miss Marple could solve any crime by comparing the killer's motive with some point of psychology in an English village, every older sleuth has the equivalent of a village. A community of experience he or she can draw on."

"Of course," Peaches said. "You might say I draw upon the confederation of the absent-minded." (Peaches knows how to make even foolishness sound good.) "Because since my experiences as an absent-minded sleuth have been written up in books, everybody sends me their memory tricks. Did you know that 83 percent of Americans believe they have bad memories for names? A scientific study showed that. And over 60 percent believe they have trouble finding things like their keys or their glasses. But that's Americans of all ages. And I, being older, have collected and developed more memory coping devices over the years. I am an expert!"

Good grief! Peaches is getting as full of herself as senior-citizen Hercule Poirot with his little gray cells! Can getting around spacey gray cells be something to crow about? That takes nerve!

Amazing what kinds of experience older sleuths draw on. Of course, ex-police-chiefs like Susanna Hofmann McShea's Forrest Haggarty can detect, especially with the help of other small-town-Connecticut seniors. How about D. B. Borton's Cat Caliban saying she's a better sleuth because she's been a mother! I guess lots of mothers would agree.

"Okay, okay!" I said. "But you older sleuths have limits. Admit that, Peaches! You can't have a convincing fistfight or sword-battle or get seriously beaten up and be back at work in two hours."

"Poo!" said Peaches. "Some of us are in great shape. Fannie Zindel, who's so full of energy she needs two authors, is a five-times tennis champion. And anybody who lives in the mountains like me has to walk up and down hills." (Peaches is rather proud of still being a size twelve.)

"But I'll admit," she said, "that mostly we are forced to battle with our wits—right? Give me an older sleuth any day for surprise twists and unexpected insight. Take Nero Wolfe. He hardly moved out of his chair, but he solved all sorts of exotic crimes with snakes and poison and I forget what else. He was a great detective, with his mind.

"But I'm not jealous of him," Peaches went on. "I'm jealous of the senior sleuths who get to travel. Such as Dottie and Joe Loudermilk in their RV van. Since they're retired, author Gar Haywood takes them to the Grand Canyon to solve murders. Why can't you take me there? There's one advantage of an older sleuth that you've ignored," she accused. "We aren't tied down. Or not as much. We can go places! Anyplace we like. We're ready!"

"So what's the drawback with being an older sleuth?" I asked. "It can't all be perfect."

"The drawback," Peaches said, "is for you, not for me. With every book, I get older. Suppose I get so old I can't detect anymore? Then what will you do?"

I just laughed. "You forget—I get older, too. And in the meantime I'll just follow the motto I learned from Mrs. Pollifax: 'Adapt, adjust, and catch your breath later.'"

Long silence from Peaches. "I don't suppose," she said, "that you'd consider getting your motto from me?"

I was grieved to read about losing Elizabeth, as I'm sure thousands of others will be too. Elizabeth was a joy, a great soul, and a wonderful friend, writer and supporter of independent bookshops. I will miss seeing her here on the Outer Banks as I have for the past 16 years.

Steve Brumfield
Manteo Booksellers

Above: Jonathan Daniels and his first wife, Elizabeth Bridgers Daniels, with their infant daughter Liz, 1926.

Right: Liz (Bibba), age 11, and 3-year-old Lucy dressed for a play at Bibba's school (1937).

In her job as a reporter for *The Redding* (Connecticut) *Pilot* in the 1970s, Liz interviewed all kinds of people, both man and beast. *Pilot* editor Sally Sanders (left) isn't at all surprised (Perry Ruben photo).

Promo photo for syndi-
cated palmistry column
(Perry Ruben photo).

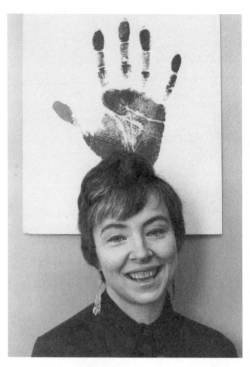

Liz talking the matchless Joan Rivers through a self-
handreading during a "What's My Line" TV appearance in the
early 1970s, as Bill Cullen looks on (Perry Ruben photo).

Liz, promoting her handreading book in the early 1970s, reads a palm during a talk at the Ridgefield, Connecticut, Community Center (Perry Ruben photo).

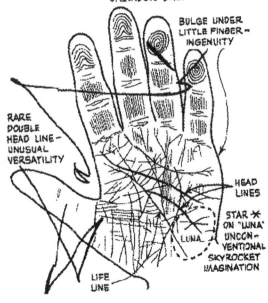

DO YOU SHOCK PEOPLE?
SALVADOR DALI

BULGE UNDER
LITTLE FINGER –
INGENUITY

RARE
DOUBLE
HEAD LINE –
UNUSUAL
VERSATILITY

HEAD
LINES

STAR ✶
ON "LUNA"
UNCON-
VENTIONAL
SKYROCKET
IMAGINATION

LUNA

LIFE
LINE

AN ARTIST WHO SHOCKED HIS CONTEMPORARIES

This is the artwork for Liz's newspaper feature on Salvador Dali—signed by the flamboyant artist with Liz's eyebrow pencil across the actual handprint (artwork by Robert Leatherbarrow).

Below: Liz frequently woke up in the morning with material in her head from what she called "sleep-think" and quickly jotted it down before going up the hill to her office and putting it into the computer. But (as you can see), only Liz knew what these jottings said!

Above: Liz receiving her Agatha award at Malice Domestic in 1995 (Lee Phan photo).

Liz's writing group in early 2001 at the Carrabba's restaurant in Asheville, their biweekly meeting place. L-R: Dershie McDevitt, Jan Harrow, Dr. Peggy D. Parris, Dr. Geraldine Powell, and Liz (photo by the waiter).

Liz and Sam the cat, in promo shot for an article Liz wrote about writers and cats interacting (John A. Miller photo).

Liz with Bailey, cover model for "Forget About Murder" (John A. Miller photo).

Photo of Liz that appeared (as "Miss August") on the International Dyslexia Society's 1998 calendar (John Warner photo).

Left: Liz at Palenque, Mexico, in her nose-flattening Mayan mode (Kitty Boniske photo). Right: Liz and Chick, Potsdam, Germany, fall 2000 (Marianne Meyer photo).

Left: Liz, Chick, and their three sons—Hart, the eldest, on left; Mark, the middle one, far right; and Worth, the youngest, next to Chick (Monika Wengler photo). Right: Liz with her eldest grandchild, Troon Squire, summer of 2000 (Jane Kinney photo).

Mostly About Food

In the 1970s, Liz's work for Acorn Press included a weekly column about food. Liz had already developed a deep interest in early-American fireplace cooking, and we were already at work on a book about hearthside cuisine, tentatively titled Iron in the Fire, *illustrated with marvelous pictures by our friend Perry Ruben. After keeping the manuscript for six months, Stephen Greene, the Vermont publisher, turned it down. "There's too many books coming out this year (1975) in connection with the Bicentennial," he wrote.*

And here is the introduction to that unpublished book:

Iron in the Fire   ·

Anyone whose childhood predates the everything-electric age is likely to remember the thrill of at least some simple fireplace cooking: toasting marshmallows, popping popcorn in a long-handle wire shaker, or perhaps the real excitement of making corn bread in a spider-legged Dutch oven on the hearth.

Fireplace cooking meant quiet gatherings of family around a cheerfully burning fire; cooking with fire or coals was not allowed to children unless adults were somewhere nearby. And while adults could enjoy the art of fireplace cooking alone as well, they usually waited for the presence of children, who had such fun roasting chestnuts in the ashes or cooking hot dogs on a stick over the fire.

Fireplace cooking required a little skill, but not more than a child could easily master. You had to learn how high to hold the popcorn-popper and how to keep the corn constantly in motion, for example. So the finished product brought special pride and pleasure when each bite was at the peak of perfection.

We knew children whose houses still included antique fireplaces complete with the equipment once used to do the family's cooking. These fireplaces were intriguing, but in nearly all cases the exact method for using the fireplace and equipment for actual cooking had been long forgotten.

A few years ago we came across a slim volume of recipes published in 1792 by Amelia Simmons, and our early interest in fireplace cooking was rekindled. Miss Simmons's simple book—the first published cookbook in America, using such unique American ingredients as Indian corn—was, of course, designed for the home-fireplace cook. Her recipes are puzzles to solve, however, for she assumed the reader had already learned to build a proper fire and use the equipment in the proper manner. In her day, you learned this in early childhood by observation, not out of cookbooks.

We knew, however, that some modern equivalents of Miss Simmons's fireplace equipment are still used by campers—the earliest exposure most of us have to fireplace cooking. At summer camp, we learned to build assorted kinds of cooking fires and to come up with such treats as blueberry pancakes cooked on a griddle or in a skillet, or gingerbread baked in a portable reflector oven.

The smell of the crackling wood and the spicy foods, indoors or out, made such meals or snacks a sensuous joy long before the first taste of the food. What marvelous smells must have wafted through Amelia Simmons's 1790 kitchen, we thought. But we knew, from our own popcorn-and-campfire days, that each fireplace implement—old or new—needs a little bit of know-how if the cook is to make the most of what the implement can do.

Once, during a power outage in a suburban town some years ago, we stayed with a family that boasted a 1790 fireplace complete with old cranes and trammels and other equipment. But the owners of this magnificent fireplace did not know how to use the equipment or even how to build a suitable cooking fire—and neither, then, did we. So we all fell back on skills learned as outdoor campers. We rigged up a reflector oven out of shiny cookie-sheets and cooked a rolled beef roast before the fire. The results were surprisingly good but not as mouth-watering as they would have been with a real knowledge of the possibilities of fireplace cooking.

Later, inspired by our chance encounter with Amelia Simmons, we were able to meet a number of fireplace-cooking enthusiasts in a number of places—people anxious to share their experiences in cooking with iron pots in the fire.

There was Flo Penland, who grew up in the mountains of North Carolina and watched her mother and grandmother make corn bread in a fireplace pot. Though Flo now lives in a modern house with a modern fireplace, she still likes to make this same kind of corn bread before the fire on bleak winter nights. It is, she said, somehow extra good that way.

Harry Boyd, who has a lovingly restored New England saltbox

house with one of the largest fireplaces we have seen, recalls seeing soda-bread and stews cooked in pots over a peat fire in his native Ireland.

Clara Platt, who is in her 80s and lives in a 1790s house in New England, recalls her girlhood in Montague County, Texas, northwest of Dallas. Her grandparents cooked before the fire, using cooking implements they brought with them from Roanoke, Virginia, by covered wagon. Clara likes to observe that land in Montague County in those days sold for 50 cents an acre.

Mrs. Carmine Nazzaro demonstrated for us an heirloom wafer iron used by her mother in their native Italy. And another friend explained how she and her family use a Swedish iron implement to make sweet crisp cookies as the family sits before the fire to talk and pass the iron back and forth. Like many pieces of fireplace equipment, the Swedish and Italian wafer irons are still available in specialty stores or from mail-order kitchen supply houses.

And then we met a whole group of fireplace cooks we call the "Re-Enacters." Members of the Fifth Connecticut Regiment, for example, who stage Revolutionary-War-vintage musters where all of the military arts—including cooking—are practiced with as much authenticity as possible. A 14-year-old member of the regiment's auxiliary baked delicious apple and berry pies in a Dutch oven over an open fire, and spectators exclaimed over the results.

While indoor and outdoor fireplace cooking are related, they are not exactly the same.

At restorations along the Hudson River in New York State, we saw re-enactments of fireplace cooking in wealthy Dutch households of early America and learned some useful safety tips about cooking with open fire.

And owners of other houses old enough to have cooking fireplaces invited us to see and photograph what they have learned and to share their excitement in bringing antique cooking implements to life.

Not that it is necessary to have an antique cooking-type fireplace—not at all. A large old colonial fireplace is useful if you want to cook a many-course meal, all in the fireplace. But an ordinary modern fireplace—or even an open-front Franklin stove—will suffice to prepare an evening snack such as roasted apples or even the main attraction at a dinner party for eight people. A turkey with chestnut stuffing roasts easily before the small fire. Any modern fireplace can be used to simmer a stew or roast potatoes.

Even without fireplace cooking utensils, the adventurous cook can turn out a savory roasted stuffed winter squash or pumpkin. With the simplest of improvised equipment, a leg of lamb can be roasted before the fire, a fish planked, or bread baked.

So we have set down some discoveries and experiences with fireplace cooking equipment, old and new and improvised, for those who:

—Enjoy trying new kinds of food or familiar foods cooked in a different way.

—Want to be ready, the night of the power outage, to prepare as good or better a dinner as could have been served if the candles were only on the table for romantic reasons.

—Own antique cooking implements and want to know exactly how these were used.

—Were all set to go out for a cookout when the rain started, or who wonder what to do with a group of young friends on a rainy day.

—Have 18th and 19th century cooking fireplaces and would like to try them out for cooking.

—Have railed at the squandering of energy when an electric or gas cookstove is running in the kitchen at the same time a wood fire is burning in the living-room fireplace, and who have wondered how the two forms of energy-use might be combined.

—Love outdoor campfire cooking in summer and would like to cook similarly indoors all through the winter months.

But, some people ask, isn't fireplace cooking a lot more work than cooking on a stove? If a whole meal of several courses is prepared at the fireplace all at once, that's hard work. Pictures of early-American cooks show them with bulging muscles from lifting all that heavy iron and big robust hardwood logs. But to simmer a stew or bake corn bread or gingerbread is little more trouble than preparing the same foods to cook on a conventional stove.

So cook when the fire is already purring in the fireplace for warmth and good cheer. Once you have the knack, almost anything can be prepared in a fireplace that can be cooked on a stove, with only a little more attention and, we think, a lot more fun and flavor.

I am so sorry to hear about Liz. I had dinner with her that last Sunday night in Anchorage at the end of Left Coast Crime, and we were talking about what we were going to do when she was up here for Malice. She was so charged up about her trip to Skagway and, as always, so full of life and good cheer. She was very encouraging to me as I head into my breast cancer surgery next week, and I deeply appreciated her wise counsel and positive attitude.
Carole Anne Nelson

Here's one of Liz's newspaper features on food, published by Acorn Press in April 1975:

Whatever Happened to the Egg in Mrs. Gorham's Cake Recipe?

Have you ever tried to put an old family recipe or one from an old book into usable form? If so, you have been bemused to see that 18th-century recipes include such measurements as gills and porringers, and list flour and sugar by the pound. Nineteenth-century recipes include "butter the size of a walnut," teacups of wine, and still often have dry ingredients by the pound.

More confusing yet, 18th- and 19th-century recipes often include that charming phrase "as much flour as is sufficient."

And even 20th-century family recipes, though in more precise measures and familiar terms, still often reflect the fact that the cook knew what she was doing partly by intuition and found it hard to put into words. For example, they say "cook until done."

We saw some marvelous old pewter measures at the Keeler Tavern in Ridgefield, but found no one there who had tried modernizing an ancient local recipe.

So we called Mrs. Benedict Gregory in Wilton, who is descended from and related to a number of long-time Wilton families of good cooks, including the Bradleys, the Treadwells, and the Benedicts as well as the Gregorys.

When we asked Mrs. Gregory if she had ever been a recipe detective, she said she had—but perhaps not precisely in the way we meant. And she told us this story:

It seems that the Mrs. Gorham, whose land is now the site of the new Wilton library, was fond of picnics. And Benedict Gregory's Aunt Frieda (Mrs. F. D. Benedict) had chickens. So Mr. and Mrs. Ben Gregory and Aunt Frieda and Mrs. Gorham frequently went on a picnic together. Aunt Frieda always sent Mrs. Gorham an egg on these occasions to make her famous "Black Cake." Aunt Frieda's fried chicken and Mrs. Gorham's cake and cold drinks and a few fixings made a picnic they all loved, and Mrs. Gregory, who loved to cook, kept asking Mrs. Gorham for the recipe for the black cake.

It was a long time before Mrs. Gorham was willing to part with the recipe, and by then the black-cake-and-chicken picnics were just a happy memory. It was no longer necessary to deliver the egg to make the picnic cake.

"Imagine my surprise," Mrs. Gregory says, "when I found there was no egg in the recipe!"

She couldn't very well ask what became of the eggs, but being an accomplished cook, she quickly determined that the molasses cake was delicious without any egg at all.

"She ate all of those eggs!" Mrs. Gregory said, adding "She was a wonderful woman but just as tight as the paper on the wall!"

So, you see, there are times when it can be enlightening if you can be a recipe detective! If a recipe you want to update is vague, the best bet is to try looking through well-written cookbooks of the period. Find the nearest equivalent. Then try variations to fit.

Here are a few of the old terms you may come across and wonder about:

- One pony—two tablespoons
- One jigger—three tablespoons
- One wineglass—a fourth cup
- One gill—a half cup
- One porringer—a cup
- Butter the size of a walnut—about two tablespoons
- Butter the size of an egg—about a fourth cup

Saleratus water is like soda, and the even earlier "pearl-ash" is used rather like baking powder. Simply use the amount of soda or baking powder necessary to the other ingredients. (More about that later.)

If you read about using a pint of brewers yeast, simply use about a package of modern yeast to each cup of liquid in the recipe. Adjust the liquid ingredients accordingly.

"Emtins" is rather like sourdough starter, or use yeast in proportion to the liquid in the recipe just as for brewer's yeast.

Here are some other clues we have come across talking to good cooks and updating some old recipes:

A kitchen scale is the surest way to find out how much to put when dry ingredients are stated in pounds and even ounces. But cookbooks have conversion tables, especially those books published in the 1920s when many still-used recipes were in pounds and ounces.

- One pound of all-purpose flour—four cups sifted
- One pound of cake flour—about four and a half cups sifted
- One pound of whole-wheat flour—about three and a half cups
- One pound of fat or most liquids—about two cups. Hence the old saying about liquid measure: A pint's a pound, the world around.
- A pound of average eggs—around 10.
- One pound of granulated sugar is about two cups, and brown sugar is two cups firmly packed. But one pound of confectioner's sugar is two and a half cups

Old-fashioned cooks made a pound cake with a pound each of butter, flour, sugar, and egg, which was rich and delicious and easy to remember! But it is an example of a recipe that will not translate to all modern equivalents. It is no good with margarine. Most old-fashioned recipes are best to try the first time with exactly the ingredients they call for. An exception is rose water. If you can't get the exotic essences like that, try sherry. It works deliciously as a substitute almost every time.

Ingredients in old and foreign recipes cannot be counted on to be exactly the same as ours. British flour behaves differently from ours, for example, explained Mrs. Robert Morton of Valley Road, Redding, when we were gathering words of wisdom from her for an upcoming column on another subject.

If the proportion of rising agent to flour seems unusual in an old recipe, it could be correct. Hugenot Torte, for example, may have more baking powder than seems justified. Doesn't work? Try it against these usual proportions of rising agent to flour: For each cup of flour you are likely to need this much rising agent:

• Two teaspoons tartrate baking powder, or
• One teaspoon double-acting baking powder or
• A half to one teaspoon of soda plus a cup of something sour like buttermilk or molasses, to raise at least a cup of flour. Often in a recipe for two cups of flour and a cup or more of sour liquid there is a teaspoon of soda plus some baking powder or eggs to add to the rising power.

For yeast recipes, follow a tried-and-true recipe for bread for the way to combine other ingredients with the yeast. Otherwise, you could kill the yeast, which is a live plant. Use one package of yeast to about a cup of liquid and be patient. It may take longer than you think to rise if it is a rich dough. A teaspoon of salt should be added for four cups flour.

Now, back to Mrs. Gregory's mother's date cake. Her mother was a Bradley and married a Treadwell, Mrs. Gregory explains, so the recipe has connections with two old Wilton families.

You will need:

a half cup butter	**a cup of sugar**
a beaten egg	**a teaspoon of cinnamon**
a half teaspoon nutmeg	**a cup of milk**
one teaspoon soda	**one teaspoon of baking powder**
a pound of pitted dates	**two cups of flour**
a half teaspoon of salt	

Cream the butter and sugar, sift dry ingredients together, cut all but four dates in small pieces and dredge them with a little of the flour. Beat egg into creamed butter and sugar, beat in flour and milk alternately in small amounts, and stir in all but four dates.

Cook at 350 degrees until done. Until done? We have not had a chance to make this yet, but here is the detective work to translate the elusive "until done." We found a cake using dried fruit in much the same manner, and using about this volume of ingredients, that cooked at 350 degrees. It varied in cooking time from about 45 minutes to over an hour. The time tended to be slightly longer if cooked in loaf pans than if cooked in layer pans.

So we would peek at the cake after about 35 minutes to be sure, and test it with a toothpick or cake tester when it begins to look done. If the toothpick comes out clean, it is done. Ice with a thin white icing, Mrs. Gregory says, and then decorate with the four last dates.

* * *

And soon Liz was writing both fiction and non-fiction about food. In the years after publication of her early mystery novels, Liz wrote a number of short stories with a gastronomical bent. Here is one of them, neatly combining Liz's interest in food with the sleuthing expertise of Peaches Dann (a lot more about whom later in this book):

A Passion for the Cook

Here in Monroe County, folks said Helen was too pretty for her own good. Our Helen's face had never launched a thousand ships and caused a Trojan war, like that gal in history. But I knew Helen's problem went more than skin deep. I didn't realize that my friend who wrote the food column for *The Weekly Word* could cause murder.

Actually, you wouldn't believe all you learn working for a rural weekly newspaper. You cover the story of some triumph or disaster, but then—because people all tend to know each other here—you learn what happens next, the final outcome. Which is often almost beyond belief.

Helen came into the office Friday morning, bringing her food column. Her eyes were wider than usual. They're green eyes, with long black lashes, and seem absolutely electric set in her heart-shaped face. Helen's skin is soft and fine like an orchid. She's slender but curvy, and there's something vulnerable about her that makes you feel you should protect her.

On Friday morning she was trembling as she sat down in the

chair across from my desk. Luckily, Friday is our most laid-back day since the paper comes out on Thursday. I had time to listen. "You're alone, Peaches?" she asked, looking all around.

Yes, I explained. Martin, our trusty editor, was out covering a fire, and our advertising gal was out selling ads. That's all of us on this paper except Tamara, our occasional photographer who snaps pictures when needed. I think of her as Tamara with the Camera.

Helen clenched her hands together in her lap to stop the trembling. "I'm afraid Charon is going to shoot me," she blurted.

Charon was her third husband, as arrogant as a baron, but, God help me, he had seemed like an improvement. Alfred, husband number one, had been so jealous he beat Helen up, always carefully so the bruises were covered by her clothes and didn't show, and for a while we didn't even know. But he did agree to a divorce and then went to California. Harold, husband number two, not only beat her up, but after the divorce and a court order to stay away, he'd still stalked her. Luckily for Helen, but not for him, he followed her across Eller Creek Road without looking both ways, was hit by a cattle truck and killed.

But Charon, who filled third place, was a nationally known artist with pictures in the Guggenheim and other museums. We were impressed with ourselves when he moved to Monroe County—to be closer to nature, he said. That went with his rugged good looks. When he married Helen, we were pleased because we thought he got the violence out of his system on canvas. His pictures, in shades of red and orange and purple and yellow, were arresting and original. One critic said they gave a foretaste of the end of the world, but in a way that kept you looking.

As she sat by my desk, Helen was as pale as if she expected the end of the world. She toyed nervously with the cup of pens next to the box of bookmarks to promote my book on memory. I'd just brought the bookmarks back from the printer.

"Why on earth are you afraid that Charon might shoot you?" I asked. That was the worst possibility yet.

"It's because of the food column," she announced, twisting her hands.

"Then stop writing it," I said. "Folks will miss the great recipes you find around the county, but they'll miss you more if you get shot." I knew she wrote mainly for her own pleasure. *The Weekly Word* doesn't pay worth a darn. Helen taught second grade to earn dependable money. She was also my long-time friend. She used to live near me in Buncombe County. Yes, I live in one county and work over the line in the next.

She said: "I mustn't stop doing anything I always do. I mustn't make any change that could get the wind up. Charon doesn't really like me doing the food column. He doesn't like the attention I get. But if I make any change in my life he has to know why, and if he finds out what's been going on—well, Charon gets wildly jealous, and he's been getting worse."

I sighed. It seemed all her husbands got worse, the longer she was married to them.

"So exactly what's wrong?" I asked. But before she could answer, our trusty editor Martin came back from covering the fire and bloomed with pleasure to see Helen. Normal male reaction. He said, "That chocolate indulgence cake recipe from the mayor's wife was positively sinful. My wife made it, and I think we both gained ten pounds." He lit a cigarette, waved, and went in his office. A relapse. Last week he'd given up smoking.

Helen beamed. Even scared white, she still loved to be told how folks enjoyed her column.

Then she said, "You know, I could use some air, Peaches. Would you be willing to go for a walk?"

She plainly didn't want a soul, including Martin, to hear what she was going to say. By now, I had to know. So I drove her down the river road to a little park where there's a walk by the water. Flowing water calms the mind.

She didn't say a word on the way—composing her thoughts, perhaps. The road is so lovely, with a rugged rock cliff on one side, now festooned with vines of little white flowers, and the broad rolling river on the other, that I was quiet, too, enjoying the ride.

We parked in an empty parking area and walked down past a sign that said we'd go in the water at our own risk, past picnic tables, to a bench near the water—water almost as musical as a fall, and muddy brown from the last night's rain. We sat down on that bench near the grassy edge of the river where a blood-red wildflower shared space with yellow daisies. Somebody, perhaps a child, had left a pile of yellow and white pebbles on the end of the bench.

Helen sighed. Then she began to talk in a rush. "It all began with that column about the peppermint sheet cake from Lou-Anne Penland, the president of the Hobbs Creek Extension Club."

Helen flicked away an electric-blue dragonfly and slowed down. "Peaches, I did like I always do. I tested the recipe in my kitchen. People do occasionally leave out ingredients. I called Tamara and told her when I expected to have the cake frosted and ready to photograph. I had invited Lou-Anne over to be in the picture. But before they arrived, just as I had that cake finished, the phone rang. It was some woman who said I'd won a bearskin rug in the church lottery. Well, that was interesting, and I couldn't be rude. I had to take the time to tell her I was thrilled."

Helen paused and looked me straight in the eye. I could tell she was coming to the dramatic part.

"When I went back to the cake, would you believe somebody had come in my kitchen and decorated it with red candy hearts and put a card with a red heart on it right by the cake? The card said, 'You're going to be mine.' It wasn't signed. I was scared silly."

A blue van drove into the parking lot above us. Oh, dear, I hoped someone wouldn't come close and shut her up.

"What did Tamara and Lou-Anne think of that?" I asked.

"Do you think I'm out of my mind?" she demanded. "I hid that card quick and pretended I'd put the candy hearts on the white frosting to make a better picture. If Charon had heard about that card, he'd have gone ballistic. That was three weeks ago."

I could see this was going to be complicated. Luckily, the person by the blue van was taking his time, letting the dog mark every bush, and staying at a distance.

"The next week," Helen said, "I locked all the doors, and I told nobody what I was going to do. I made lemon-sesame chicken, the recipe donated by Mattie Belle who works in the library. She hates to have her picture taken, so I said I'd just use a picture of the chicken beside a pile of books. Nobody knew when Tamara was coming to take that picture, except Tamara, of course.

"I arranged the chicken and the books on the dining room table. The doorbell rang, and I went to let Tamara in, but she wasn't there. I looked both ways and called her. No Tamara. Then I noticed a package on the doorstep. I opened it and there was nothing inside. So I ran back to the dining room, and there by my chicken thighs was a page torn from an old book about medieval chastity belts. You know, those nasty metal belts that a man could lock on his wife as he went off to the Crusades to make sex impossible until he got back with the key."

Yes, I knew. I had always wondered how a chastity belt could be the least bit sanitary.

The blue-van man was walking toward us with a dog, past the cement picnic tables. But he was not close yet.

"There was a note, too," said Helen. "The note said, 'I want you just for me.'" Angrily, she took a pebble and threw it in the water with a splash.

"Did the handwriting look at all familiar?" I asked.

"It was written on a typewriter or a computer, I guess. On plain white paper like anybody could get." Helen threw another pebble hard into white water where the river flowed over a rock.

"But how did someone get in my house? How did they know my

schedule?" Her voice rose in panic. "The doors were locked. My God, suppose Charon saw that note? Or saw the man who brought it? Charon was right over in his studio behind the house, lost in his work the way he gets. If he saw the note he'd think—he'd be sure— I'd been with that guy.

"And when he wasn't painting, Charon spent the week cleaning his guns. He'd given up smoking, I'd been begging him to do that, but it made him nervous. At least when Martin quit he didn't clean guns. Charon made me very nervous."

I could tell. The water sound was not enough to soothe her.

The man with the dog had luckily stopped a good ways off for the dog to do his business against the sign that told what was not allowed in the park.

"Who has a key to your house?" I asked.

"Nobody but my sister and my cleaning woman, and I trust them both absolutely. Sis has six kids, and sometimes she has to get away. She can come to my house anytime and sit down and read a book. She sits in the kitchen. She says she likes the way my kitchen smells." Helen allowed herself a small smile. "Sis wouldn't make me trouble."

"But either one could have left that key where someone could copy it," I said. Helen's twin sister looked almost like her and yet she wasn't as sexy. She had a sturdy air that made you think she could take care of herself. I had to admit she was not the type to leave a key where someone could copy it. And her sister's husband was dependable too. "Dull but kind," Helen called him.

Now the man from the blue van came right toward us, walking a German shepherd. Ah, yes—Alfred Battle, our white-haired and rugged retired county commissioner. I remember he once winked at me, pointed at his white hair, and said, "When there's snow on the roof there's fire in the furnace." Not too much, I hoped. He stopped and glowed with pleasure to see Helen. He was polite to me but I saw where his attention went. "What a lovely surprise to see you-all here," he said.

We chatted a moment and then I said, "We're just taking a brisk walk." We got up and left him looking startled at our getaway. We headed toward a path that went off into the wooded part of the riverbank.

"He has the same cleaning woman I do," Helen said. "And he's a friend of my sister's. Oh, this is awful. Now I'm going to suspect everybody I know!" Sunlight through the leaves above us dappled her face.

"Your valentine man may be somebody who has been watching you from a distance, someone you don't know," I told her. "Why didn't you tell me the column was getting dangerous, right off?" Poison ivy climbed a tree that edged the water. Somehow that seemed appropriate.

"I didn't tell anybody," she said. "I was so afraid Charon would find out. And if a stalker can't get to you one way he'll try another. By this week I was really scared. So I made Coupe Bugatti."

I didn't see the connection, but I waited. We passed a gently sloping place—obviously for boats and rafts to be pulled in or out of the river. Fortunately, at 10 A.M. there were no boats.

"This week I've written about Lawrence Whittaker, a writer who once interviewed Ettore Bugatti, the great car designer and maker. Lawrence got the recipe from a millionaire collector of cars who he also interviewed in connection with the story. Hey, pretty uptown for Monroe County, don't you think?"

That obviously still pleased her, scared or not.

"Now, this recipe is so simple and quick that I figured I could throw it together and photograph it so fast that the man who's bothering me wouldn't have time to make trouble," she said. "I'd be done when he thought I had just started."

Helen stopped and rested against a tree that leaned out over the water. Luckily no poison ivy there. "All I needed was the best coffee ice cream, dark rum, simple syrup, whipped cream, and shaved bitter chocolate," she said. "And Lawrence Whittaker said I didn't even need to make the simple syrup. That would have taken a while, boiling it up and waiting for it to cool. He said his shortcut was to use pale clover honey instead, and the taste was virtually the same." That did sound good.

"I told no one what I was going to do, except Tamara who had to take the picture. I mixed the honey with one third as much rum. That took two minutes. I put two scoops of ice cream in each of two tall coupe glasses, and put the glasses in the freezer compartment. One minute. No problem so far. When Tamara arrived, I planned to pour some rum syrup over each coupe. I then planned to do something sacrilegious to the memory of Bugatti, but I was doing this to photograph, not to win a gourmet prize. I did not whip heavy cream myself. I planned to use the kind that comes in a pressurized can and make a mound of whipped cream on each coupe. I grated the bitter chocolate in a little grinder I have, and planned to put a generous sprinkle on each portion. Total time, ten minutes. No interruption from that crazy man. The doorbell rang. I hoped that this time it would be Tamara and I thought, *Hoorah, I'm home free!*" Helen threw one more pebble she'd brought with her into the water. They were her exclamation points.

"But Tamara was holding a bouquet of yellow roses and she

said, 'This was hung on your mailbox. There's a card.'

"I was angry. 'Some nut has been pestering me,' I told her. 'Please, for God's sake, don't tell anybody. Charon gets jealous.' Well, I had to tell her something." Helen was so upset she couldn't stand still. We hurried on. She couldn't stop talking, either.

"After Tamara left, I read the card: 'I'll pick you up in front of your house right after you test the recipe next week. You can put a sign in the kitchen window which says YES or NO as you start to cook. If you don't come I'll kill you and then kill myself. Our bodies can be in the picture on page one.'" She turned and faced me so suddenly that I almost bumped into her. "What will I do? This sounds too crazy and I'm scared."

I grabbed a young tree and got my balance. "Maybe it's an ugly joke," I said hopefully. "But I think you need to call the sheriff, right now."

"I wouldn't dare! Then Charon would certainly hear about it. You know Charon is so talented. But most great artists are a little unbalanced."

I figured that was an exaggeration even if Vincent Van Gogh, whose work now sold for millions, did cut off his ear.

She stayed planted in front of me. "And Charon has told me that if I'm ever unfaithful he'll shoot me."

I was appalled. "Helen," I said, still holding onto my tree, "forgive an old friend's bluntness, but you need some counseling. If you marry a destructive man once, that can be a mistake. But you've done it three times. You need help." For the first time I noticed the cicadas, like a loud buzzing in my ears.

She didn't even get mad. She said, "All right, if you'll help me through this without the sheriff, I'll do it. Help me find out who is this man who's sending me notes, and if this is a real threat or a joke. Help me to do it before Charon finds out."

"Call the sheriff," I said again. I know how stubborn Helen can be, so I knew she wouldn't.

"Listen," she said, "the sheriff is the worst one. He hugged me at the Fire Company fund-raiser last month. Charon had fits."

I sighed. "All right," I said. "I'll think about what you can do."

Now, Helen would be better off if she weren't so sexy, and I'd be much better off if I weren't so inventive. Because the idea of setting the trap came to me, as if the sound of rushing water could inspire my thoughts. And the trap seemed like such an interesting idea that it would be a sinful waste not to go ahead and do it. I should have refused to help.

"Are you sure you want to take the chance that this nut won't do something dangerous and unexpected?" I asked Helen. "Why should he wait for next week?"

"Because he's obviously fixated on the cooking column," she said. She began to walk again. "Maybe it's the man who got so mad when there was a typo and he put a tablespoon of salt in the chicken salad with white grapes and pecans, instead of a teaspoon. Everybody else had enough common sense to know it must be a typo. But he did it and doubled the recipe for a family reunion. Oh, he was mad."

And suddenly I thought: Why, it could even be a woman who was mad at Helen and trying to make trouble, maybe a woman who wanted Charon for herself! Man or woman, my idea would show that person up!

I sat down on a boulder and Helen sat down uneasily beside me. I said, "You know, I have a recipe that I've put on bookmarks advertising my *How to Survive Without a Memory*, now that the paperback edition is out. I went to the printer to pick up the bookmarks on my way to work this morning. The recipe is for cookies you can forget but not burn."

She gave me a why-are-you-wasting-my-time? glance.

"Next week, you can run my recipe, and we'll catch your tormentor with it," I said. I had one of the bookmarks in my pocketbook. I read it out loud:

Special Occasion Ginger Cookies
(that you can't forget and burn)

Ingredients:
> **2 egg whites**
> **2/3 cup sugar**
> **1 teaspoon vanilla**
> **1-1/3 cup roughly chopped pecans**
> **a half cup chopped crystallized ginger**

Directions:

Preheat oven to 350 degrees. Beat egg whites almost stiff, add two tablespoons of the sugar. Beat very stiff, then slowly add the rest of the sugar, then vanilla while continuing to beat. Fold in the ginger. Then fold in all but about two tablespoons of the nuts. Drop by spoonfuls onto cookie sheets covered with foil or waxed paper. Sprinkle cookies with reserved nuts. Put cookie sheets in oven and TURN OFF THE OVEN. Cookies are done when they are firm enough to come off sheet in one piece. Don't open oven to test for at least two hours, as oven will lose heat. Makes two dozen.

"They sound good," Helen said, only a little impatient. "But how could they be a trap?"

So I explained. "What I don't say in the recipe is that you can leave these cookies in the oven a long time, even twelve hours. You can really forget them, and they'll still come out fine. So you don't have to photograph these cookies at the time the stalker will expect. You can creep around and stalk him and find out who he is."

I regret to tell you Helen's eyes sparkled. She enjoys risk.

Of course, I worried about her when she went home. But even if I called the sheriff myself, what could he do? He didn't have the staff to shadow Helen all week.

After work, I drove past her house. All peaceful. I parked down the road in the mouth of an old wood road, out of sight of the main road, and walked up the mountain in back of her house. The top of the first rise overlooked her kitchen window. Pretty quick, I found a spot with a fallen log to sit on and a lot of cigarette butts scuffed out near it. I looked at a butt. Camels. Good lord, Martin smoked Camels. But he would never—would he? From where I sat, a watcher's presence would be masked by bushes, but binoculars would have picked out Helen's every move in the kitchen. I shivered.

I noted the lay of the land. Charon's studio was separate from, and in back of, the white clapboard house. The house looked 1920s. The studio was natural wood and modern with large glass skylights on the north side. The watcher from the hill could have seen Helen in her kitchen as clearly as if he stood right outside the window, and see Charon if he left his studio. He could not have seen a car parked in front of the house, but he could have seen Tamara's car drive up.

I heard crashing through the bushes, and froze. Thank goodness it was only a black dog with wagging tail. But it made me aware I shouldn't hang around near a place where a possibly deranged chain-smoker felt at home.

On Tuesday, Helen was set to test the recipe. No further communication from the valentine man.

I told Tamara not to go take a picture, but if anyone asked her if she was going, to say that she was.

Helen put the cookies in the oven and a YES sign in the window and then came out into a spot that you couldn't see from the mountain log-and-cigarette place, and we hid across the street in the bushes.

That's when everything went wrong. We saw a blue Volvo park in front of the house. "That's Sis's car," Helen said, amazed. "Would she pull a joke like this? No, she has a book under her arm. She's coming to my house to get away and read! Oh, help!"

We ran after her into the house. But not quick enough. We

heard two shots before we reached the kitchen. In the kitchen we found Sis shot in the heart. Oh, lord, this was dreadful! Sis who looked just like Helen, with a book on gardening still clutched in her hand. Helen screamed with horror and put her arms around her dead sister lying on the floor. Frantically I looked around for the killer. We could be next.

I found him outside the shattered window. Charon lay still with a pistol in his hand. He'd shot himself in the neck. Didn't he know enough to shoot himself in the ear, or did his hand slip? There was blood all over the place, raw red as one of his pictures. He was alive, though barely. "I knew she cheated. I proved it," he half gasped, half gurgled, and then he stopped breathing.

I can't tell you how desperately I wished that he'd merely cut off his ear.

Or how desperately I wished I had somehow persuaded Helen to call the sheriff. Or figured out that Charon hadn't really given up smoking.

It was Charon who'd cheated—slipped off and smoked while he spied on Helen.

I shuddered. My friend Deputy Wynatt says I'm murder-prone— and he's right. If someone is going to get killed, I'm going to be there. That negative thinking was not going to help. At least sometimes I prevent a death. I had saved Helen. I could feel good about that. I had not saved her sister.

As for Charon, the seeds of his own destruction were in him, I think. I was sorry. He would have been pleased, however, at the obituaries that called him a true original and a great artist. He would have loved the way his work went up in price.

The most amazing part of this story happened next. Helen mourned for Sis and Charon both. She said it was her fault for not noticing that Charon was heading for a breakdown. She should have figured out a way to help him. The excellent Asheville shrink she visited had a hard time talking her out of obsessing about that.

But she decided she would marry her brother-in-law. "He's dull and that's what I need," she told me. "And he's kind, and he needs a mother for those kids. And furthermore," she said, "raising six children should keep me so busy I won't get into trouble." I prayed that was true.

Of course, Helen never wrote the food column about the cookies. We were so upset about Charon and Sis that we forgot and left the cookies in the oven all day. But when Helen remembered and took them out, they were just fine. She put them in a cookie tin. They keep.

Three weeks later she came by the office and presented us with the tin of cookies. "I can't bear to eat these," she told me, "because everything else went so desperately wrong the day I baked them. Only the cookies turned out right."

I bit into one with my afternoon coffee. It was crunchy, spicy and absolutely delicious.

* * *

And this story, written for The News & Observer *in Raleigh, North Carolina, contains a recipe for carrot cake—as well as a fairly gruesome murder. The story is notable for Peaches Dann's rather public encounter with the Demon Rum, which she insists is a memory-aiding device:*

Of Poetry and Death and Carrot Cake

It may seem romantic in a terrible way when you read about poets like Sylvia Plath, so sensitive they kill themselves. But when you bump into the possibility nearby, it's ugly. Even so, I would not have gotten drunk except for memory. You see, I'm absent-minded and the author of a book called *How to Survive Without a Memory.* I need memory strategies.

I'm a reporter on the paper here in Monroe County. That's one reason I jammed on my brakes at the house of Leo Blount, our local

I was in a writing group with Liz during the early 1980s and recently sent her an e-mail after visiting her web site. We had not communicated in years, but she replied promptly and graciously. She told me about her upcoming trip to Alaska, which was of particular interest to me because my mother grew up there.

Liz was writing Kill the Messenger *while I was in her writing group. After it was published, she autographed a copy for me, writing "I look forward to YOUR book." That book—*More Than Petticoats: Remarkable North Carolina Women—*was published this past spring.*

Liz was a major inspiration to me, having started her fiction-writing career somewhat late in life. I am 50 years old, and have finally started working seriously on my first novel, fulfilling a life-long dream. Liz may be gone, but her spirit and inspiration live on.

Scotti Cohn

poet and colorful curmudgeon, when I saw cars with flashing lights parked in front. He'd been found dead in his old Ford with the exhaust pipe rigged to pump carbon monoxide into the car. Leo, who, just the day before, had brought to our office a poem about spring, and a coffee cake he picked up at Samantha's restaurant.

You see, Leo made a habit of coming by the paper with news tidbits, but mainly to complain. He wanted the world to behave better. He told me his will left everything he owned or might inherit to activist causes such as the Civil Liberties Union or Greenpeace, not one cent to his stupid relatives.

He looked like a lion with indigestion. Shaggy and scowling. That helped me remember his name: Leo the lion. The first time he ranted about the tax rate, I was startled as he shook his fist. Then I learned he was blowing off steam, and lonely. His wife left him after loud fights. He called his only son a wrong-headed fool. Leo's wealthy father sent him money and contempt. Retired captains of industry don't expect an only son to devote his life to poetry, even though Leo had a national reputation.

"Are you sure it was suicide?" I asked Sheriff's Deputy Wynatt when he dropped by the office the next day.

He squirmed. "That's the official word. But it seemed strange he had a recipe for carrot cake stuffed in his pocket with a note on it from you saying, "Enjoy! This is extra moist.""

"But Leo never cooked," I said. "No one would give him a recipe. He ate his meals at Samantha's."

"Exactly," Wynatt said with a big thank-you-for-noticing smile. "Something is fishy."

Deputy Wynatt claims, strictly off the record, that I have a sixth sense about murder, just like his cousin Mindy has the sight. I claim I just have an unfortunate reputation for having solved murders, which makes folks think I might again.

"That recipe was crumpled like Leo had pulled it out of a wastebasket," Wynatt said.

"Or like he stuck it in his pocket fast, without time to fold it up," I mused. "Poor Leo. Maybe he knew someone was about to kill him and he grabbed that recipe as a clue of some sort."

I was thinking my imagination might be carrying me away, but Wynatt nodded approval. "Perhaps he thought you'd know who you gave it to."

"Maybe," I said. "I've shared it with several people. I have a feeling I gave it to someone recently who I wouldn't expect to cook. Oh!" I cried. "I took the recipe with me to the reception after the Olds' wedding, to give to my cousin Mary."

I sighed. "But I gave it to someone else."

Wynatt nodded encouragement.

"I don't drink much, but I was tired and I'd skipped lunch, and all of a sudden my head was whirling from champagne, and right then I found the recipe in my pocket and wondered why it was in my hand, and someone said, 'What's that?' When I explained, that person took it. I have a feeling it was somebody I don't like, somebody, well, evil."

"Ah!" Wynatt said hopefully.

Right then, my handsome husband, Ted, with the unruly hair came into the office. He's a journalism professor. Very logical. We clued him in.

"If the liquor hadn't gone to my head, I bet I could remember who it was," I groaned.

Ted laughed. "But you're forgetting your own memory trick," he said. "It's in your book: To help remember, you duplicate the circumstances of the first occasion. If you smelled lilacs, smell lilacs again. Experiments have shown that if something happened when you were drunk, you can help your memory by getting drunk again."

And that's why I found myself at home with Ted and Deputy Wynatt—two men who should be dedicated to my well-being— deliberately getting me drunk.

Ted brought out white wine. "Unfortunately, I don't have anything stronger, but if you drink this fast—"

I chugalugged a glass. I felt a buzz. But nothing came to mind except the bride, glowing. I bolted down another glass. I felt dizzy. No useful memory came, but I felt wildly cheerful.

"Oh, dear," Ted said. "I thought I had more wine! You just drank the last glass."

"I have a secret weapon," I giggled. "Moonshine: on my memento shelf. I never meant to drink it, but that jar helped me find one killer already! It's lucky!"

So Ted got the little jar of white lightning and I took a sip. The top of my head flew off. Still, no face came. I hiccuped. I took a larger gulp. My throat was on fire. My head began to whirl. A fuzzy picture began to form. I could hear the violin played at the reception.

"It's a man who wears super-stylish clothes," I said. "It's somebody who feels the world owes him plenty." I took another gulp. "It's Leo's son, George." Then I got sick.

After three cups of coffee, Deputy Wynatt took me to tell the sheriff.

At George's house they found an unlicensed gun and a letter from his grandfather saying he wouldn't lend George money. "And I may be old and sick but you can wait your turn until your father dies to inherit."

I guess George hoped that with Leo dead, Grandpa would leave his money straight to him. The autopsy showed Leo was drugged before he died. Probably at gunpoint, at his son's house, put in his own car in his own garage, and gassed.

Leo died, but his poetry would live. I made a carrot cake and took it by the sheriff's office, a thank-you gift for nabbing Leo's killer. The sheriff asked one favor: "Please remember to send my wife the recipe."

And here's the recipe, which The News & Observer *published as a sidebar:*

Super Carrot Cake

4 eggs, well beaten
2 cups brown sugar
1 and 1/3 cups vegetable oil
2 cups all-purpose flour
2 tsp. baking soda
2 tsp. baking powder
2 tsp. cinnamon
1 tsp. salt
3 cups grated raw carrot
1 cup chopped walnuts
2 tsp. grated orange rind
3/4 cup crushed canned pineapple, drained

Beat eggs, add sugar and cream together. Blend in oil. Sift dry ingredients and add to mixture. Fold into the batter the carrots, walnuts, orange rind, and pineapple. Half fill a greased 6 by 12 or 9 by 9 inch pan. Bake at 350 degrees for about 50 minutes. Frost with lemon cream-cheese frosting. Refrigerate.

Will happily leave the refrigerator long enough to go to a picnic if not left in the hot sun.

Lemon Cream-Cheese Frosting

8 ounces cream cheese
3 tablespoons butter, preferably unsalted
1 and 1/2 cups confectioner's sugar
half teaspoon vanilla extract
1 tablespoon lemon juice
2 teaspoons grated outer rind of lemon

Have butter and cheese at room temperature. Cream together. Sift in confectioner's sugar while beating smooth. Stir in vanilla, lemon juice, and lemon zest. Spread on cake.

* * *

Years after Liz moved from Redding to North Carolina, her old friends in Redding asked her to contribute a recipe to a new edition of the Mark Twain Library Cookbook, and (her eye on a chance to promote Peaches Dann) she was happy to comply:

Rosemary for Remembrance

That's what Shakespeare mentioned—rosemary for remembrance. And folks in those days thought the pungent herb did improve memory. So Peaches Dann, my absent-minded sleuth who specializes in memory tricks, likes to make Rosemary Chicken, on the off chance that it'll help and also because it's good! She makes two versions: fast and crispy, or slow and luxurious.

Fast & Crispy Rosemary Chicken

This is what Peaches fed her frightened young cousin who feared she was jinxed after the poor gal came upon a body with medieval magic symbols painted on it. Equally good on ordinary occasions.

1 roasting chicken
a little olive oil
one tablespoon powdered rosemary
a sprig fresh rosemary (optional)
peeled onions, scraped carrots
a half cup dry white wine

Preheat oven to 400 degrees. Rub chicken first with olive oil, then with powdered rosemary. Yes, it will resemble Cajun blackened foods, but the taste is different. Place a sprig of fresh rosemary in cavity if desired. Roast for fifteen minutes. Surround with oiled onions and carrots. Pour on white wine and roast for 45 minutes more or until thigh juices run clear when chicken is stuck with skewer.

Remove chicken. Make sauce by adding two tablespoons of flour to the pan juices and browning slightly, and then adding half a cup of white wine and a cup of chicken broth.

Good served with baked potatoes and garnished with parsley. Arrange all on a nice oval platter, with sauce on the side.

No-Hurry Chicken Rosemary

This is what Peaches makes when there is plenty of time to soak the herb in wine.

one chicken cut up
butter or olive oil
one tablespoon rosemary, preferably fresh
three-fourths cup white wine
salt and pepper
sauteed mushrooms as desired

Crush rosemary and steep in wine at least several hours at room temperature. Season chicken with salt and pepper and brown slowly in butter or oil. Add strained wine. Cover and simmer forty minutes, or until tender. Add sauteed mushrooms, the more the better. The friend who gave me this recipe uses canned mushrooms, but I think the fresh are much more luxurious.

I just returned from the memorial service for Liz at her church in Asheville. I am still in shock that this has happened and happened so quickly, but I want to share something I overheard that is the essence of Liz Squire. It seems the emergency room doctor was working with Liz and making the decision to put her in ICU because of skyrocketing blood pressure. Meanwhile, Liz was engaging him in a conversation about the types of books he read. When he said he liked mysteries, Liz dispatched her son to the car to get bookmarks of her latest book. That is so Liz.
Anne Underwood Grant

The Peaches Dann
Short Stories

Peaches Dann, Liz's beloved absent-minded sleuth, made her novelistic debut in 1994 in Who Killed What's-Her-Name? *The following year, "The Dog Who Remembered Too Much," which had won Liz the coveted Agatha award for best traditional mystery short story at the Sisters in Crime convention that year, appeared in an anthology edited by Carolyn G. Hart,* Malice Domestic 4. *Here it is:*

The Dog Who Remembered Too Much

"Mama's gone, Peaches," Lola said to me, "and I need your help." I held the phone tight, and a shiver of sadness went through me.

I knew Lola meant that her wonderful eighty-three-year-old mother, Bonnie Amons—my next-door neighbor—had died. Lola liked soft-pedal words—"gone" or "passed on" for died, "indisposed" for vomiting all over, and so forth.

Bonnie's death was my fault. Now, why on earth would I feel like that? I'd been good to Bonnie; I even helped train her dog. "I heard she was much worse the last few weeks since I've been away from Asheville," I said. I looked out into my sunny garden where a robin took a morning dip in the birdbath. Bonnie's garden adjoined mine on the right. That blooming apple tree was on her land.

"She'd been declining," Lola said. "Even her mind was going. She talked about changing her will, to leave Doc James everything she had if he'd just get her well. Of course, she couldn't do that without a lawyer." Suddenly Lola sounded smug, but then properly sad again. "You're never ready for loved ones to go, are you? And I arrived to look in about eight this morning and. . . ." She sighed.

I figured there was no easy way to say what she found. But she hadn't called me right away. My watch said quarter to ten.

Strange, I thought, that Bonnie got so sick so fast. Three weeks before, she'd been a little vague about time, she'd been almost blind, but there was still a lot of spunk in the old gal. She did have to take heart medicine, but otherwise she was full of ginger. Still, she was eighty-three. And nobody lasts forever.

"And now," Lola blurted, "somebody is trying to shoot George."

"Shoot George?" Why on earth would anybody want to shoot my neighbor's little black-and-white volunteer dog? I say volunteer because he simply appeared a year or so ago. And Bonnie couldn't bear not to feed him, so George—which is what Bonnie named him—moved in and became her mainstay.

"But everybody loves George," I said. "What on earth happened?"

"Right after I found Mama"—silence while she pulled herself together—"Peaches, she had plainly passed on. I found her and then I called Doc James and Andrea Ann." Andrea Ann was Lola's older sister.

"George barked to go out and I let him out and then I heard a gunshot. But thank the good Lord I hadn't closed the door tight, and George came running in and had one of his shaking fits."

I knew it didn't require a gunshot to scare the dog. He had those shakes with new people, especially men, and especially men wearing boots. Somebody had mistreated that dog. But somebody had been good to him and trained him right, because he was an affectionate little dog who would sit or come on command. I figured we'd never know the whole story.

"I didn't see a living soul," Lola said, "but the mountain is in back of Mama's house here. Somebody could shoot down from among the trees and then slip away."

"It's probably some crazy mean kid," I said, "with a new gun. What do you want me to do?"

I said that bit about a kid to ease her mind, but I found myself wondering: Was there someone from that dog's past who wanted him out of the way? Silly idea, I told myself. But the idea grew: Was there some guilty secret the dog knew? Oh, come on! What imagination! First I'd asked myself if it was my fault that Bonnie died because I wasn't around to look in. Then I wondered if a little dog knew guilty secrets. But I never entirely dismiss my wild ideas. Some of them turn out. If you have a lousy memory, and I admit to that, sometimes you just know something without remembering the little signs that made you know it. I file my strange ideas under "Way Far Out," but I don't erase them.

"People will be coming and going here," Lola said, "paying respects to Mama. Would you take care of George till I get time to take him to my place?"

"And are you going to keep him for good?" I asked.

"I don't know," she said. "Mama would want him to have a good home, but Victor doesn't care too much for dogs." I didn't like Lola's husband, Victor. Why did my wonderful friend Bonnie's two daughters both marry stinkers?

Unsuccessful stinkers. One from the city, one from the country. Andrea Ann's Arnold had run a tired trailer park out in the county where he grew up, except he'd finally sold it and put a down payment on a house near Bonnie's (which is to say, near me) and announced he was going to be a salesman. Now they were neighbors. And Arnold had to shave more often. Funny thing, though, Arnold had always had bedroom eyes even without shaving. Gave every woman he met the once-over like he was checking her out for sex, like his imagination was extra good in that department. Carnal Arnold. From the day I met him, I'd remembered his name that way.

Lola's husband, Victor, had a craft shop in Asheville. He'd always shaved. In fact, he overdressed. Slick Vic. He wore suits with vests to work. But most of his mountain-type "handmade crafts" came from Korea. He couldn't understand why, in an area with so many real and beautiful crafts, his shop didn't do well. Also, Victor was selfish and wanted to be the center of everything. And Lola was, I am sorry to say, a doormat. A mealy-mouthed doormat. Victor and Lola were made for each other. But not for a little dog with boot-kicks and God knew what else to get over.

"I'd like to have George," I said. "He has character. I'll come get him right now."

"Now, where has that dog gone?" Lola groaned as she let me in the front door. Why on earth had she worn a pink satin blouse to drop by her mother's in the morning? It went with her teased hairdresser hair and her carefully painted rosebud mouth. On a woman of fifty-plus. No doubt Slick Vic liked it.

We traced George to Bonnie's room, where the unmade bed looked so forlorn. Doc James must have arranged for the funeral home to come and get the body. Lola seemed too upset to have thought clearly and worked that out. Doc was getting a little senile himself. At least, I didn't think he'd come to see Bonnie as often as he should. But Bonnie would never change doctors.

George stuck his little black nose out from under the dust ruffle when he heard me and gave the single bark which means hello. "Good dog," I said to encourage him.

I looked around the room and choked up. The picture of praying hands, as worn as Bonnie's, hung as always on the wall above the old brass bed. Across from it was the plain bureau with Bonnie's hairbrush and comb and the old crazed mirror that had belonged to her mother. On the bedside table was a framed picture of the two girls as kids, Lola and Andrea Ann. Pouting in Sunday dresses. Also a glass of water, Bonnie's bottle of heart pills, and a box of dog biscuits. Everything was just like it had been at my last visit when I'd slipped in early before I left for my plane. I was glad I'd said that good-bye.

I walked over and picked up the pills and sighed. Heart medicine almost killed my father. As-much-as-you-need can save your life. More-than-you-need is deadly poison. "Lanoxin" (Digoxin), the label said, Rite-Aid.

"Bonnie changed pharmacies," I said out loud. "I used to get her pills for her sometimes from Barefoot and Cheetham when I got my thyroid pills." Who could forget a name that made a picture like Barefoot and Cheetham? The two are actually old mountain names. Several in the phone book.

"Rite-Aid is a chain, so it costs less," Lola said primly. She stood near the bed nervously, watching me. Twitching like she wanted me to hurry up.

George edged out from under the bed. His small straight tail began to wag. He fastened his bright little black eyes on me.

"Bonnie really counted on George," I reminisced. "He even helped her remember her pill." Silence. Lola didn't like to admit that before the dog came, her mother sometimes forgot to take her heart pill at all. Which was dangerous. So I had come to the rescue.

I take pride in the fact that my friends count on me for memory tricks. In fact, I'm writing a book called *How to Survive Without a Memory*. My only problem is that sometimes I forget to take my own advice. But the dog-pill trick really works. A dog's stomach can tell time as well as an alarm clock. Give him a treat at the same time two or three days running, and he'll come ask for it on the button after that. Especially if he's a hungry type. And before George showed up on Bonnie's doorstep, goodness knows how long he'd been hungry.

George nudged my leg to be patted. I stroked his velvet head.

"Yes," Lola admitted, "George was a help, although my Victor was always afraid the dog was going to give us fleas."

Fleas! I'd taken on the job of seeing that George never had any. Bonnie's daughters never took time for that. Lola was always off at Victor's beck and call.

Andrea Ann, who was a trained nurse, did look in more often. She kept an eye on her mother, now that they'd made up a long-standing fight. You see, Andrea Ann had thought her mother had ruined her marriage by not lending her money. A dumb idea, but Andrea Ann had spells of dumb. And she had a talent for getting mad. Angrier Ann. She had evidently forgiven her mother, but she wasn't about to take on dog care.

Sometimes I wondered if Andrea Ann had any warm feelings—even for people, much less dogs. She'd told me that when she was a child she'd dissected small animals—mice, chipmunks, and once (to my horror) a squirrel—because she wanted to know what was inside. Which maybe made her a better squirrel nurse, especially since her patients were anesthetized while she was with them. Human interaction was not required.

I don't think Andrea Ann knew how to show love. And Lola wasn't much better. George was the one who quivered with love whenever Bonnie came near. Who jumped with joy when she fed him. George knew she'd taken him in and saved his life. Fleas indeed!

"Why, George told your mother by his bark whether a friend or a stranger was at the front door. He went crazy over strangers."

"And she felt safer that way, Peaches," Lola admitted, shrugging those satin shoulders.

"And George may be small and scared of strangers," I added, "but he can be fierce. He used to come steal my cat's supper. Now I put it on a high shelf."

"Mama called him a feist." Lola eyed his bowed legs, white chest, and funny little black body. "But he looks like a mongrel to me."

Out in the country, feists are kind of a breed. Not all exactly alike, but all small and fierce when they need to be. That's where the word *feisty* comes from. The dictionary says so.

"It's our mountain thriftiness, I guess," I said. "To breed a fierce watchdog in a small size that won't need much to eat."

George came out from under the bed and began to bark. Someone at the door? Andrea Ann should certainly be here by now. We went to look. No one was there. George raced back into the bedroom. He stood by the bed and barked. All of him quivered, and he pranced up and down, stamping first one front paw, then the other.

"Oh! It's time for your mother's pill!" I could have cried. He was barking, as always, because it was time for the treat that Bonnie gave him each time she took a pill. George wanted his dog biscuit. I gave him one for old times' sake. I looked at the pills. "Take one at 10 A.M.," the label said. And sure enough, the clock said ten. George was going to have to be deprogrammed so he didn't bark every day at ten o'clock.

I picked him up and he wriggled with delight and licked my nose.

"Where's Andrea Ann?" I asked. Now she and Arnold lived just a few houses down the street, and Lola said she'd called her sister before she called me. Andrea should have arrived.

"She said she had to get dressed," Lola said. "She and Arnold."

Arnold the new salesman. Shallow and insincere. He'd kept trying to talk Bonnie into selling the large tract of land with a lake and a little cabin on it, out at the edge of town. But she was attached to that place. Carnal Arnold was too thickheaded to understand that. Or maybe he and Andrea Ann had wanted to borrow the money that Bonnie could get by selling the land. They tended to gamble. They'd been on vacation to Acapulco and Atlantic City and I forget where else.

You might think I don't like anybody, the way I talk about Bonnie's girls and their men. I like most everybody. But something had gone wrong with those girls. I never knew their father. He was gone by the time I moved in next to Bonnie. Maybe he was the bad apple. Bonnie refused to talk about him.

"Do you think your father is still alive?' I asked Lola. "Do you need to let him know?"

She glared at me. "That," she said, "is not your business." At the same moment, Andrea Ann walked in the door. No pink satin for her. Nurse's white and laced shoes. Andrea was the practical type. Dumb spells and all. Her mother said she never wasted a thing. Even saved odd bits of string. She glared at me too.

So I took a hint and went home, carrying little George against my shoulder.

I put my old barn coat on the floor for him to lie on. Silk, my cat, who used to belong to my mother, came through the cat-door. My father didn't really want Silk, and I seem to inherit animals. Silk and George were friends from outdoors. No problem. I poured myself some cornflakes, added milk. I did some wash. I answered two letters.

George was restless. He knew something was wrong. He kept going to the door and asking to get out. He didn't know how to use the cat door. "You've been out," I said, remembering the gunshot, "and it nearly killed you." I looked out the window. I saw Lola talking to Carnal Arnold on her mother's front porch. Even from a distance I could see her preen and him leer. A car drove up and out got Victor. A traffic jam. About time that joker got there, it was early afternoon.

All of a sudden George began to bark again. It wasn't quite his stranger-at-the-door bark. But insistent. He didn't go to the door and hop up and down to get out. Still, I glanced outside. Nobody. I looked at the clock. Two o'clock. Not the right time for the pill routine. What on earth was he trying to tell me? I gave him a dog biscuit. He stopped barking.

Then I heard a thump on the side of the house, over toward the bedroom—the side away from Bonnie's house. I went in the bedroom to investigate. Both animals followed me. I looked out the bedroom window, past the stained-glass cardinal fastened to the glass. Nobody in sight on that side of the house. Though there was a hedge. Someone could have slipped behind that. Nothing seemed to have fallen in the bedroom. The picture of an old man playing a mountain dulcimer hung securely in place. So did the picture of the barn owl. No explanation for the noise. Only then did it occur to me that that thump was designed to get me out of the kitchen. That someone actually banged the side of the house.

I hurried back into the kitchen, and George began to run toward the cat door. I saw what he was after—a big piece of juicy raw hamburger. I ran so fast, I grabbed it before he did. I wiped the floor with my sleeve before either animal could lick any juice. I put the meat in a square freezer box and called the police department.

I was lucky to reach an old friend, Lieutenant John Wilson—whom I call Mustache, for obvious reasons. "I hate to hear from you," he said, "in case somebody else has been murdered." He said it like a joke. But of course, it wasn't. I've been mixed up in several murders. Not, thank God, on the wrong side.

"You're right. My next-door neighbor, Bonnie Amons, has been murdered," I said. "If you'll get right over here, I can tell you how to prove it, even though she was eighty-three and everybody thinks she died of natural causes. Or," I said, "I can give you the proof if you come at five-thirty."

"I can't come now," he said. "I can't even talk long now. I'd have to send somebody else. I'll come at five-thirty or quarter of six."

"Nothing is going to change before then," I said. "But don't be late."

You can bet I took good care of George for the rest of the afternoon, and Mustache arrived as promised, about five-thirty-five.

"Okay," he said, "tell me your theory. I bet it's something that nobody but me would ever believe. But I've had practice." He sighed. I know he wishes I wouldn't get mixed up in strange deaths. Like finding my poor aunt Nancy in the goldfish pond or stumbling on the fact that a serial killer was coming up I-40 our way and had my father on a list. Mustache wishes I wouldn't throw him curves. He has an orderly side that wants the world to make sense. You can tell by his crisp blue suit. No wrinkles. And by his straight firm mouth and intelligent eyes.

On the other hand, if he stuck to the tried-and-true way, he probably wouldn't have that scar next to his eye. He probably wouldn't have that wry manner—that was kind of nice. "Why do you believe that your neighbor, Bonnie Amons, was murdered?"

I introduced him to George. "This little dog belonged to Bonnie

Amons, and he was trained to bark for a dog biscuit at ten o'clock every morning," I said. "That reminded her to take her heart pill."

George eyed Mustache's feet. No boots. George stood his ground.

"Now, someone had trained this dog to bark for a dog biscuit more times a day than Bonnie was supposed to take pills. Today he's barked at ten and two, and I'll bet he'll bark at six. That would make a regular pattern." Even my friend Mustache looked doubtful. Mustache looked at the kitchen clock. Quarter of six.

"And then, if you want to be sure of the whole pattern, let your police gal who works with the drug-sniffing dog keep George for a day and see," I said. "If she gives him a dog biscuit after he barks for it, he'll keep on barking at regular intervals, and you can use that for evidence."

"I might laugh at that evidence," Mustache sighed, "except I know you. But we need more. That dog-alarm-clock stuff could be laughed out of court."

"Well, I'm willing to bet an autopsy on Bonnie Amons will show she's been taking more Lanoxin than she should, maybe three times as much," I said. "The amount will match the number of times a day that George barks in a certain way. I showed Bonnie how to train this little dog to bark when she was due to take her medicine, but now her daughter, Andrea Ann, has trained the dog to bark more often. And I believe the overdose killed my friend."

"Well, you know about heart medicine, all right," he sighed, pulling at his mustache, "since the attempt last year to kill your father with it. So you think this Andrea Ann killed her own mother?"

"Sure," I said. "Andrea Ann had a fight with her mother because Bonnie wouldn't lend her money. Then Andrea Ann made up and helped nurse her mother. Maybe just in order to kill her. Andrea Ann is a little strange. But very determined. She didn't like to live in a trailer park."

"But how could anyone prove Andrea Ann was the poisoner, even if the autopsy and the dog check out? And we can't even ask for an autopsy without some proof that something is wrong." He chewed the end of his mustache. "I hate to let you down," he said kindly, "but this one may be too preposterous if all you have is the dog and speculation."

"Luckily," I said, "Andrea Ann thought the dog could incriminate her by barking too often. She thought I'd figure out what happened. She had one of her dumb spells. So she gave me proof.

"Here," I said, "is some hamburger laced with poison. I'm sure of it. If you look in Andrea Ann's refrigerator, I think you'll find unpoisoned hamburger that matches it. Andrea Ann never could bring herself to waste anything. She may possibly have thrown out the poison, but she can't have thrown it far.

"She's needed to be over at her mother's house with her sister, looking innocent. She could slip out while her sister was busy flirting with her husband and drop the poisoned meat into my kitchen, the louse. But she didn't have time to go far away. And she didn't expect to have to use poison. Earlier she had shot at George, but she missed. Then she probably poisoned this meat with what she had handy—some household pesticide. You'll find the evidence. I have faith."

But Mustache was staring at the clock. The hands said six. George was lying quietly on the floor by my feet. I sighed. So okay, my imagination led me astray. But I didn't believe that. George yawned.

And then he stood up and began to bark. He jumped up and down and ran back and forth. He stamped his feet.

I handed Mustache a dog biscuit. "Here, you give it to him," I suggested. He did, and George wagged his tail and stopped barking.

I am happy to say that when Mustache got himself a hurry-up search warrant, there was hamburger in Andrea Ann's fridge, and it matched. Modern science can spot those things. The rat-poison box was still in her garage. She was overconfident. So sure that once the dog was dead, nobody could spot those extra pill-barkings. So sure she could prevent us from discovering the secret of the dog.

Mustache found one thing I missed. Andrea Ann was going to three different pharmacies to get Lanoxin, using stolen and forged prescription forms she got from her nursing job.

As for George, he settled in with me and is a big help. I used to take my thyroid pills when I thought of it. Or else I didn't. Sometimes it was hard to remember. Now I take them every day at ten o'clock.

* * *

Liz was often asked what she imagined Peaches Dann to look like. Despite her earlier allusion to Goldie Hawn as her ideal screen portrayer of Peaches, here's what Liz wrote to a friend:

Peaches has a slightly heart-shaped face and short wavy brown hair. Actually, it's beginning to be gray, but Peaches figures brown goes better with her clothes. She has twinkly eyes and sometimes a wry grin. She's rounded but not fat. Her hands—which will be important in the next book—have squarish palms, tapered fingers with slight knots or knuckles at the lower joints, and large thumbs. She's medium tall.

The next short story in the Peaches group is very loosely based on
Liz's uncle Robert Bridgers, who moved from Raleigh to Asheville in
the 1970s. Liz had helped pack up Robert's belongings for the move,
but when he opened his trunk in Asheville, Robert couldn't find his
bottle of aspirin. Liz had thrown out the ancient yellowed pills,
remarking that they not only looked awful but smelled awful.

Never one to waste anything (like her Uncle Robert), Liz turned the
seemingly trivial bit into this intriguing mystery story, which
appeared in Jessica Fletcher Presents . . . Murder They Wrote II.
This story has an awful lot of Liz's Uncle Robert in it. I think he
would have been pleased.

In Memory of Jack

Because I bought a dozen candy bars from Billy Read, I was able
to fulfill my Uncle Jack's last wishes.

It's hard to say no to Billy. He came in the kitchen door, gave
me a hero-worship smile, and put some Mars Bars and Reese's
Cups on the table. He said, "What I like best about that book you
wrote is the part about how you can remember something better if
you see a real shocker of a picture in your head."

It's nice to have an avid admirer thirteen years old. It's different.

"That system really works with names," he said. "I have a new
teacher. Miss McCarson. McCarson is like My Car's On. So I see her
under the front wheels. That's neat."

Billy is our neighbor who likes books and wears thick glasses.
He needs heroes, male or female. Enter: me. He was all dressed
up, in good slacks and tie. "I'm selling candy," he said, "to raise
money for our eighth-grade trip."

In his teenage, awestruck tone, he added, "and I think it's wonderful you can do two things at once. You write books and you solve
murders."

My book, I hasten to add, is not about murders. It's called *How to Survive Without a Memory*, by me, Peaches Dann. It's a subject I know well, and I didn't really write it for teenagers, but why not? They do tend to be absent-minded.

Billy squirmed with admiration. Kind of sweet. "And I read in the paper how you saved that girl who was tied up and locked up, and you found out who killed her sister." He beamed. "And she wasn't much older than me."

I *have* solved murders, though not on purpose, exactly. My mountain relatives and friends are just plain accident-prone. They get killed and accused like you wouldn't believe. Maybe because I'm related to half the population. At least on my father's side.

"I'm reading a book about famous murders too," he said, ignoring his mission with the candy bars. "I just see shocking stuff in my head and I can remember all the ways there are to get killed."

Good grief, was I that ghoulish as a kid? Well, I did like blood and thunder.

". . . Like plain old hanging." He grabbed his necktie and held the loose end up above his head to imitate that. I opened my mouth, couldn't think of a thing to say, and closed it again.

He picked up the bread knife from the kitchen table. ". . . And stabbing." He pretended to plunge it into his chest.

"And fancy kinds, like strychnine poisoning. Where the person thrashes around"—he arched his body back and forward—"and then they die with this 'risus sardonicus'—I like those words, which mean a hideous smile. And their eyeballs are rolled up in their head and bulging, too." He made a face that was hideous and grinning worse than death. It was an image to remember, all right.

"But didn't you want to sell me candy?" I asked, and I bought a dozen Mars Bars quick to end the conversation before he cut himself or his eyes got stuck. I figured I could take some candy to my Uncle Jack, who needed spice in his life. He loved chocolate.

The following Thursday I went to visit Uncle Jack. I just had a feeling that was the right day. Maybe he told me something and I forgot it and it just hung around in my mind like intuition. I knew I should go then.

Jack was my only nearby relative on my mother's side. I told you I have a million kin on Pop's side. But my mother's folks have moved away from here, chasing opportunity. Only Uncle Jack stayed near Asheville, living in a shack out in the country. He grew a small garden and called himself an old hermit. Like Thoreau without philosophy or a pond, my husband said, sounding like a college professor, which he is. Still, Jack didn't have a single enemy that I knew of.

I went by Uncle Jack's whenever I was down his way, off the road to Paint Fork, not far from Asheville. He had the gift of making you feel like there was nobody he would rather see in the whole world. I was sure he was lonely, in spite of the million birds that flocked around his house because he fed them even in summer.

As I drove onto the dirt drive that leads to his weathered wood cabin, the sun was shining. The birds were calling back and forth in the trees, an irregular symphony. I got out of my car and paused to hear.

Then those birds flew up in a flutter and streamed away as a woman banged my uncle's back screen door. She came running out, screaming, "Oh, God, he's gone." I stood still in surprise. She ran right over to me, past a white Cadillac parked in the drive. A white Cadillac of all things! She stopped, gulped a couple of times, looked me straight in the eye, and cried, "This is terrible. I loved him. I loved them both."

A red bird, confused, flew right across in front of her. I felt his wind. I was confused too.

"But I couldn't marry either one," she cried. "I couldn't do it. And now he's gone!" That part is etched on my mind because it seemed so absolutely strange. "Strange" is a memory aide, par excellence.

Now, I may be bad at names, and also faces, but I was sure I had never seen this woman with the triangular face, small mouth, and large lustrous eyes before in my life. And how could Uncle Jack be gone? I was alarmed. He never went anywhere.

You see, something went wrong for Jack. My mother said it all began back in school where he almost flunked out. But he wasn't stupid, he just couldn't fit a mold. One of his brothers became a lawyer and the other became a doctor, which made that even harder. But he was seventy years old now. He could relax.

So what on earth was wrong now? Jack found a place for himself. He looked after an aunt. She had nurses, but he did errands. She died and left him enough to manage in his shack in the woods.

Still, he hadn't had a girlfriend in years that I knew of. And here was this hysterical woman in rich-city-folks country clothes. Designer-type denim, a huge leather bag, Birkenstocks, southwestern silver and turquoise dripping from her neck and ears. Her body was shaking but it still looked like art work: composed, painted, curled, manicured, massaged, whatever. She was also petite and pretty, though she must have been at least 65, maybe older.

I guess I looked sympathetic. She threw her arms around me, engulfed me in heady perfume, and wept on my shoulder as if I was her mother. I'm not old enough, for goodness' sake. I'm only 56. But

I was sorry for whatever was wrong, and alarmed.

"You expected him to be there and now he's not?" I asked. "He knew you were coming?" I couldn't keep amazement out of my voice.

"Yes, yes, I wrote. And he wrote back. He expected me at two o'clock." She and I both looked at our watches. It was two-twenty.

"And now he's dead," she cried.

Dead! I couldn't move. She had me in a going-down-for-the-third-time hug. "He was always my friend," she sobbed on my shoulder, "even when I wouldn't marry him—even when I never saw him. I knew he was there. He never could keep a job, and I need looking after. Well, I do! But now he's dead."

Dead! I managed to pull loose and started to run and see what had happened to Uncle Jack.

"No!" she cried. "Don't look! It's terrible. Don't go." She clasped her silvered throat as if she might choke.

But I had to go. I ran down the dirt drive past blooming daisies and tall grasses, pulled the screen door open, and looked into the shadowy room. And there, next to the worn couch where he often slept without even bothering to remove his jeans and shirt, was Uncle Jack, contorted on the gray wooden floor as if he had died writhing. He had such a terrible grimace on his face that right away I saw Billy Read, the candy-bar boy with his whatever-sardonicus, his horrible smile. My uncle's eyes were rolled up in his head just like Billy said, and bulging too. Strychnine! I felt sick.

But I needed to be sure he was dead. I knelt down and felt. No pulse. I couldn't believe this. Uncle Jack never hurt a soul. Not on purpose. So who could want to hurt him? Why?

But wait, I told myself. Suppose this was a heart attack? I didn't believe it. Suppose he killed himself? He wasn't the type. He was spartan, but in his way he enjoyed life. He certainly enjoyed his birds.

So call the sheriff, I told myself, choking back tears, but Jack didn't have a phone. Besides, I needed to look around.

By the reclining chair where he always sat, and where one contorted hand now pointed, the small glass-topped table that his mother had loved lay on its side on the floor. The glass had cracked. He'd said she'd warned him over and over not to break it. That thought made me choke up more.

The Paris ashtray he'd brought back from the war always sat on the table, but it was on the floor, too. With cigarette butts scattered all over. Somehow, Jack did okay in the army. He used to tell me how he meant to look up his old army buddies after the war, but then he never did.

Had something from that time come back to haunt him? Why so many cigarette butts? Had he been nervous and smoked double-time? Or had someone else smoked too? I looked closely. All were his cork-tipped kind of butts.

In the corner near his chair stood the big brass-bound black trunk that had belonged to his father. I couldn't open that without touching—never corrupt a crime scene—so I took a chance that the undisturbed dust on top meant it hadn't been opened lately and left it alone. I knew the trunk held a German gun he'd managed to bring back from World War II which probably didn't work. "I could have gotten in trouble for bringing that back," he used to say and shake his head and chuckle. His photograph albums were in there, too, showing how good-looking he was as a young man, with that widow's peak and rebellious dark eyes with long lashes. A heartbreaker.

Was that why this carefully made-up woman had come back to find him? She said she'd loved him! But she didn't fit.

Out the window, I saw his big bird feeder, a tray on a pole. A lone black bird had ventured back and pecked at seed.

My eye fell on his rock collection on one windowsill. Oh, he loved to tell about that. As a kid he hiked a lot and collected quartz and such. And he loved to tell how he'd almost stepped on snakes a couple of times. "I should have looked where I stepped more carefully, but I never did." Always a storyteller, Uncle Jack.

The champagne-bottle lamp on the table at the end of the couch looked out of place in his rustic room. He'd said he gave a party for his best girl and some friends right after the war and they drank the champagne. "And at that party I introduced her to the rich good-looking guy that she upped and married. I wasn't very smart, was I?" And yet, as I say, my Uncle Jack wasn't exactly dumb. He had an open library book cover-up on the arm of his chair. A new life of Robert E. Lee.

I heard a sniff, and saw the city woman standing in the door, quietly crying and watching me. Her makeup was smeared now, distorting her face. Reminding me of his. I had to stand close to him, the room was so small. I shuddered. And I suddenly had the oddest feeling that this woman was sad, and shocked—but not surprised.

So why did I remember Uncle Jack's bee story right then? He'd told it to me a million times—how he was walking down the road and he saw a man off in a field all done up with a helmet on his head and a veil over his face, and long pants and a long-sleeved heavy shirt and gloves, and so Uncle Jack walked over to see what was going on. And the man began to wave his arms and act very strange, so Uncle Jack went even closer, and it turned out the man was working with bees. "And—do you know?—I could have been stung to death by those bees, and the man was trying to tell me that, and I was too dumb to realize!" He liked to laugh at himself. About how he wasn't clever at looking out for number one.

So had he done something careless that enraged someone to the point of poison? And what did this woman know about it? Why didn't I go right over and ask her? But I wanted to look around first. I let my eyes go back to his poor contorted body. Who could my uncle have infuriated to the point of murder? Uncle Jack never went anywhere. Not except with a neighbor to the grocery store or sometimes the laundromat, or to the bookmobile that parked just down the road. You don't poison somebody because he doesn't return a library book on time. I hope not.

The city woman went right on sobbing. She didn't seem to want to talk. Neither did I.

I looked at the old brown throw-blanket on the end of the couch. Jack never wanted anything new. He said the throw belonged to his grandmother. It was full of holes but "I like what I'm used to." That's what he said when I tried to get him a new one for his birthday. He didn't ask for much. He didn't have anything that anyone would want to steal. It wasn't fair for him to be dead.

The bathroom door was open, so I stepped in. His old brown and white terry-cloth robe was on the hook on the back of the door. A brown bath towel hung on a rack at the end of the claw-foot enamel tub. By now, that tub must be a valuable antique. But he wouldn't have sold it. He was used to it. A couple of tissues and a wrapper from some Tums lay in the bottom of the dented metal wastebasket. The medicine cabinet hung open. His few bottles of medicine sat on the shelf. Not that he ever used them. Like I said, he was a spartan. He ignored pain.

Once, a few years back, when I dropped by, he was down with flu. I said I'd get him something for his upset stomach, but all he'd let me get him was a cup of tea. "And put the Tums on the table, and if I don't feel better in a while I'll take one." I noticed he had an ancient-looking bottle of Pepto-Bismol and an antique-looking tin that said BAKING SODA. I remembered the soda tin. When I was a kid I saw him put two spoonfuls from that tin into a glass of water and drink it down, and I asked if it was instant orange soda or some other kind. And he just laughed and said baking soda helped an acid stomach and wasn't sweet soda at all. And I thought that was so strange.

On the day when he had flu, I said his medicines looked kind of old and I'd get him some new ones. "I don't waste things," he said.

He sounded angry. "You leave those there." And now the antique Pepto-Bismol was still there, but no Tums and baking soda. There was some rubbing alcohol, some aftershave lotion which Ted and I gave him the Christmas before, a box of Band-Aids, and an ancient-looking bottle of iodine.

I came back to the living room, and the woman was no longer in the door. I looked out and saw her down the drive a little way, sitting on a log, still crying. She stared hard at me. I decided she wasn't going to run away.

I cased the small lean-to kitchen—nothing out of place there. I went in Uncle Jack's bedroom. A sweater for our cool mountain evenings hung over a chair. A few holes in that too. On the table under the window, I saw a box of letters, maybe about twenty. My fingers itched. But I knew I should leave the crime scene as it was. Still, one letter was open on the table. The second page was on top. I could read that.

"Don't say you're almost scared to see me again, Jack. You've been my friend all these years. And now that I am alone I need my friends. I remember you with such nostalgia. I'm glad that you remember me when you feed the birds, that you think how I love birds. I'll be by at two on Thursday, and we'll reminisce."

It was signed "With Love, L."

How long had it lain there? Why was he almost afraid to see her? And did it matter if anyone but my uncle knew the woman was coming at two o'clock?

Now I was afraid the woman might leave. I ran out, but she was still sitting on the log.

"Nothing looks disturbed inside," I said. "Except near his body. Did you touch anything?"

The woman seemed to relax a little and raised her blotched face, and I thought: *Why, she's relieved at what I just said. That's odd.*

She said, "No."

Then I remembered myself and said, "I'm Peaches Dann, Jack Harrison's niece."

"We have to call the police, don't we?" she said. "And they have to talk to me because—" she choked up again. *She's afraid*, I thought. Could she have done this? And now cry crocodile tears?

"We have to call the sheriff, not police," I said. "We're out in the county. I'll call from the house down the hill. You'd better come with me."

She got in my Toyota, leaving her white Cadillac. Perhaps she didn't trust herself to drive. "Where are you staying?" I asked as we headed toward a neighbor's house. "You may have to stay over."

"I was only passing through."

Next I did something which may prove I'm nuts. "You cared about my uncle," I said. "Why don't you stay with us." I said that to this woman about whom I knew nothing at all, not even her name, this woman I'd have never met if I hadn't brought my uncle candy bars. She might perfectly well be the one who killed my mother's brother. But I felt no woman who loved birds could be all bad.

Of course she told me her name then: Lulu Girder. Lulu. Yes, that matched the L. on the letter.

Lulu! The girl who went with the bottle of champagne! Suddenly that came back to me. My uncle used to say, "Her name was Lulu, and she was a real lulu!" To him that obviously meant a real winner. Maybe a hot babe. I wished her last name—Girder—didn't rhyme with murder, but that did mean I wasn't likely to forget it. Billy would have been pleased.

The county sheriff I had known well had been defeated for office several months back, which was just as well because he didn't like me. The sheriff's men who arrived were new to me. I told them everything I'd noticed, and that my uncle had no enemies at all that I knew of. They agreed that, yes, as the next of kin, they'd keep in touch with me. Good. I needed to be absolutely sure what killed my uncle.

They questioned Lulu and asked her to stick around. And so my invitation was accepted.

Lulu was no trouble as a houseguest, I'll say that. She knew how to pitch in and help snap the beans or pick the blueberries in the yard. Oh, she appreciated nice things. She spotted the Persian rug Ted's great-aunt left him. The great-aunt whose husband owned the largest brickyard in South Carolina. And Lulu seemed to be a nurturer. She pulled a thorn from my cat Silk's paw. But mostly she sat on our terrace, listened to the birds sing, and retreated into a book. Whatever was around: *The Kitchen God's Wife* by Amy Tam or a mystery by Margaret Maron. She sat and read for hours like someone recuperating from an illness.

She could have been recuperating from murder. But I didn't want to think so. I liked her. Still, I had an odd feeling she was waiting for something. Was it something she expected from me? From the sheriff? What?

She told me the basics of her life. She'd grown up in Asheville, met Uncle Jack as one of the boys coming back from World War II. Left Asheville when she married, lived in Atlanta. No children. Now her husband had died. She was wandering, not sure what next.

"Jack and I were so young when we met," she said, as she and

Ted and I had breakfast on the terrace. "Twenty-three didn't seem young then, but it certainly does now. Jack was kind," she said, sipping her coffee. "I never heard him say one mean word. A rebel, yes, impractical, but never mean. He was terribly good-looking. And he worshiped me. That may sound vain," she said, fluttering eyelashes, "but it's true." She smiled a dreamy smile at the clematis vine with white star flowers at the edge of the terrace.

Ted excused himself. He said he had to finish digging the hole and plant the two-foot-high quince tree he'd bought at Penland's nursery the day before. He winked at me. "I like your quince jelly."

After he left, Lulu reached out and touched my hand and said, "You have to understand that I loved your Uncle Jack," she frowned. "But I also loved Martin Heller."

What? "Martin Heller? Who was that?"

"I don't know how you can love two men at once." She sighed. "But I did. Martin wasn't like Jack. He was trouble. He couldn't control his temper. If you hurt Martin Heller, he had to get even. He actually went to jail for breaking a friend's nose."

I'd remember that name: He was a real hell-raiser, a Heller.

"I was a crazy kid," she said. "I had to fix people. I had to love the ones who needed to be loved. We actually hung out together, Jack and Martin and me. But I couldn't marry either one. So then I met Harold, and he was kind, and he was practical, and he was rich, and he asked me to marry him. And I didn't love him so I knew he must be okay."

Suddenly this all fit together. "Jack introduced you to Harold," I said. "At a champagne party."

"Yes," she said. "Poor Jack. He took it hard." Tears glistened in her eyes. She dabbed them with her napkin. "But we stayed friends. We wrote now and then. My husband was a little dull. And I cheated on him." She glanced at me to see if I was shocked. I'm always too busy trying to figure people out to be shocked.

"I'm not proud I cheated," she said. "He was important to me. He took care of me. And I disappointed him. So it was nice to have a friend like Jack, who still thought that I was wonderful."

But he was "almost scared" to see you again, I thought—that's what it said in the letter. Because Uncle Jack still loved her? Or why?

"Was your husband jealous of Jack?" I asked.

"He was a very jealous man, but why of Jack? Jack became a friend. I needed a friend."

"And this other man you said you loved? This Heller?"

She sighed deeply. She plucked a daisy by the edge of the deck and began to pull off the petals. "I've always believed Martin killed himself." She threw the daisy down as if she was angry at it. "Martin drove his car into a tree right after I married Hal." She waited for me to react, but I outwaited her. "He was so damned angry to learn I'd picked another man, that he killed himself," she said. "I sure have my regrets."

Killed himself! Both of the men she loved died violent deaths. Poor Lulu. Or was this woman by my side the kiss of death. There were people, I'd heard, who needed to kill what they loved. People who looked as friendly as Lulu.

She was silent for a long time, staring into the heart of the clematis as if it had an answer for her. I finished my pancakes. I watched my husband digging a deep hole for the quince tree. He believes it's important to put in fertilizer below the plant. To prepare the soil just right. I thought how lucky to have a husband who likes to make things grow, instead of two dead lovers and a husband who died disappointed.

I glanced at Lulu. She must have been a lovely young girl with those lustrous blue eyes and small gentle mouth. Wide-browed like a kitten. She was toying with her pancakes, not eating much.

Finally Lulu spoke again, eyes sorrowful but hopeful. "Jack believed that Martin hit that tree because he was drunk."

That would be less painful for Lulu. Yes. "How would Jack know?"

She began to twist and shred her paper napkin. "Jack wrote me about it," she said. "Martin came to see Jack right after I married Hal, and brought some bottles of red wine in a grocery bag. Brought the whole bag inside because it was hot outside in his car and he didn't want the milk to sour." She sighed. "Jack was so funny he wrote me all the details. Lord, that was fifty years ago! Martin told him they'd both lost me, so they should be friends, they should get drunk together. Jack was touched. So Martin drank a lot of red wine, but Jack couldn't drink much. Red wine upset his stomach, always had. But he wanted to be friends, so he drank a little. Then he couldn't find soda to settle his stomach. Just the empty tin. But Martin had soda in his groceries. He gave the box to Jack. 'Which proved he really was my friend.' That's what Jack wrote me. Little things touched Jack. And he was horrified that Martin went out from his house drunk and drove into a tree." Her napkin was now in shreds. "Jack felt he should have stopped Martin. But no one ever could stop Martin from what he meant to do."

"And that is why the soda, which he put in his old tried-and-true baking soda tin, was one of my uncle's mementos," I said. I laughed. "A very odd memento. The one he never talked about. But he wouldn't let me throw it out."

Later that day as I washed lettuce and Lulu cut up chicken for salad, Deputy Frank Robb from the sheriff's office called to tell me that the lab report showed strychnine had killed my uncle Jack. So I was right. I shuddered. "There was not a bit of strychnine anywhere in the house. Not even a glass that had had some in it," he reported. "No clear fingerprints but his and yours. Frankly, we're baffled."

I came back and sat down at the kitchen table. I told Lulu the news. She went dead pale.

And I realized I knew who killed my uncle.

I jumped up and went to call Chuck Sprinkle at the Weaverville Pharmacy, who knows about such things, and ask him a few questions about strychnine. Yes, he said strychnine would keep potent for years and years mixed with baking soda in a tin.

Then I confronted Lulu. "You stole my uncle's soda," I said. "He never threw it away. He never threw anything away."

She began to tremble, so she put the knife down. She put her small plump hands flat on the table to steady herself.

"Strychnine was mixed into the soda," I said. "You removed it for that reason."

She blinked several times. Blue eyes furtive in their mascara rings. Desperately trying to think of a good lie, I thought. I was disappointed.

Then her shoulders slumped. She seemed to fade. Blonde hair washed out, skin shriveled beneath her makeup, eyes watery blue, hands clasped as if each was afraid to be alone.

"I killed him," she whispered. Then she sat straighter and said it out loud. "I killed him."

"Why?" I asked.

"I killed them both." Her voice cracked like a teen's. "It was my fault. I could have prevented what happened. With Martin, I should have known."

She rocked back and forth in her chair. She swallowed. "Martin called me and began to yell that he would never forgive me for 'leading him on' and then marrying another man. I should have known he would do something wild. I knew what he was like and I loved him anyway. I felt weak when he kissed me. I can still remember." She pursed her lips. She sighed. "But I never felt safe with him. I felt safe with Jack." She cried a little. To get my sympathy? No, I felt her tears were real.

"And when Martin said that he was going to go get drunk with Jack because I'd done them both in, I should have known. 'That fool, Jack,' Martin screamed at me. 'It was just like that fool to introduce you to the perfect man to marry. Stinking rich. And stinking respectable. Goodbye!' He hung up in my face."

Her eyes looked straight through me, back to the past. I knew she didn't hear the two finches calling to each other across the lawn, or see the small green inchworm that had landed on one of her hands. Those hands were holding the table again as if it might run away. "Martin," she said, as if the word was a curse.

"And so, what happened?" I asked.

She blinked and came back to the present. She brushed away the inchworm. "Martin knew red wine gave Jack a stomachache," Lulu said unhappily. "We all knew that. Red wine or nerves. Either one. So Martin gave Jack red wine and soda."

"Wine and soda?"

"Martin brought the red wine and also the poison mixed into the baking soda, and I'm sure he told Jack he needed to take some soda when his stomach hurt. He was so damn clever. If Jack already had soda in the bathroom, Martin probably threw it out. And Martin was persuasive, he really was. He meant to poison Jack and kill himself. I'm sure of that. To get even with Jack and make me feel bad."

"But he didn't wait and watch Uncle Jack take the strychnine and soda," I said, "because Uncle Jack didn't take it. Thank God. He had the habit of trying first to sleep off whatever hurt. And then he got to taking Tums instead of soda. He liked the flavor."

She shook her head amazed. "So why. . . ?"

"And when, after all these years, he expected you—when he was so nervous about this meeting that he smoked a whole pack of cigarettes—he got a stomachache. And he wanted to be his best with you. He had no time to sleep it off. And he was out of Tums. The empty container was in the trash. So he took some soda and he died."

"Yes," she sobbed, "and as soon as I found him dead, it all slipped into place. And I knew. And it was my fault because I should have known sooner. I should have known when Martin said goodbye he meant the big goodbye. I should have written Jack to throw away that soda Martin gave him. What Martin gave my Jack was death. And Martin killed himself because of me." She shook, a child-woman in her rich-woman clothes. I felt a surge of fury at this Martin, but not at Lulu.

I squeezed her hand tight. "No," I said. "He killed himself because he couldn't live with himself. Anymore than you could live with him. He killed himself because he was angry at the whole world. That's not your fault. And you don't need to keep protecting him. He's dead. He can't be tried for murder. You didn't need to steal that poison to protect his name."

"And Jack—" she sobbed.

"He died expecting you," I said. "And perhaps hoping for more than was really possible. He had a few minutes of pain. But, basically, he died happy."

She stared at me, wide-eyed, incredulous. "You're generous, like Jack."

I felt like crying myself. "I'd like to do what he would have wanted me to do," I said. "He would have wished for you to be happy."

And then I did something that wasn't like me at all. It was like Uncle Jack. Generous and a little bit reckless.

Lulu was crying so hard I didn't think she could hear me. "Stop that!" I called out. She almost choked, but she stopped.

"Now, if you take that soda tin to the police," I said, "you may be charged with withholding information. You could even be a prime suspect for murder, since you were the last one to see Uncle Jack alive. And you certainly had the means."

She nodded unhappily.

"If you don't take that soda tin to the police, and if you dispose of it forever—in an incinerator, for example—then if by some chance an innocent person should be accused of the murder, we have no way to prove otherwise. So I want you to write down the story of Jack's letter to you about Martin's visit and the red wine. Just that part, no admission of anything, and sign it. I'll put it in my safety deposit box in case of need. And then," I said, "you might take that soda tin from wherever it's hidden, and the glass and spoon—you must have those—and put them in one of those plastic bags that are a problem because they don't biodegrade in the dump," I said. "And when Ted comes in to lunch, you could drop the poison in that hole that Ted has dug for the quince tree and put a little dirt on top so Ted won't notice.

"And then you need to forgive yourself, because you never meant to cause hurt." I gave her a big hug for Uncle Jack.

Later, when Ted finished planting the quince and tamped the dirt around the bush, I admired the lovely job. "It looks so at home, you'd think it had been there forever," I said. A red bird perched on top and began to sing.

I almost cried. But then at the same time I almost laughed. Because I thought how bug-eyed Billy Read would be to know that murder can lie in wait for almost 50 years. And that an accessory to hiding evidence lived right down his street in my house. I must never tell Ted. He'd be shocked.

"It's always a fine thing," Ted said, "to plant a fruit tree that's useful as well as ornamental."

"Yes," I said. "Let's say we planted it in memory of Uncle Jack."

Like the rest of you, I am stunned by Liz's abrupt death. She came late to the mystery field, but she loved it and soon carved out her own space. Modest and self-effacing, it would have been easy to overlook her among our splashier and more self-confident colleagues. But those who knew her soon came to treasure her wry dry wit, her genuine interest in others, her selflessness in volunteering to do the jobs no one else wanted and to do them well. On a purely selfish level, our chapter of Mystery Writers of America will sorely miss her steady hand on our newsletter.

Like her character, Peaches Dann, Liz was also notoriously absent-minded and she collected so many mnemonic tricks that friends kept urging her to write a book about them. I still use her suggestion about putting my car keys with something I mean to take along with me when I leave, whether it be milk I've stuck in a friend's refrigerator on the way home from grocery shopping or a plant from their garden.

She was always ready to welcome newcomers to our ranks. She read our hands, she read our hearts, and like you, mine is very heavy today as I try to comprehend our loss.

Margaret Maron

In the words of the blurb introducing this story in Malice Domestic 10, "Peaches stumbles across something more in the compost heap than mulch."

Down the Garden Path

Almost every Saturday I take a morning walk and I stop and hear about the adventures of little Mimi's friend named Pompadori. Pompadori rode tigers and elephants when the circus was in town, and among other amazing accomplishments, she knew how to fly. But even so, last Saturday I was startled to hear that Pompadori found a body in the compost heap.

I must tell you about Mimi. She's five years old, and one of those kids you find yourself pulling for. She has what I can only call presence. She stands sturdily on her feet like she intends to survive no matter what. She wears overalls and cheerful T-shirts with hearts or teddy bears or some such on them, but occasionally mismatched socks. Most notably, her eyes are sad and wise and naive all at once. Her best friends are a black dog of many breeds and Pompadori, who isn't even real. Mimi and the dog named Fritzy play in her front yard, and greet me eagerly when I walk by.

"Mama says I make up stories and tell lies, but Grandma says that I'm her angel," she'd once told me.

"Stories don't have to be lies," I told her. "Some people get paid for making up stories."

She'd liked that.

Still, it's hard to sort out the truth when I talk to Mimi. I've noticed there do seem to be rules. She tells the truth when she talks about her grandma who she visits once a week. Grandma reads to her, Mimi says, and obviously that nourishes her imagination. I've met Grandma. She's a salt-of-the-earth type.

Mimi makes up stories around the things that worry her or scare her. Like her mother.

"Mama drinks a magic potion," she told me. "Mama becomes a sleeping beauty." I figured that was her way of saying her mother was an alcoholic. "When my papa was here, my mama was a witch, so he went away. I'm glad she's not a witch with me."

The compost heap was my connection with her mama, Mabel—that, and saying "Hi" to Mimi. Otherwise I hardly knew Mabel. I remembered her name because it's like Maybe plus L. And maybe she could be as colorful and rotten as neighborhood gossip said. Maybe she did raise L. But Maybe not. A would-be pop singer, I heard, but not successful enough to cut the mustard; an alcoholic and a nymphomaniac with a nasty temper. So said my unfavorite neighbor, Nina the Whiner. I wait and believe what I see.

I enjoyed the compost connection. Right after she moved in last year, Mabel contacted us neighbors and offered to trade us organic vegetables for our grass clippings, vegetable peels, and other compostables. Sounded good to me. Four of us, including Nina, took her up on it.

But Mabel never came to collect these herself. She'd hired a gorgeous young man about twenty years old to work in her garden, and he came by once a week for the pickup. (Maybe he was Mabel's lover. Nina had suggested that. If I wasn't happily married, I might have been tempted.)

Now, in July, the young man brought me perfectly beautiful squash and cucumbers and beans and more. So I wanted to have kind thoughts of Mabel.

I told Mimi that I thought Pompadori might have made a mistake about the man in the compost heap, and I continued my walk down to Beaverdam Lake and back. A lovely walk with pine trees and my neighbors' yards in bloom. When I came back, Mimi was waiting in her yard nervously pulling the petals off a daisy. I noticed the dog wasn't with her this Saturday. That was unusual. Mimi took hold of my arm, and I could feel she was trembling.

"There's a man in the compost heap, and Mama is sick, and bad Mrs. Broken Face yelled at Monk," she said. Strange words from a child who looked as gentle and pretty as an angel on a Christmas card. Except for those intense eyes.

Mrs. Broken Face was our neighbor Annie, who has a birthmark. Monk was the gorgeous young gardener, a poet, no less. Asheville attracts poets.

I call our neighbor Annie the Fannie. Annie was nastily divorced and fading pretty, and she switched her tail like a high sign. She comforted herself with men. And Monk delivered her vegetables.

"Where is Monk?" I asked Mimi. A man that good-looking is obviously the opposite of a monk as in monastery. Opposites help me remember names too.

"We can't find Monk," Mimi said. She took hold of my arm again and pulled. "Mama is sick." Mimi's eyes said *Help!*

So I let her pull me around in back of the white clapboard house. I had an ominous feeling that I was going to need to do something. But what can you do about a person who drinks and doesn't get help? What can you do to help her child? Oh, I'd brought by a friend of mine who's in AA and loves to garden. A contact if Mabel ever wanted that. But, as I say, except for eating her vegetables, I hardly knew the woman.

Mimi pulled me to the stone terrace overlooking the vegetable garden, and there sat Mabel drinking tea. Mabel with her slightly disheveled long red hair, and slightly bloodshot eyes. Behind her, just beyond the terrace, were rows of beautifully cared-for shining red tomatoes and yellow squash and dark green kale and much more, in softly turned rich black soil. I told myself that no one with such a garden could be all bad.

She leaned back in her white wicker chair and nervously adjusted a designer denim jacket. She raised her eyes and stared at me as if I were a ghost. "What the hell are you doing here?" she asked. "You're the third one."

Behind her, down at the end of the garden, was the large compost heap with grass clippings and vegetable peels and such included. Inspiration for a wild tale? Or what?

Mabel poured herself some tawny liquid from a large brown teapot. I realized it wasn't tea. More like scotch whiskey. Even if she did pour it into a cup.

Belatedly she remembered manners. "Would you like some tea?" she asked. "There's some in the kitchen." Her voice was only slightly slurred.

I said, "No, thank you," and sat down. Mabel took another gulp of whiskey and said, "I'm glad you're here!" She said it like it was a revelation that surprised her.

I told her how I enjoyed the squash and tomatoes. Then I asked, "I'm the third what? The third one to visit you this morning?" Her mind seemed to be on something else. She didn't answer.

Mimi sat in a small wicker chair just her size and twisted her hands together. "Mrs. Big Foot yelled, too," Mimi said.

I love her names for our neighbors. She meant self-righteous Laurie down the road. Laurie weighs about a hundred and eighty pounds and she does have big feet. She minds everybody else's business with a heavy hand. I knew she'd called social services to try to get Mimi removed from her mama. And yet Laurie's own daughter, Laura Sue, was a tramp in spite of Mama's best efforts. "If that Monk makes a pass at Laura Sue, I'll give him what-for!" she'd said. Yes, heavy-handed. I, myself, called her two-ton Laurie since *lorry* is what the Brits call a truck.

"Was Laurie here this morning?" I asked Mabel tactfully.

"Nobody was here!" she cried. She smelled afraid, a sweetish smell that mixed strangely with the scent of whiskey. What had happened here? I was the third what?

Mimi held onto her chair tight. She was scared too, but in a different way. I couldn't quite put my finger on the difference. "Monk said he'd make me a paper bird," she said. "But he's not here."

I knew Monk better than I knew Mabel since he was the one who came by for my clippings and delivered the vegetables. He was all charm, and looked so young. He didn't just rely on his amazing good looks: good bones, sexy muscles, glowing skin, luxurious hair. Magnificent even in old cut-offs and a T-shirt and high-topped black work shoes. Magnificent, but his eyes were appraising and greedy and needy at the same time.

"I hear you've written a book," he'd told me sweetly, "all about memory tricks. That's wonderful! I have trouble remembering names and numbers, myself. But I have a trick that always works. I write what I have to remember on my hand." He glanced at me for my approval.

"That way I don't have to stop and look in my little book," he said, pulling a black address book out of his pocket. Odd that he had a notebook on the job. Maybe to jot down poetry ideas. A pretty drawing of a bunch of flowers came out with it, primitive but eye-catching. He grinned. "The Kid drew that: Mimi. She's a real little artist. She did it just for me," he said proudly.

He put back the black book and the drawing. "I learned that hand trick from my mother," he said. "She's a surgical nurse. If she absolutely has to remember something during an operation she puts a bandage on her hand and writes on the bandage. I just write on myself." He held up his left hand.

I had said that was a new trick to me, and I had thanked him as warmly as he'd plainly needed.

Now I looked around Mabel's garden. Why wasn't Monk here? This man who needed admiration even from a little child.

Mimi said Annie and Laurie had been here, yet her mother denied it. Hey, they were both members of the compost club. And Pompadori said there was a man in the compost heap. Pompadori who wasn't even real. Somehow, what I was hearing almost fit together in a nightmare, but not quite. At least one member of the compost club had been left out. Nina the Whiner. Nina whose husband traveled, and she complained about that non-stop. He was a smart man. He'd managed to get a phone number that even I could remember. Our call numbers plus 5555. Said it helped him when he did business at home.

I'm not sure why I asked what I asked next. "Was Nina here this morning?"

"No!" Mabel cried. "That woman . . . is a slut. I wouldn't let her even . . . come in my yard!"

Mimi ignored that. No comment about Nina from Pompadori. "Fritzy dug up the man's shoe," she said urgently. "Mama put Fritzy in the cellar."

And Fritzy was nowhere in sight.

"Mimi heard my brother," Mabel said, enunciating slowly. "My stupid brother . . . who eats fast food . . . said that I am such a fanatic about my vegetables . . . that when I die . . . I'll leave my body to a compost heap . . . so Mimi made up one of her stories."

I prayed that was true.

Mabel was drinking her whiskey at an alarming rate. Two butterflies danced around us. She didn't even seem to see them.

I turned to Mimi. "If I go down to the compost heap and look and I come back and tell you that there is no man in that shoe, will you believe me?"

All she said was, "Go look!" She was trembling again.

"You stay with your mama. She needs you," I said. So Mimi went over and stood close to Mabel, frowning with worry when Mabel began to cry. From whiskey self-pity? Or something more?

I walked past Mabel gulping her "tea," past rows of glowing purple eggplant with its peppery smell, several kinds of tomatoes, bush beans, parsley, dill, and cilantro. I picked a sprig of dill as I passed and crushed it and sniffed the wonderful sour odor that spoke of pickles that could be. I looked off at the blue-green mountains. I didn't want to hurry to confront . . . what?

And I had an odd thought that whatever was wrong might be the fault of our wonderful mountains. You see, Asheville is a place where people come with the impression that they can fulfill their dreams here. Maybe it's the view of mountains, one behind another, or something in the air. Creative people flourish here and always have. Thomas Wolfe wrote books here. Bela Bartok wrote music here. Potters, artists, writers, musicians, and new-age healers fill the hills and hollers. But unless you can bring your job with you, it's hard to get the kind of work you want here. And in this place of high hopes, the ones who don't blossom can get bitter. I was the only one in our compost club who wasn't bitter. An odd concentration, but that's how it was. And bitter can lash out. Was that somehow related to a dead man in the compost? If there was one? Or was the dead man only the fantasy of a lonely little girl's imaginary friend?

The compost, in its man-sized weathered wood box, stood just past a tall row of Romano pole beans. The beans hid one end of the box from view. The end I could see did not sprout a shoe. Good. But the compost seemed disturbed, with the new clippings unevenly mixed with the old. I walked closer. And there in the other end of the heap was a black shoe, really a work boot, like the ones Monk wore, stuck out of the heap of organic stuff in the box, ominous and ugly. I felt cold in the bright sun. The boot was sole-outward, as if the rest of the wearer could be under the tossed salad of new peels and clippings and black rotted compost. I shuddered involuntarily. On the ground by the box was a shovel with bits of compost clinging to the business end. There was also something brown that could have been dried blood on one edge of the shovel.

I walked back to Mimi and leaned down and kissed her on the top of the head.

"I didn't lie," she said.

"No," I told her sadly, "You didn't lie."

I put my hand on Mabel's shoulder, trying to pull her to enough sobriety to hear what I said next. "I'm going to call Mimi's grandma to come get her," I said, "because the best thing Mimi can do for you and for herself is to be safe and well, and I'm also going to have to call the police."

The shock cleared Mabel's eyes, at least for a moment. I didn't know what to expect. Hysterics? More denial? I braced myself.

She took hold of my hand, and for one moment a look of raw anguish twisted her face. She said the last thing I expected. "Thank you."

"Go," she said to Mimi. "I want you to go." Then she raised her cup, which she had just filled, and downed it to the last drop. Her head fell forward onto her arms.

Mimi came with me reluctantly, looking back over her shoulder every minute, but she came. She showed me how to punch one button on the phone to get Grandma. I just said, "This is a neighbor. There's an emergency here. Please come get little Mimi."

She didn't even pause to ask questions. She just said, "I'll be there in five minutes."

I suggested Mimi go get Fritzy from the basement. She said she'd get her suitcase too. It was packed from the last visit. As soon as she was gone, I called the police. I gave the address and said there seemed to be a dead man in the compost heap.

The dispatcher said, "If this is a joke, ma'am. . . ."

I said I wished it was a joke and gave him my name.

I went upstairs and I admit I was nosy. I checked Mabel's bedroom with the unmade four-poster bed and the picture of a smiling Monk, framed on the dresser. Also another picture of Monk and Mabel together, holding up some huge tomatoes. Also two shirts that looked like his were hanging in the closet. Yes, score one for Nina.

When I came back, Mimi was in the front hall by a red suitcase. She was hugging Fritzy. Obviously Mimi knew something was terribly wrong, but she said, "Grandma is coming," and smiled. Grandma was at the door almost by the time she'd said it.

I said, "I believe the police are about to arrive."

Mimi and the dog ran to Grandma and she put her arms tight around Mimi. "My angel," she said. "You'll be safe with me."

"When you get a chance, call me," she said to me, giving me a card with her number. Her whole aim was obviously to get Mimi away as fast as possible, and to upset her as little as possible. A wise woman.

Before they could leave, I leaned down and gave Mimi a quick hug, dog and all. "Angels are strong," I said.

Luckily the first policeman who came was a friend of mine. The one I call Mustache because he has one. I led Mustache toward the compost heap, past Mabel who was sleeping, led him to the man-sized weathered wood box, just past those Romano pole beans. Mustache inspected the boot and shovel, pulled out his cellular phone, and called for backup.

We stood away from the box where he could keep an eye on Mabel and the compost all at once, but she was out like a light.

Mustache asked me what I'd seen and heard and I told him what had gone on in this house since I arrived. Then he asked, "So what do you really think happened?"

Thank goodness Mustache doesn't resent the fact that sometimes partly by luck I figure out the answer, the way I did about my neighbor's dog who remembered too much and solved a murder.

"I won't be sure what happened here," I said, "until you uncover the man whose foot is in that boot and I see what's written on his left hand."

Mustache did a double-take. "But how do you know there's writing if you haven't seen the body?"

"Just a hunch, based on a remembering trick." I told him about Monk and his mother in the operating room. Monk who was probably beyond hope from any operating room.

I figured the left hand in the compost heap would show whether three women killed Monk, or whether it was four.

When the backup team arrived it seemed to take forever to photograph the scene, then carefully uncover the body. Yes, it was poor Monk. I identified him and wished he'd died some more poetic way. Poor Monk who needed to be admired—I wished he hadn't been draped with rotting lettuce. I noticed the huge gash on his head with bits of rotted vegetable and grass sticking in the dried blood.

At last his left hand was free and clear and wiped clean. I recognized the number written on it. Yes, it ended with 5555.

"Four women killed him," I told Mustache.

He blinked with shock, as if he thought I meant it happened in an orgy. Well, I guess police come across all sorts of strange deaths. I remembered the story of the woman who made a date on the Internet to come to Asheville to be killed, and came and was killed. I shuddered. "So why did Mabel lie? And say nobody came here this morning? And even accuse her daughter of being a liar?" I mused out loud.

Mustache grinned. "You're going to tell me."

"Because," I said, "Mabel knew Annie and Laurie were links in the chain that led to murder." Then I explained what I believed took place. "Poor Monk needed to be admired so badly," I said, "that he did or said whatever you wanted. He said he liked your book or he said he loved you. Whatever. Mabel wanted him to be her lover. Exclusive rights. After all, he worked for her. Her neighbor Annie wanted the same thing, and Laurie's daughter was after him, I think." I sighed and thought how handsome but how young he'd been. "I don't think he knew how to handle all that. So first Annie came and told him off in front of Mabel." I could picture that. And how angry Mabel got when she learned the Annie connection. "Then Laurie accused him of chasing her daughter, which made Mabel madder.

"The last straw must have been when poor Mabel saw our

neighbor Nina's phone number written on his hand, and figured he was going to make out with Nina, whose husband is in Brazil.

"Three rages at a man who desperately needed admiration was more than he could bear. I bet he said, 'I quit.'"

"Which was his right," Mustache sighed.

"Which added to Mabel's drunken rage. She hit him with the shovel, probably didn't mean to kill him, then was too drunk to get the body far, so she buried it in the compost heap. She was also too drunk to know what to do when Mimi discovered the shoe."

Mustache grinned. I don't know why I amuse him so. "I'll be interested to see," he said, "if our scientific deduction comes to the same conclusion."

Later, as I read the story in the paper about poor Monk who'd been hit over the head with a shovel and buried in the compost heap, I was profoundly sorry. And basically I'd been right. Rage did it. Rage, the great American twentieth-century sport. More often seen on the road.

But I was grateful that Mimi was with her grandma, who believed what Mimi said. Mimi was going to have a tough time with what had happened, but with someone to love and cherish her, I thought she was tough enough to survive.

And I thought about that shining garden. That garden didn't fit with the ugly sick part of Mabel that could destroy the ones she loved. I like to believe that it fit with the Mabel who could finally see what was hopeless and could not be prevented: her own arrest. But could also finally sense what could be saved and helped to grow, and that, thank God, was Mimi.

* * *

This, the last Peaches Dann short story Liz wrote, is generally thought to be her best. It is included in an anthology edited by Jeffrey Marks that was nominated for an Anthony in 2001:

Ode to a Dead Gardenia

"Edgar Allen Poe would have loved this house, and especially the garden," I said to my cousin Robert, the English professor. The place depressed me so much that I had to say something halfway cheerful.

"Yes, Poe would have felt absolutely inspired by this garden," Robert said bitterly, as he brushed away a trailing frond of wisteria hanging down from a smothered tree. "He would even have liked the mystery that may ruin all our lives."

As we walked toward it, the graceful lines of the big old house with fluted columns across the front made it seem to cry out for help. It must once have been white but now was splotched dirty gray. A window shutter hung at an angle, and several were missing, and all around the house were the remains of a generous garden now grown up in tangles. The house stood almost in the shadow of an office building on one side, and I'd noticed a sign in front of the house on the other side which said FUTURE SITE OF THE LOOMIS BUILDING. Too bad that nice looking house, which even had a swimming pool, was going to be torn down.

"Raleigh is growing fast and our Aunt Camellia keeps getting higher and higher offers for her house," Robert said, pointing at the old mansion. "It's on a huge lot, and the last offer was over two million dollars."

I whistled.

"But as I told you, even though we are all broke, Aunt Camellia says that while she's alive she'll never sell. She says there's a reason. But when we ask why, she clamps her mouth shut." Robert sighed. "Even though she's seventy-three years old and has such bad arthritis she can hardly climb the stairs. Even though she can't afford to keep the place repaired. And then there's the problem of Cammie. She'd like to help with that, too. Cammie is her namesake and her goddaughter and her heir. But right now Aunt Camellia doesn't have a cent to spare."

I'd just seen Cammie when we got the key to the house. She wrenched my heart. She was beautiful, dark-haired, maybe forty years old, and confined to a wheelchair with multiple sclerosis. That sometimes goes into remission even after years, but they couldn't count on it. Cammie had given me a warm smile and held out her hand. The hand shook slightly, but the smile held steady. "Robert says that maybe you can help us."

Well, I am a newspaper reporter. I have even stumbled across the solutions to murders occasionally up in the mountains where

— 149 —

I live. But this mystery about the house, God willing, was nothing like that.

I'd held Cammie's hand so firmly that it didn't shake. "I'll do what I can," I'd said. Behind her, on a shelf, was a wedding picture of Robert with Cammie all in white, both beaming. That was the past. Also a picture of Cammie in her wheelchair with three little children smiling up at her.

Now Robert was working two jobs to pay for sitters and nurses so Cammie could stay at home with him and the kids. He even moonlighted driving an armored truck because that paid well— because it was dangerous work, I thought with a shiver.

A brier from the edge of the path scratched my leg. "Aunt Camellia hasn't given you a clue about why she won't sell?" I asked.

Robert pulled a brier loose from a trouser leg. "Once, she said her husband, Claude, wanted to sell that house, and she'll never do what he wanted to do. That's crazy, now that he's dead." He sighed. "And she won't even consider a mortgage because the bank might foreclose. That's what happened to the people who owned the house before her husband bought it."

"Is she losing her marbles?" I asked.

Robert shook his head. "She's eccentric but she's sharp as a tack. She's in the hospital today for tests—that's why I have the key to feed the cat. But it's physical stuff. She's been having dizzy spells. She'll be out tomorrow."

I hoped he'd told me the whole story. People can sometimes ignore ugly things when they convince themselves that it won't matter and will make life smoother.

The red-brick path led to the front door—a double door with paint peeling like all the rest of the house. He unlocked the door and let us into a hallway with rooms on both sides and a sweeping circular staircase to the next floor.

"Wow," I said, "this must have been something!" Now, the white paint was dingy yellow and flaked. This certainly seemed like the house of somebody who didn't care. And yet I saw that even if the house might be in bad repair, it was scrupulously clean.

The high-ceilinged rooms to the right and left of the hall, and two more across the back of the house, were empty. "Aunt Camellia has sold most of the antiques," Robert said.

Huge mirrors over the mantels showed only us, looking puzzled. We went up the circular stairs and, on the next floor, found a portrait staring at us, a well-painted man in a Civil War uniform.

"That's Aunt Camellia's great-grandfather," Robert explained. "This house originally belonged to Aunt Camellia's family. They lost it to taxes after the Civil War. Claude managed to buy it back when the new owners lost it during the Great Depression. Some folks said she married Claude for the house, and that's why she didn't mind going off and looking after her mother in Nashville for three months once and leaving him alone. I think she just felt she had to do it. She's big on duty."

Only two rooms upstairs were furnished. One was a bedroom, one seemed to be a study. I thought I heard a footstep in the distance. "Does this house have a ghost?" I asked, half joking and half serious.

"Not that I've ever heard," he said shortly.

We zeroed in on the two rooms Aunt Camellia lived in. These were sparsely furnished with necessities—a bed, a bed stand, and a bureau in one and a desk and a few chairs in the other.

"What are we looking for?" I asked, but Robert said he didn't know. He just felt sure there must be a clue somewhere in the old house. That was his only hope.

I began to have a feeling that someone was following us. Old houses can creak in strange ways. Perhaps it was only that—but I asked, "Did you lock the garden gate behind us?"

He frowned. "No. But we're here. And there's not much to steal."

I kept my ears cocked.

We looked through the clothes in the closet. They were mostly in shades of violet. Obviously her favorite color. All a tiny bit musty. We found nothing, even in the pockets, except for a rumpled handkerchief with lace around the edge.

On Aunt Camellia's old-fashioned mahogany dresser stood a large bottle of gardenia perfume. She must have really liked that scent to have such a large bottle. Or maybe it had been a present from an admirer long ago. The bottle was dusty as if she never used it now. *Odd*, I found myself thinking. Nothing else in the room was dusty.

And why gardenia perfume for a woman named Camellia? Camellias have always intrigued me. My aunt in Charleston had a camellia bush, and the pink flowers looked as if they should be delicate and smell delicious, but they were long lasting and without scent.

We went into the study. "Aunt Camellia writes poetry," Robert told me with some pride. "There are notebooks with her poetry here. And a few magazines where her poems have been published."

The notebooks and magazines were in a pile on a rolltop desk.

I turned to Robert: "I'm going to look through the drawers—okay?"

He looked embarrassed and said, "Considering how worried we are. . . ." His voice trailed off.

I looked in the dresser drawers and was surprised to find a legal document in the top right drawer. LAST WILL AND TESTAMENT, it said. I hoped her lawyer had a copy in his safe. Aside from being creaky, this old wooden mansion was probably a firetrap.

"She read us the will," Robert said. "We know what's in it."

Skipping the legal language, the heirs mentioned were her niece Camellia (Cammie) and someone named Jewel Parkham. Cammie and Robert got the house and the portrait of the general. Jewel Parkham got the furniture, "and I wish it could be more."

"Jewel Parkham is the nurse who raised Aunt Camellia," Robert explained when I asked. "She was married to a preacher but her husband died and she went to work for Miss Camellia's father as a kind of housekeeper-nurse. Jewel must be in her mid-nineties by now. Her granddaughter is on the city council: Dorothy Parkham. She's a lawyer, specialty real estate."

I noticed the notebooks on top of the desk, and something made me stop and skim through Aunt Camellia's poetry. A few poems were rather old-fashioned but others were quite fresh. I was impressed. One poem was about gardenias. I would have expected it to be in praise of those lovely white flowers, especially since Aunt Camellia had gardenia perfume on her dressing table.

Even the title was odd: "Ode to a Dead Gardenia."

> If you do not touch me
> I bathe you in perfume,
> which is too sweet.
> I stay ivory as heavy cream.
> If you touch me, I turn dark as a bruise.
> I will be a curse, until you die.

I remembered I'd worn a gardenia to my high-school prom. When I took my corsage off, I touched the flower petals by mistake and saw how soon they darkened.

I shivered and was not sure why.

Now I heard the creaking noise. So loud this time I knew it was more than old-house noise. Someone had followed us! In fact, the door opened and there stood an African-American woman, bowed with age. Her hair was white and she leaned on a cane, trembling.

Robert rushed to get a chair for her. "Jewel!" he cried. "You came up all those stairs." He was tense with alarm, and I could see why.

The old woman all but fell into the chair, out of breath, leaned back and shut her eyes. Her right hand dropped the cane and clutched her heart. "I came up slow," she whispered.

Gradually she began to breathe normally and opened her eyes.

"I'm not gone yet!" she announced. "There's spunk in this gal yet."

"But why have you come here?" Robert asked in a worried tone.

"I went to see your Aunt Camellia in the hospital," she said. "My granddaughter took me. I saw your car here and you folks at the door. My poor Camellia is scared sick. She's scared they'll take this house for taxes."

Good grief. If Aunt Camellia's stubbornness meant they took the house for taxes, that would be a real catastrophe.

"I raised that girl," Jewel said. "After her mama died, there was just me. Oh, her father was there, but he was mostly busy. Now I hate to see her so scared. That's why she's sick. She's scared sick. Scared to sell and scared she'll lose this house if she won't sell."

It was incredible to me that seventy-three-year-old Aunt Camellia had a baby-nurse who was still alive and worried about her—who was maybe the only one she felt safe to tell. Tell exactly what?

"This has to do with a gardenia, doesn't it?" I asked. That was a pretty wild guess, but if a gardenia was going to curse her until she died—well, it must figure in.

Jewel gave me a sharp look. "I've never told," she said. "I've been good to that girl and she's been good to me."

"But maybe you could help us understand," Robert said, "if there is anything we can do. This is not like before. We're desperate, and so is Aunt Camellia. My friend here is absolutely discreet. She's helping us."

Jewel gave me another piercing glance. "You're our friend?" she demanded.

"Absolutely," I said.

She continued to look me up and down. Finally she took a deep breath and said, "All right. I'll trust you." Then her words poured out.

"That Lulu woman liked to wear a gardenia behind her ear. Oh, she was good-looking with red hair and the kind of curves men want. And she was spiteful. Said she didn't like women, only men. I'd come over to get the house back in shape the day before Miss Camellia was coming back from seeing to her mama in Nashville. I heard that Lulu woman talking to Mr. Claude. Used to be that folks like her treated us blacks like we weren't there. They'd say anything in front of us or with us in the next room. Forgot we were around. It was downright interesting." She smiled a wry little smile.

"Mr. Claude told that Lulu woman that he couldn't see her anymore—that everything was finished. Had to be.

"That woman said she wouldn't let him loose. She said she'd tell Camellia what they'd done and Camellia would leave him. She'd see to that."

"And were you there when she confronted Camellia?" I asked, fascinated.

"No," she said. "That mean-talking woman disappeared and nobody missed her. Some said she'd gone to Knoxville.

"But I worked for Miss Camellia. Even if she was grown she still needed me. And I needed the work. My daughter was in college at Shaw. I was so proud of that. The day after they said that woman left for Knoxville, I found a dead gardenia lying in a corner of Camellia's room. So dark and bruised, you'd hardly know what it was. I picked it up and Camellia saw me and turned pale as a ghost. I said, 'You killed that woman and I don't blame you.' I had to know.

"Well, she gave up and told me. That girl came by at night when Mr. Claude was out at a meeting and told my poor Camellia what she and Mr. Claude did and began to tell her all the details of what they did, like no lady ever would, and my Camellia slapped her. That hussy went wild and choked my Camellia. But Mr. Claude had come home. They didn't even hear him. He hit that Lulu with the poker from the fireplace. Hit her right on the head where it crushed that gardenia. That's why it was all black when I found it."

"He killed her!" I gasped.

She gave me a speculative look. "He saved Camellia."

But suddenly I wondered, *Was all this a lie to cover whatever really happened?* Loyalty shone strong in Jewel's face. Loyalty to the child she raised, even if it wasn't her own child.

I thought I heard the stairs creak again. I should have said, "Is someone coming?" But I wanted Jewel to finish her story so badly that I told myself it was nothing.

"Mr. Claude told Camellia she was no good at telling a lie. That girl never was. So he told her he didn't want her to know what he did with the body. She had to swear to stay in her room. She says she did it. She swore not to look out the window, and she didn't. But she did look at the clock. He left about ten o'clock. He came back before eleven. She figured he must have buried that body somewhere in the garden."

"But that would have been crazy!" I said.

She stared me down. "I guess Mr. Claude did what he felt he had to do. The next day he signed up for a cruise to send my poor Camellia away from here. Her and her sister. To be out of a question-asking place, if anybody missed that Lulu. Before they left, he must have managed to get that Lulu's bags from the motel where she was staying, ready to move in with Claude as soon as she scared Camellia off. Must have got rid of the car, too."

"But then," said Robert, "why on earth would Claude want to sell the house? Someone might find the body."

The old woman laughed. "It was Camellia who said Mr. Claude wanted to sell. I never heard that man say a word about it when he was alive. After he was gone, she said he'd wanted to sell."

I looked out the window into the tangled garden. I didn't believe the body was there. And in a shallow grave, at that, if he took less than an hour to bury it.

"Was Claude smart?" I asked.

"Absolutely brilliant," Robert said. "He was a contractor, but he also made and lost three fortunes in real estate. Unfortunately he lost the last one just before he died."

"Then the body is not in the garden," I said, "unless he thought he had some really foolproof hiding place."

"Don't matter if the body is in the garden," Jewel said. "Miss Camellia believes it's there. She'll never sell. And I don't know what she'll do about the taxes."

The door opened again. Oh, boy, someone had heard the whole story and it was my fault for not speaking up.

A young African-American woman in a stylish gray silk suit and red pocketbook and heels hurried into the room. "Good morning," she said to us. "I'm Dorothy Parkham." She turned immediately to Jewel. "You should have told me about this house, Grandma," she said. Ah, the councilwoman. The real estate lawyer. She'd followed her grandmother here.

"That was none of your business," Jewel said. "Miss Camellia helped your mama get an education. So your mama could help you. But I knew if I told you her secret, you'd try to make her sell this house no matter what."

The councilwoman smiled. "Not by blackmail!" she said. "But it sounds like she's in trouble! She says she won't sell it while she's alive. But she knows it'll be sold when she dies. What difference does it make?"

"When she's gone," Jewel said, "they can't ask her questions. Like I say, that girl can't lie."

The councilwoman sat in the one remaining chair and tossed her head. "I have a client who wants to buy this house," she said. "I think I know how to persuade Miss Camellia to sell it."

"Oh, Lord," Jewel cried, and her hands flew up in front of her as if to ward off trouble. "What have I done?"

But Robert was interested. "How can you make Aunt Camellia want to sell the house?" he asked.

"This piece of land will be worth more every year. This town is growing like crazy," the councilwoman said. I could see by the twinkle in her eye that she was pleased with herself. "Now, Grandma, you stop looking that way and have faith. My client wants this property for an investment. He can buy on the basis that Miss Camellia lives here until she dies. He can begin to pay her for the house while she's alive. She can live in that house and be comfortable!" she said.

Jewel burst into tears. "Lord be praised," she gasped.

Robert stepped forward and grasped the granddaughter's hand. "I can't tell you what this will mean to us all!"

"Us all, including me," the councilwoman said. "I'll get a good commission."

"But what should we do about the murder?" I asked.

They all said it together: "What murder?"

On my next trip through town, I called Robert to see how things were going. "Oh, you'll have to come by," he said. "Aunt Camellia has invited Cammie and me for tea to see what she's doing to the house and garden. And, yes, she's also helping us, God bless her. Meet us there at three."

I found that changes had already started. I walked around the house and admired them. The blinds were rehung straight and a crew of men was pulling down a small ugly porch on the back which didn't seem to go with the house. Obviously a later addition. The flower beds by the house were weeded, though the edges of the huge garden were left wild. Oddly, that was an attractive effect. The front door was painted, but the rest of the house was still gray with age. One thing at a time.

Robert met me at the door and led me to a room on the first floor, easily accessible to Cammie in her wheelchair. There, around a small table with a lace cloth, were Cammie and Miss Camellia and Jewel. I bet Jewel appreciated the lack of stairs almost as much as Cammie did. She beamed and winked at me. Miss Camellia, in a lavender dress that complemented her gray-blue hair, poured tea from a silver tea service she'd managed to hold onto because, she said, it was her great-grandmother's. The very tea set they'd buried to hide it from the Yankees. I guess that really did happen sometimes.

"We are all beholden to Jewel," Robert said, "for figuring out a way to save this house."

"Jewel is so smart," Miss Camellia said, smiling so her wrinkles looked like many laugh lines. "She asked her granddaughter if there wasn't a way to get money for this house while I still lived, a way that guaranteed that I could stay here. And that smart girl came up with a way."

Jewel winked at me again. So Camellia didn't know her secret was out.

"Robert showed me your house while he was feeding the cat. It's a lovely house," I said. "I notice you are very fond of gardenia perfume."

"Oh, that," she said. A faraway look came into her eyes. "You know, nobody is perfect, and long ago my husband gave that perfume to another woman. I kept it there to remind us to work at being true to one another."

Oh, boy! I bet that husband walked the straight and narrow path.

So everything was finally all right then, and everything was going to be all right now. I was glad.

But just then, a workman in old overalls broke in without a by-your-leave.

"Ma'am," he said to Miss Camellia, "we've found something."

I worked to keep my face blank. Miss Camellia blinked, startled.

"Under that old porch, we've found a great big old block of cement. Must be eight feet long. And thick. Not going to fit in the flower beds you want by the house." Now the workman's eyes lit up. Did he suspect as I did that a body was in that cement? I felt cold.

No one said a word. Our poker faces did us proud.

"Now, my brother is pulling down that house next door," the man in overalls said. "He's got his heavy stuff there today. He's filling the pool. Now, the easiest way to get rid of this ugly block of cement—unless it's something you want—is to get him to drag it over to the pool."

I'm proud to say not one of us let out a sigh of relief.

Miss Camellia smiled graciously. "Yes, tell your brother that cement block is his for fill for the building next door." Maybe she couldn't lie, but she could sure keep her cool.

I told myself we were camellias, not gardenias. We would endure.

Like many learning disabilities teachers, I had enjoyed meeting Elizabeth (Kansas Learning Disability Association—Elizabeth was our keynote speaker), hearing her speak about her memory problems, learning compensatory techniques from her, and reading her mystery books which incorporated her coping strategies. I will miss her and her talent, humor, and spirit.

Susan Geoffrion Neverve

On Writers and Writing

Over the years, Liz wrote a number of pieces about writers and writing. Many a time when she was working at her computer, her cat Sam would be sitting in her lap. So it was natural, when the North Carolina Literary Review *asked her to describe her life as a cat owner, that Liz would be thinking in terms of equating cats and writing:*

Cats

I have a black cat with a white chest and face who looks like he's wearing a tuxedo. No bow-tie, however. His name is Sam. He sits inscrutable as an English butler and watches me write about murder and mayhem. Sometimes his tail twitches. I wonder if he's heard that old expression: The butler did it.

Like all cats I ever knew, he loves to sit on manuscripts. It's as if he thought they might hatch.

At the moment, I'm writing about an absent-minded sleuth who uses memory tricks to solve crimes. I have not yet thought of a trick to help me or my sleuth avoid tripping over a cat when we walk along with our minds in the clouds.

In addition to my Sam, I'm friends with several farm cats who come by to visit me. All of them are trying to teach me to keep my mind on where my feet are going. They get right under my feet, and yowl with annoyance when I trip. It's a conspiracy.

Cats seem to know they can teach a mystery writer like me a lot about her trade. First they dramatize contradictions: that special abilities don't necessarily show at a glance. Anyone who's seen how a cat and a dog react to a rattlesnake knows that. The dog barks and announces the snake. That's helpful. Then he runs around yapping, and acts like he's going to charge in for the kill. If he does, he's likely to get bitten. Dogs are not fast enough to outmaneuver snakes. That's what my neighbors say out here in the country.

So when our rattlesnake appeared, I thanked the dog for warning us and then called up a neighbor with a reputation for knowing what to do about snakes. I locked the dog in the house. I went back out to find the coiled rattler and my cat staring each other straight in the eye.

A cat named Silk is the only witness to the first murder in *Who Killed What's-Her-Name?*. That's the first book in my series about Peaches Dann, the absent-minded sleuth. Silk doesn't tell who the killer is, though she gives hints. But I have the feeling with cats that they might not tell even if they could talk. Not unless it suited them. Cats make their own moral judgments.

Silk is in a tale I wrote for a Sisters-In-Crime collection of short stories. I discovered when I wrote that story that Silk, who used to belong to Peaches Dann's father, was going to move in with Peaches. So she'll obviously be in later books in the series. Cats do that. They decide when and where they will appear.

Now to get back to the great desire cats have to make me watch where I'm going, I bet I could use that in a later book in my series. My sleuth could literally fall upon a clue. Or she could be jarred into consciousness just as she needs to be wide awake and watching out. Or then again—but who knows. It's the unpredictability of cats that's interesting, right?

* * *

Liz was nominated for an Anthony Award in 1995, same year she won an Agatha for the same story. Here is her account of the night at the Anthony Awards dinner at Bouchercon, at which she sat (and presumably ate) with bated breath:

On Being a Nominee

You've heard of jet lag. There is also Bouchercon lag after the world's largest mystery convention. Takes a while to snap back from the non-stop action. At Bouchercon in St. Paul, I had added suspense. I was an Anthony nominee. The Anthony is the award given to an array of mystery categories from best first novel to best magazine. I was thrilled to be nominated for best short story along with so many mystery writers I admired. It would be even more of a thrill to win that dagger stuck in a block of wood, with a bright red pool of "blood" on the wood. Great to set it on the table in the living room, and say in an offhand way, "Yes, a story about my absent-minded sleuth won this."

"Kind of like the sword in the stone in the King Arthur stories?"

a friend asks. Not exactly. No blood on King Arthur's sword.

There was lots else going on at Bouchercon besides awards. Well over a thousand people registered. You have to search for your friends. All the most dedicated mystery fans and a great many authors are there: fellow North Carolinian Margaret Maron, Steve Womack from Tennessee, Teri Holbrook and Kathy Trocheck, Sisters in Crime from Atlanta. Margaret has already won every prize there is. Steve was up for a Shamus for the best private-eye paperback original, and won an Edgar a while back. Good luck, they said. Lots of folks on hand I haven't seen since the last convention: Joan Hess, Carolyn Hart, Annette and Marty Meyers. "Mystery folks are family," says one fan.

On Thursday, there's a Black Mystery Writers Symposium. Walter Mosley keeps us laughing as well as thinking. There's a theory that mystery writers are more cheerful and witty than any other congregation of writers because they have already murdered all their enemies—at least in print. Saw Rob and T. J. MacGregor at the authors reception later in the evening. Rob won an Edgar this year.

Friday means interesting panels on every subject from Location to Virtual Murder. I am going to be the MC of a panel, but not till Sunday. People will not be reminded that I exist on Friday when they vote for the Anthony. They will forget my short story, "The Dog Who Remembered Too Much." Perhaps I should have worn a T-shirt with the title on it embroidered in sequins. That sort of thing goes through a nominee's mind. Too late. I go out and visit bookstores with a group of authors who call themselves the Thundering Herd, organized by Keith Snyder, a young up-and-coming writer.

My publisher gives a splendid cocktail party. Because lines in the hands of famous folks like Salvador Dali are clues in my upcoming book, *Whose Death Is It, Anyway?*, I read prospects and talents from the hands of guests. I've had practice. I used to do a syndicated feature on the hands of famous people. I enjoy myself. I forget about the Anthony.

At the banquet I wish Teri Holbrook good luck. She's up for an Anthony in Best Paperback Original category. Toastmaster Jeremiah Healy introduces guest of honor Mary Higgins Clark and tells how her new contract makes the national budget of Bulgaria look like peanuts, but she remains a regular gal. That's to cheer up all us types whose contracts are more like peanuts. There's hope. Mary tells us about the young fan who wrote she enjoyed Mary's books so much she even read the boring part. We laugh a lot and have a fine time.

Then the Anthonys are announced. No, I didn't win. My friend Gar Anthony Haywood got the dagger for his story "And Pray Nobody Sees You." I admit it's a great story. Margaret Maron says I'm not allowed to win but one prize in one year. That's to comfort me with the fact that my story won the Agatha at Malice Domestic.

If the other nominees weren't such talented folks, the Anthony wouldn't be such a great prize would it? And God bless Dennis Armstrong, Bouchercon chairperson, who topped a great convention by having small daggers made for all us nominees. So I do have a dagger in my living room. All I lack is the official block of wood with the pool of "blood." When I was a kid, we had an expression for demanding a lot: "What do you want, blood?" Of course. All us mystery writers want blood.

I was greeted by this story when I picked up the paper yesterday. I broke into tears and continue to grieve. Elizabeth is an inspiration to all of us who deal with dyslexia and work with others dealing with the same. Elizabeth was a celebrity at two conferences I hosted. I have a signed copy of Remember the Alibi *and will treasure it forever.*

Jonathan Jones

About Dyslexia, Psychics and Other Stuff

In the mid-1960s, Liz made a fascinating discovery about herself. She had been taking our son Mark to Dr. Harvey Tuckman in Westport, Connecticut, for eye exercises to correct dyslexia and realized—while observing one of the exercises—that she herself was dyslexic. But she didn't go public about this for many more years. She had, however, written a novel about a young girl's efforts to cope with dyslexia—and a rewrite of this novel became Memory Can Be Murder, *third in the Peaches Dann series. Liz then made a conscious decision to go public with her own affliction (she hated it when it was called a "disability").*

· As part of her effort to promote Memory Can Be Murder, *Liz made a number of speeches to groups under the auspices of the Learning Disabilities Association. Here is a speech she made in April 1999 to a bookstore audience during an LDA convention in Philadelphia:*

Murder Is So Final

I've never murdered anyone or been murdered or solved a murder, and yet, in writing mysteries, I write about what I know. Of course, I've sometimes wanted to murder someone—but I never have, because murder is so final. You can't apologize later. But the things you want to do—and don't want to do—can be grist for the fiction mill.

Mystery is a great genre because absolutely anything that adds to the suspense or the puzzle can be grist for that mill.

If the sleuth has something within himself that he has to get around, that adds tension. Even Sherlock Holmes had a problem—he was a drug addict. Agatha Christie's Miss Marple was a spinster at a time and place where married women got the respect. Dick Francis has written one book where his sleuth has an artificial hand and, of course, he's terrified because one of the people he's up against keeps trying to destroy the sleuth's remaining hand. This makes for electric tension.

The fact that I'm dyslexic has been a great boon to my mystery novels. What most people have heard about dyslexics is that they sometimes see things backwards. My sister gave me a T-shirt that says "Dyslexics of the World, Untie." And you may have heard the definition of an agnostic dyslexic—someone who lies awake at night wondering of there's a D O G.

In my book *Memory Can Be Murder,* the young protagonist helps solve the murders when she realizes she had seen something backwards.

But there's more to it than that. Unless dyslexics use the right method, they may not be able to learn to read. I was lucky that my family kept trying one thing after another until they hit on phonics, which worked. Dyslexics have trouble spelling. Thank goodness my computer and my husband can spell.

Nowadays there's expert help for anyone to get around these problems, and in fact there are folders right in this bookstore that tell where to get help.

Dyslexics can also have trouble with non-meaningful memory, like names. I can't remember worth a dern without using mnemonic tricks. This glitch has become useful, maybe even with a little help from Above. When my husband and I were living in the Middle East, we visited the Church of the Holy Sepulcher in Jerusalem. While my husband went around taking notes for a story he was working on, I decided to visit the low-ceilinged vault that is revered as the Tomb of Christ. As I was about to enter, a young priest whispered to me that any prayer I offered at the tomb would be answered—guaranteed. I entered, crouched low, and asked God to make me a better person. I stood up and hit my head on the ceiling!

One day I was in a bookstore like this, promoting my first mystery that was not part of the current series. At one point during the talk, I dropped all my notes on the floor and had no idea what to say next. So, quick—make a joke. "You'll be happy to know," I said, "that my next book is going to be called *How to Survive Without a Memory.*

At least five people came up afterward and said, "When you write that book, please let me know—I want to buy one." And I was super-listening. These folks weren't just polite—they were serious. I was onto something. So I wrote a mystery about a sleuth who was writing a book called *How to Survive Without a Memory* and solving murders with her memory tricks.

For example, in *Remember the Alibi*, my sleuth uses the telephone memory trick to help escape the killer. That's the one where, if you absolutely have to remember something when you get home, you call yourself up and leave a message on your answering machine. She solves a murder because she forgets her pocketbook and goes back for it just when the killer has let down his defenses. And so it goes.

My sleuth, Peaches Dann, uses my memory tricks, and readers send in their own tricks, jokes, and excuses. Laughing improves memory. Excuses really help. An amusing excuse means panic doesn't set in when you forget. Panic is terrible for your memory—and bad for sleuths in every way.

One problem I discovered early on: I first made the sleuth as unsure of herself as I used to be. Bad idea. A sleuth has to have admirable qualities. So I was forced to stop and think. What admirable qualities would grow out of having to get around a flakey memory? Actually, they are about the same as the strengths you can gain from getting around dyslexia or any other learning challenge. Determination, for example, and inventiveness.

A bad memory nudges you to be a good judge of people, since you often have to depend on them for information. Forgetters have to develop intuition. Intuition helps my sleuth not only to solve murders but prevent a few in *Whose Death Is It, Anyway,* for example.

Using talents to get around what you might call un-talents means learning about strategy. Strategy is useful in any facet of life. Of course it helps in solving crimes. It helps trap a blackmailer in *Is There a Dead Man in the House?.*

I was so pleased when I figured all this out that I almost took down the sign over my desk for slightly bad days—the sign that says "Mind out to lunch—back in ten minutes." Or the sign for really bad days—the one that says "Of all the things I've lost, I miss my mind the most." I felt smart. I felt virtuous. Why, I had all these good qualities—just like my sleuth. At least, some of the time.

Of course, sometimes I forgot.

Each of my mysteries has other elements beside memory tricks. House restoration, handreading, medieval memory tricks, rattlesnakes—and even my great-grandfather's tombstone.

I'd like to leave one thought with you—the one my mysteries forced me to learn. Whatever you've had to get around in your life has probably added to your talents—perhaps in ways you do not even know yet.

Another thing my sleuth and I have learned is that great numbers of Americans feel as if they can't remember well enough—especially as they get older. That's why so many memory jokes are about older people. Like the story about the two older people sitting on a park bench, and one said to the other, "We're old friends and I know you won't mind if I ask you a question: Was it you or your sister who died?" We people who learn memory tricks when we're young are all set when we get more mature.

A woman saw her mother in the grocery store one day, walking around and tapping, first her forehead, then her chest, then her stomach, and then down below. "Mother," she said, "why on earth are you acting that way in the grocery store?" Her mother said, "Why, I'm just remembering my list—a head of lettuce, breast of chicken, navel oranges and Fantastic!"

* * *

Liz was frequently called upon to read hands—which she always insisted enabled you to discern tendencies, not to predict the future. This started in 1970 when she was promoting her book on handreading and was revived in 1997 when Whose Death Is It, Anyway? *first appeared. And there was always interest in how Peaches used handreading to solve that mystery, and what Liz really thought about the subject. Here is a piece Liz wrote combining her thoughts about palmistry with Peaches's thoughts, with a segue into a short course in handreading:*

The Mystery in Your Hands

Does absent-minded sleuth Peaches Dann believe a hand can predict murder? No. She agrees with me. Handreading is knowledge that is accumulated through the ages like the use of healing herbs. So your hands can show a great deal about you, but Peaches and I believe your future is not frozen.

In *Whose Death Is It, Anyway?* Cousin Fern from California is teaching Peaches how to read hands. Fern has a collection of famous prints from Mark Twain's to Eleanor Roosevelt's to Salvador Dali's. In a roundabout way, these prints plus a line an old book calls "the mark of murder" become clues to why a young girl disappears, and to bloody murder.

In real life, hands can hold clues to character, prospects, and talents. Peaches thought you might like to read your own. Also try reading the hands that celebrities wave on television or hold up in the press.

Thumbs give some of the simplest, surest clues. Who has the larger thumbs in proportion to the rest of the hand, you or your favorite other? The one with the larger thumbs usually makes the plans, and probably wins more arguments depending on the rest of the hand. The famous tend to have large thumbs. Watch your TV screen and see. Note Oprah Winfrey. A large thumb is basically one that comes higher than the middle of the first section of the index finger when held close to the finger. The owner tends to plan ahead and follow the plan. If your thumb is small you may lack strong willpower.

Notice all that hedging: "tends to," "is likely to." Qualities in a hand get balanced against each other. For example, if a hand is weak and flabby, a large thumb would lose importance. If a hand is well marked in other ways, a small thumb might denote a person who gets ahead through intuition rather than determination. Sorry. The world is not simple.

You can read the shape of the thumbs too. Double-jointed thumbs that curve back in an arch suggest the ability to get along with all sorts of people. Notice Henry Wallace's thumb. That shape could mean "watch out for extravagance" if there are wide spaces between the bases of the fingers.

Whoever gestures with his hands as open as a starfish tends to be open in all ways. He who often holds his hands closed is likely to play his cards close to his chest. Maybe he's been burned. Notice our president's hands.

Try lines. Few lines, with the heart, head, life, and fate lines clearly marked, means you are a person who keeps his or her eye on the main issues, are not likely to get lost in complications. Deeply marked lines suggest you feel things deeply. You adore what you like, really dislike what you dislike. Many fine lines suggest you are extremely sensitive.

If your hand is most highly padded and lined on the index finger-thumb side you actively pursue your ambitions. If the little-finger side of the hand is more highly padded and/or lined, your energy goes more towards perception. You are intuitive. If the base of the palm is the developed area you probably have instinctive warmth and earthy imagination, and if your hand is firm you love physical action like a racecar driver. If the middle third of the palm bulges, you likely fight for what you want. Note Salvador Dali's hand. If the top third is the more padded or lined part, mental energy is your forte.

If your hand has tapered fingers with rounded tips, a basically oval palm, it's conic. This means versatility and love of beauty, but needs a large thumb to carry projects through.

The square hand has a squarish palm and fingers that are basically rectangular. The owner wants a place for everything and everything in its place, and is often a scientist. Ross Perot, who uses expressive hands to make his points, has square hands.

The philosophic hand is long and bony with knots at both joints of the fingers and the palm usually contains many lines. The philosophic person likes to look at all sides of a question, is often wise, but sometimes contradictory. Eleanor Roosevelt was an example of the philosophic hand at its best.

The spatulate hand is broader at either the top or bottom of the palm—shaped like a chemist's spatula. The fingertips flare too. This hand shows the need for constant action, as in the hand of a woman sports-car racer.

Your hand may be a mixture of these types. Each finger contributes meaning. If the index finger is longer than the ring finger, that would tend to mean the person could take authority. Teachers, lawyers, business leaders tend to have longer index fingers. Artists of all sorts, expert salesmen, gamblers tend to have longer ring fingers.

Extremely serious folks have the long middle finger large out of proportion.

The little finger large in proportion to the rest of the hand usually belongs to someone quick-witted and intuitive at best, fast-talking at worst. The little finger is long if it comes higher than the second joint of the ring finger like Salvador Dali's print does.

But what about particular lines? you say. Specific line positions have meanings. At least one is known to be connected to a genetic condition. A symptom of Down's Syndrome is one horizontal line across the hand instead of two. But some brilliant people like Franklin Roosevelt's vice president, Henry Wallace, who was also a pioneering geneticist, have the single line. Other clues need to be added in. As we learn more and more about genetic markers, more of the ancient art of hand reading may turn out to be genetic clues.

Not all is genetic however, because lines change. Broken, wavering and frayed lines, a sign of stress, may become well-marked again.

If you are like my friend Allene who sometimes says "Hello, Elizabeth" before I speak and when I haven't telephoned her for a month, tradition says handreading can help that psychic spark to flourish. But there's a great deal revealed by hands in themselves.

By and large, a balanced-looking hand with clearly marked lines is a sign you are in balance with yourself. A strangely shaped hand with broken lines shows you are one of those who needs to learn to use what you do well to get around what you do badly.

Absent-minded sleuth Peaches Dann, who has to use her excellent ingenuity to get around her terrible memory, wishes you luck!

* * *

For many years, Liz had an interest in psychical research, psychic phenomena, and false memory syndrome. The latter became the central factor in Remember the Alibi *and led to Liz's membership in the False Memory Syndrome Foundation. Here is a piece Liz wrote celebrating the formation of the Foundation for Research on the Nature of Man at Duke University: It appeared in* The News & Observer *in Raleigh in the 1970s.*

Got a Hunch?

Not long ago, a man dressed in ghostlike shrouds walked across the front of a screen in a crowded British movie theater. He was a researcher in psychic phenomena—and what he wanted to find out was if anyone in the theater would see exactly what crossed in front of the screen.

After the show, the researcher took a poll of the audience. Thirty-two percent of the people saw nothing at all. Others saw a

> *I had no idea Liz was in her seventies. I thought she was much younger. The last time I saw her we sat and discussed, among other things, whether or not multiple personalities actually exist or whether they are merely a convenient defense tool. We both agreed that it made for an interesting plot whether true or not.*
>
> *David Hunter*

polar bear, a friar, and a young girl in a summer dress, a fault in the movie screen, or some other moving object—except one man, who correctly reported that what he saw was a man dressed up in a ghost costume.

The experience of this researcher—who found that people tend not to see clearly what they do not expect to see—is indeed the experience of the whole field of extrasensory research. Scientists have felt that extrasensory perception, or E.S.P., broke their physical laws. Some others have felt it was against common sense. For E.S.P. occurs when we neither see nor hear nor smell nor taste nor touch in the normal way, nor figure something out by logic or common sense, but "just know."

And the subject becomes much more complicated when what we "just know" pays no attention to time and space—when one twin knows what the other twin is doing, even though they are hundreds of miles apart, or when a man "just knows"—in considerable detail—how an airplane crash will happen, before it happens.

North Carolina has traditionally had a large number of reported occurrences of psychic phenomena—or at least unexplainable phenomena—in the mountains. Yet even here future-reading and mind-reading, for example, have seemed to need a lot of proof. Proof has been supplied more abundantly in the new Research Triangle laboratory. Hopefully, laws to explain E.S.P. will be found too.

Such experiences have been reported since antiquity. King Croesus, in the sixth century B.C., tested seven oracles in seven different cities by asking each to tell what the king was doing on a particular day and to send the findings by king's messenger to the palace. Just one oracle gave an accurate description—down to the kind of pot the king's lunch was cooked in.

Lincoln told of a premonition of his assassination, and Mark Twain told of a dream that foretold his brother's death.

Since the 1870s, societies that have explored such strange happenings have collected details of extrasensory experiences and have conducted ever more careful research into them. But since exploration and nuclear fission have become commonplace, research into psychic phenomena has surged.

North Carolina's place in this new science reflects a growing serious interest in the extrasensory world and more open-mindedness on the part of younger scientists. The heightened interests extend to the man in the street, and even to the Broadway theater.

Noel Coward's *Blithe Spirit*, a play about a ghost, was about as far as the theater could go for several decades. But now, the lyricist of *My Fair Lady* is at work on a musical comedy about a "wildly extrasensory" girl. The show is called *On a Clear Day You Can See Forever*, and according to its author, it is based on records of actual cases kept by parapsychologists.

Serious work in exploring the extrasensory goes on at a number of American colleges, including the University of Virginia and the College of the City of New York. Letters pour in seeking information. The American Society for Psychical Research once received a letter from a child in elementary school: "My class is studying communication," he wrote, "and my friends are reporting on television and the telephone. Where can I find what I need for a report on extrasensory communication?"

The interest is not just in America. The Russians heard a rumor that experiments in mental telepathy were being conducted on the U.S. nuclear submarine *Nautilus*. As quickly as possible, the Russians published a book on their own experiments in long-distance suggestion.

The Russian experimenters had expected they might prove that telepathy is based on radio-like waves moving from one man to another. This would have fit the Russian resistance to supernatural explanation of psychic phenomena. So, the experimenters put the person who was doing the suggestion inside a special Faraday cage that screens out radio and other electromagnetic waves, and put the person to whom the suggestion was to be sent inside another such cage.

These experimenters reached the conclusion that not only was there evidence of mental telepathy, but that it could not be "mental radio." This touched off a heated discussion in the Soviet Union and sparked new activity at a special Leningrad University parapsychology laboratory.

In Canada, departments at two universities conducted an experiment with a psychic healer, who believed his power to heal passed between hands. He held wounded mice in his hands for 20 minutes twice a day while another group of wounded mice went untreated in this manner. By the end of 14 days, wounds on the treated mice became slightly—but measurably—more healed than wounds on the untreated mice.

This psychic healing is related to E.S.P but different. It is what old-school people called mind-on-matter and what parapsychologists call telekinetic effect. Healing tests are closely related to the dice tests at Duke, which measured mind over matter by testing the ability of the mind to influence the roll of dice. The psychic power so measured is called psychokinesis, or P.K. Like E.S.P., P.K. is stirring worldwide interest.

In India, traditional home of floating in the air by mind power (levitation), the government is sponsoring development of a large parapsychology research center where such ancient traditions can presumably be tested. These projects and new research centers are merely a sampling of worldwide activity.

While scientific interest in extrasensory and P.K. is centered around provocative new findings, most of us are more likely to become interested after an impressive personal experience. When I started writing a newspaper feature and book on handreading, everyone immediately told me of their psychic experiences. Handreading does not require a dramatic form of E.S.P., but many expect that it does, and claim me for a fellow psychic.

A woman explained how she had foreseen her husband's heart attack in a warning dream, and made him go to the doctor for what he thought was merely a bad attack of indigestion. The result was that he was given treatment in time to prevent serious aftereffects of the attack.

A young salesman I know suffers agonies because he cannot decide whether to tell his knowledge of the future and frighten his friends or keep it to himself and wonder if he could have helped prevent some of their troubles. I began to realize how many Americans have experiences they need help to explain. As interest in the extrasensory mounts, some of these people are helping researchers.

Recently, the Associated Press reported how a Massachusetts teenager could read a reporter's scrawled notes blindfolded, and he had been trying to help police find a lost child through psychic impressions under hypnosis. In the Middle Ages, a girl reported to have powers like these might have been called a saint, but her chances of being burned as a witch would have been even greater.

But in 1964, that teenager's course was to volunteer herself for scientific research. Researchers believe volunteers are valuable because a complete study of individual men and women who apparently can break the laws of time and space can help them learn what kind of person knows the "unknowable" and why and when and, eventually, how.

Even stories about E.S.P. experiences help investigators, especially where there have been witnesses or written evidence, for example, of a dream before it came true in lifelike detail. What these stories have in common can furnish important clues. For example, in a great many stories, the apparent sender of a psychic impression is in a highly wrought emotional state, often in great danger or even about to die. The man or woman who receives the impression is relaxed or even resting. A typical example is the mother who jumps up from a nap sure that her child is in great danger, and she finds him out of sight and earshot of her bed about to fall off the roof.

Findings about E.S.P. are likely to tell us more about man than why hunches work, some experimenters believe. Highly creative writers, artists, and musicians appear to have more psychic experiences than the average man does. This may mean that creativity and E.S.P. are closely related in the ways in which they work.

North Carolina's new Foundation for Research on the Nature of Man, of which the parapsychology lab will be a part, may help to unlock new understanding of the kind of mental energy available to a Shakespeare or a seer. This might be as revolutionary as the splitting of the atom, and with any luck, much easier on our nerves.

* * *

Liz constantly urged beginning writers not to waste anything and to use all their life experiences in their work. There's a perfect example in this exchange of letters between the Connecticut court system and Liz:

Using What You Know

STATE OF CONNECTICUT
COURT OF COMMON PLEAS
DANBURY, CONNECTICUT

TO: *Mrs. Elizabeth Squire*
Starrs Plain Road
Redding, Conn.

SUMMONS FOR PETIT JUROR

You are hereby notified that you have been drawn for jury duty in this court and you are hereby summoned to appear before the Court

of Common Pleas at Danbury on March 22, 1976, at 9:15 a.m. at
which time you will give your attendance according to law.

THE REDDING PILOT
Redding, Connecticut

March 3, 1976

Dear Ms. McNamara:

I have been called for jury duty on March 22 but find I have to be out of town at the annual meeting of a family business of which I am an owner. Therefore, I hope I may appear after March 30.

I am a reporter on *The Redding Pilot*, which is sometimes short-staffed. But in early April or early June it would be possible for me to perform jury duty without undue difficulty for my co-workers on the paper.

When I do serve, I would like to do a series of articles for *The Pilot* and its sister papers on what it is like to perform jury duty, and at that time I would like to talk to someone about background material for these articles.

Sincerely,
Elizabeth D. Squire

(And so, in due course, Liz wrote a three-part series for the Acorn Press papers. "Never waste anything" was her motto.)

I'll never forget the sparkle in her eyes and the lilt in her voice when she talked about her work. Or, indeed, when she talked about anything. Liz always seemed to be having a good time, whatever she was doing, and she brought such enthusiasm and energy to it all. Just being around her made me feel better; if I can use such a trite phrase, she had such a positive aura about her, you simply couldn't help but respond to it. She also had a bit of the bulldog in her when it came to promoting her work, a quality I'd like to emulate, but I doubt I could ever do it with the blend of tenacity and graciousness that Liz managed. She was truly a marvel to behold.

Dean James

Here is the first chapter of Liz's last novel—the one she was work-ing on at the time of her death. Liz, as we have seen, never wrote out-lines for her novels, and never divulged the ending. She knew where this novel was heading—even if we cannot know that. The working title for the novel was:

The Ultimate Catastrophe

I don't like snakes. I don't even like to write stories about them for the *Weekly Word* where I sit at a large old wooden desk and wel-come those who bring in news. But Vernor Rice shuffled in with such a pleased grin I couldn't help grinning back in spite of what he told me. I also shivered.

"This dern dry weather is driving snakes down the mountain for water," he said. "I read in your paper last week how that tourist was bitten in the woods and Barney Jones found her dead. She must have been bit and lost too. Called Barney up and we agreed that snakes are bad this year."

I made a note to watch where I walked.

Vernor wears faded overalls and denim shirts. He's a big man, in his seventies, with that I-love-the-world smile, but his teeth are tobacco stained and he goes outside to spit snuff. You might not guess that he's a kind of an expert about old-fashioned nature lore. He knows how to plant by the moon signs or foretell a hard win-ter. Plainly, I'd have to write a little item about thirsty snakes.

"Of course more snakes will please snake handlers," he said cheerfully, thrumming a shoulder strap. "I've heard a preacher from Georgia is setting up a service around here to test for true faith."

"Where? When?" I asked. I'd certainly have to do a story about that whether I liked it or not.

"Only a rumor," he said with a shrug. "Don't worry." He beamed reassurance. His voice, which I heard was an asset to his church choir, rang with enthusiasm. "I'll be by when I know more about snakes."

I was glad that gentle Ellie Mangle came in and changed the subject, even if Ellie could tangle any subject in knots.

"It's a pleasure to visit your nice quiet newspaper office where nobody is being murdered every five minutes," she said, as she handed me the Methodist church news. Ellie often started a thought in a way that didn't seem to make sense, but if you waited till she finished speaking, it usually came clear. I waited. The September breeze outside had rumpled her hair, and she brushed back her bangs from her eyes. Her slightly-too-long hair added to her air of cheerful vagueness. She looked straight into my eyes and spoke slowly the way she must do with her nursery school students.

"And I want to talk to you because I need air-conditioning," she said.

I write about everything from church fairs to County Commission fights to the sheriff's latest arrest to tourists dead from snake bite. I have nothing to do with air-conditioning. I waited.

"You see," she sighed, "Henry Knorr—that's my neighbor—is eighty, and he was lonely all by himself, and so his daughter gave him two peacocks, and they hatched more peacocks. They sound like someone screaming, like someone being murdered in the distance, every five minutes. He doesn't care because he's deaf, but I wish he had chickens." I continued to wait.

"And that's why I want you to give me advice about a book I'm writing," she added.

What?

"I need to air-condition my house so I can close the windows and won't hear the peacocks, so I need to finish this book quickly and make some extra money, and you wrote a book about your own worst fault and sold it, so I'd be so grateful if you'd help me out."

Well, that was true, my *How to Survive Without a Memory* was doing well. And writing it had actually improved the way I cope with my own flaky memory. That's why I have Post-it reminder notes in assorted colors all over my office, for example, and a large wall calendar with spaces to write in for each day, and I've trained my new dog to remind me of things.

"My book," Ellie said, "is going to be called *How to Cope With 1001 Catastrophes That No Well-Run Household Would Ever Have.*"

Now that was a title I could remember. I could use that book. And as for the peacocks, I'd once read a book called *Murder With Peacocks*, but in this case, I could see that they were just a catastrophe for which my friend Ellie needed a solution.

"Does your book tell how to cope with snakes?" I asked. Maybe I could add that to the dry-weather story and give it an upbeat twist.

She blinked. "Not yet," she said. "I'll put in a chapter about that. But I need your help."

And there was something about Ellie that made me feel I ought to help her out. I happen to know she's about 28, but, standing there by my desk, she looked young and unscarred and innocent. With that fluffy brown hair and baby fine skin, she looked as soft as a kitten, without a bit of catlike guile. She looked like she had never had to deal with a serious problem in her life, though that wasn't true. When she was 26, her husband, Fred (unfortunately I remember him as Dead Fred), ran his motorcycle into a ditch and was killed. She has landed on her feet and supports herself teaching nursery school. Dead Fred is a good mnemonic because it's a little shocking. You see, things stick in your mind better if they are shocking or funny, and it helps if they rhyme.

But what kinds of problems—well, aside from the peacocks—could Ellie have to cope with now besides kids knocking over jars of finger paint? I was curious. I looked at my "In" basket. It was nearly empty because the paper comes out on Thursday, so Friday is my relaxed day. On Friday, I'll agree to do anything.

"Come and have lunch with me," Ellie begged. "Fred encouraged me to write this book. He said, 'Ellie, express yourself.' He was so good to me. And today is our anniversary. I thought it would be good to work on it on our anniversary." She blinked back tears. Still grieving. Well, two years is not so long, and a good husband is a treasure to lose.

"We can talk about my book over chicken salad," she added, standing straight.

That cinched it. Ellie is a super-cook. I buy her double-fudge brownies at cake sales whenever I get the chance. Besides, I like her. "I'd love to come to lunch," I said, "if you'll promise no catastrophes today. I'm not in the mood."

She smiled so broadly that the corners of her eyes crinkled. Tears banished. "Of course not," she said, "and even if something should go wrong, my guardian angel will see us through. He looks after me, especially in emergencies." Her brown eyes were wide and moist with belief.

Well, you know what they say in the newspaper business: "Believe nothing you hear and only half of what you see." That's without further proof. Some of my colleagues have forgotten that rule, but it's still my motto.

"How do you know you have a guardian angel?" I asked dryly.

"I have a friend who sees things like that," she explained matter-of-factly. "My guardian angel is an Indian chief."

Oh. I revised my mental picture from feathered wings to a feather headdress. I guess I looked skeptical.

"Don't you believe in guardian angels?" she asked.

"I'm not in the believing business. I'm in the finding-out business," I said. "I don't necessarily believe you have an Indian chief for a guardian, but I don't believe it's absolutely impossible either. The universe is full of constant wild surprises. Even this county is full of surprises," *like maybe snake handlers*, I thought unhappily. And if by some wild chance guardian angels were parceled out to the ones who needed them most, Ellie, naive and alone as she was, should certainly be high on the list.

"I'll drive and we can talk on the way," she said. "I have to come back this way after lunch anyhow."

"So either two of us or three of us, if you count your guardian, will proceed to your house," I said, "and discuss *How to Cope With 1001 Catastrophes That No Well-Run Household Would Ever Have.*"

All I expected besides chicken salad was to hear the cries of Ellie's catastrophe. I've heard peacocks. Their calls are high and piercing and sound like "arlp!" in a desperate kind of way. Almost like "help!" and yet they are just having a nice peacock chat. I could stand a little of that.

"So, tell your guardian chief to make sure that nothing spoils our lunch," I said as we left the office. I thought I was just making small talk to keep her cheered up.

Well, I was feeling bad about leaving Elizabeth Daniels Squire's Peaches Dann series off my list of humorous mysteries, when I thought . . . surely, of all people, Liz would understand someone forgetting something.

When I read my first Peaches Dann mystery, it was a gorgeous spring day. I read some, and then it warmed up outside, and I went and did some yard work. And almost the entire time I was outside, I was thinking about the book, and Peaches, and wondering what would happen next. Elizabeth Daniels Squire was a gifted writer with a real and memorable voice. One I am so sad to learn is now silent.

Liz was a charming woman and a real Southern Lady in the best senses of the phrase. Her social grace was evident even in the briefest of meetings.

I am grateful to have met her and to have the wonderful gift of her writing to brighten dark times. Like this one.

Mary Miller

AFTERWORD

The foregoing chapters record with great affection a generous sampling of Liz's writing over the years. In the course of attending writers conventions and signing and speaking at libraries and bookstores around the country over a 20-year period, Liz made many hundreds of friends, many of whom shared with her family their thoughts on learning of her sudden and somewhat mysterious death on February 25, 2001.

Here is the obituary prepared by her office for newspapers published on the following day:

Elizabeth Daniels Squire, Mystery Author, 74, Dies

Elizabeth Daniels Squire, 74, of Maney Branch Road, Weaverville, NC, died unexpectedly Sunday morning in Santa Rosa, California, where she had stopped on her return from a business trip to Alaska.

Mrs. Squire was the author of eight mysteries and was at work on a ninth at the time of her death. She had been attending a mystery writing convention in Anchorage and had conducted workshops in Skagway, Alaska, with creative writing groups in the junior and senior high schools there.

A native of Raleigh and a graduate of Ashley Hall School in Charleston, SC, and of Vassar College, Mrs. Squire was the daughter of Jonathan Daniels, former press secretary to President Truman, and a granddaughter of Josephus Daniels, editor of The News & Observer in Raleigh, Secretary of the Navy in the Wilson Administration, and ambassador to Mexico during the Roosevelt administration. She spent most of her life writing for newspapers, and a newspaper publisher was the victim in her first mystery, Kill the Messenger, published in 1990.

Since then, Mrs. Squire published seven mysteries in the Peaches Dann series, all of which are in print and several of which have been published in large-print editions. She also authored a number of short stories, one of which won the coveted Agatha award.

In addition to her fiction-writing, Mrs. Squire had served as chairman of the board of trustees of the Weaverville Library and as a director of the News & Observer Publishing Co. in Raleigh. From 1966 until she moved to North Carolina in 1979, Mrs. Squire was a staff reporter for the Redding, Conn., Pilot. She was a member of the North Caroliniana Society, Sisters in Crime, and was a past chairman of the Southeastern chapter of the Mystery Writers of America.

Mrs. Squire is survived by her husband, C. B. Squire; three sons, Jonathan Hart Squire of the Beech community, Mark M. Squire of Sebastopol, California, whom she was visiting at the time of her death, and Worth P. Squire of College Grove, TN, as well as seven grandchildren. Her sisters, Adelaide Daniels Key of Asheville, Dr. Lucy Daniels of Raleigh, and Dr. Cleves Daniels Weber of Maui, Hawaii, also survive.

A memorial service for Mrs. Squire will take place at Grace Episcopal Church in Asheville on Tuesday afternoon at 2 o'clock. Memorials may be sent to the Asheville-Buncombe Community Christian Ministries at 30 Cumberland Ave., Asheville, NC 28801.

* * *

Here is the homily by our old friend the Rev. Charles E. Johnson, delivered at the memorial service in Asheville for Liz on February 27, 2001:

A Remembrance for Elizabeth

It is with gratitude and humility that I accept the honor of celebrating with a homily on the life of a wise and wonderful woman: Elizabeth Daniels Squire.

With gratitude because her family and my family in Eastern North Carolina lived together with mutual respect and friendship for more than 100 years. With humility because, though of course I didn't know Elizabeth for 100 years, each year that I did was as rich as a decade. Elizabeth was truly a wise and wonderful person impossible to praise sufficiently.

As a guiding compass for the homily, hear these words from the 2nd chapter of Ecclesiasticus as found in the Apocrypha in the New English Bible: "If you aspire to be a servant of the Lord, prepare yourself for testing. Set a straight course, be resolute, and do not lose your head in time of disaster. Bear every hardship that is sent you, and be patient whatever the cost. For gold is assayed (and refined) by fire."

Elizabeth lived and ended her days on earth refined: she exemplified refinement in every sense of the word.

A lady of refinement is never haughty or arrogant—she is sympathetic and sensitive and she is appreciative of the feelings of others. In a word: She is kind.

Elizabeth was fortunate in having a husband who shared her values and appreciated those values in her. Happily, she was also the mother of children who blossomed with extraordinary vigor, supported by her wisdom, by her patient tolerance of their spirited independence and by her wise and patient insistence that independence be ultimately crowned with a genuine sense of personal responsibility. She is blessed in her children as they have been blessed by her.

Three pillars of Elizabeth's character deserve particular mention:

(1) She was courageous. She didn't shrink from facing what had to be faced. Elizabeth was dyslexic. I'm not sure anyone can truly appreciate what a burden and a challenge dyslexia was to Elizabeth. The pain was made sharper by her own sometimes-frustrated desire to become an author. The fact is that she accepted this burden, bore it without complaint, and triumphed—becoming a published writer who delighted many readers with her mystery stories.

(2) She had a remarkable sense of humor. Along with dyslexia, Elizabeth had a real problem with memory. In dealing with this problem, Elizabeth exhibited one of the real strengths of her personality, and one of the most lovable. She was always able to see the humor in a situation and appreciate it even though, and sometimes especially if the joke was on her.

The titles of her books make no effort to conceal her memory problem. I'll mention just one. The title? Who Killed What's-Her-Name?

There is in one of her books an episode which deals with her heroine (could be Elizabeth) on her way to deliver a frozen dessert to someone. She stops her car at her father's house for a short visit en route. She temporarily deposits the dessert in her father's refrigerator. She leaves in time to get to the house of the friend who is awaiting the frozen dessert. But she arrives without the dessert. It is still in her father's refrigerator. Elizabeth's reaction? Good! She has hit upon a new remedy to include in her new book on how to deal with memory lapses: When putting a dish in the refrigerator not your own during a visit, be sure to put your car keys alongside the dish. You cannot leave without it.

(3) A third quality (and this by no means exhausts what could be said about Elizabeth)—but it is a very important quality—was a special kind of joie de vivre, a joy of living, which was in no way selfish. She simply without words invited people to be happy. It was almost as if she was magically free from any desire to grab happiness primarily for herself. Without mentioning anything about it, her spirit seemed to send out the message that we were enjoying a happy time together—and she was always quietly delighted when she saw others happy.

There was nothing exactly definable about this quality—rather, the proof of it was that, in a mysterious sort of way, she made other people happy—they liked to be around her. They came to love her. What a wonderful way to be! Her quiet happy spirit makes of this an occasion not for mourning but for serene celebration. For I truly believe I know her spirit and that her spirit is glad (as only Elizabeth knew how to be glad) that we are happily here together. You know, I feel that she is inviting us in her own way now to share with her a few moments of her eternal happiness.

Let us conclude with a Scottish prayer that Elizabeth admired, and then with a psalm from the Scottish Psalter, "The Lord's My Shepherd," which I will sing a capella.

* * *

And in the days and months since Liz's death, many messages of condolence were received by her family. Fellow mystery-writer Anne Underwood Grant wrote the following tribute for the Hendersonville Times-News:

It Was Her Last Unselfish Act

A few short weeks ago, my friend and fellow mystery writer, Elizabeth Daniels Squire of Weaverville, died suddenly and unexpectedly. Her death was a shock to all who knew her because Liz was someone we thought would live forever. Seventy-four at the time of her death, Liz could run circles around those of us several decades her junior.

Mystery writers are unusually close and supportive compared to other fiction writers I've known. Within other genres, oftentimes writers are into one-upmanship, isolationism and elitism. They backbite without provocation. Mystery writers, as a whole, go out of their way to help each other through the tangled maze that is the current publishing industry.

Liz was always the first to show newly published mystery writers the ropes. She had a theory she shared frequently about why mystery writers are, with few exceptions, such nice people.

"Compare what we do to romance authors," she'd say. "All day they write about love and beauty and romantic interludes. Then look at what we write about." She always grinned at this point in her telling. "My theory is that we put our evil parts onto paper every day, leaving our goodness for the real world to experience. As for romance writers, no wonder they're so hard to get along with!"

Liz lived a life of accomplishment. Her family founded The

(Raleigh) News & Observer *and for the last several hundred years, has wielded influence rarely paralleled in North Carolina.*

Her grandfather was ambassador to Mexico; her father, press secretary to President Truman. Few people knew Liz was one of those Daniels; in fact, I never heard her mention her heritage. She graduated from Vassar in spite of a lifelong battle with dyslexia. She tackled her dyslexia the way she approached everything—directly and lightly, as if somehow the difficulty was a gift from God. A couple of years back she was the keynote speaker to the annual gathering of the International Dyslexia Association.

She used her handicap to inspire kids to embrace words and the books they come wrapped in. "If I can be published," she would say, beaming to a classroom full of dyslexic youth, "just think what you can do!"

At the time of her death, Liz was returning from two weeks in Alaska, where mystery writers had gathered for a conference known as Left Coast Crime. Her second week there, she had agreed to fly by seaplane out into the Alaskan bush, to an island called Skagway.

While in Skagway, Liz spent each day in the schoolhouse or the library where she shared her love of books and taught creative writing to kids who never imagined they'd meet a real author.

Her trip to Skagway was the last unselfish act of a woman who lived her life unselfishly. A true ambassador for the mystery world, an inspiration to both kids and adults with reading difficulties and a light-hearted friend to all of us who knew her well, Elizabeth Daniels Squire has a place in our hearts forever. The road ahead is lighter and brighter because she lived.

* * *

My sons and I buried Elizabeth's ashes in the Maney Branch Cemetery, which adjoins our farm in northeastern Buncombe County, North Carolina, and placed over them a headstone with the following inscription:

Elizabeth Bridgers Daniels Squire
July 17, 1926 - February 25, 2001
"Respect the real deep-down differences in the way people's minds work, including your own. And if some folks think that's outrageous, so be it."—E.D.S.

The inscription was taken from a piece Elizabeth wrote for Deadly Women. *The entire short story, "The Older They Get. . . ," appears earlier in this book.*

And, to close, here is a poem by Liz:

Hope

As the tide of hope goes out, each wave still rises
But makes a lower water-line on the shore than the wave
      before.

It is important to believe in love, isn't it?

But when two people bring each other pinched white faces
      of pain
Where once there was the flush and sparkle of expectation,
It is important to remember that love can exist, did exist,
      will exist,
But it can't be pinned forever in one place, like a butterfly
      on a pin.

The pin kills it.

A strangle-hold pulls love down to death, like a panicked
      swimmer drowns a would-be savior.

Hope that love will revive dies more slowly.

Hope that love grows somewhere must not die.

Like God, love is not dead. I hope.

INDEX